Mesmerized
An Ellora's Cave publication, 2003

Ellora's Cave Publishing, Inc.
PO Box 787
Hudson, OH 44236-0787

ISBN # 184360965

ISBN MS Reader (LIT) ISBN # 1-84360-662-3
Other available formats (no ISBNs are assigned):
Adobe (PDF), Rocketbook (RB), Mobipocket (PRC) & HTML

MESMERIZED edited by Briana St. James.
Cover art by Darrell King.

What the critics are saying

"MESMERIZED is an anthology that is more than just a book. This anthology brings readers three dynamite authors who know how to please their readers, set the pages on fire, create worlds that we never want to return from and always leave us anticipating more. It is one heck of a hot, steamy and intriguing time while reading MESMERIZED. Jaci Burton, Sahara Kelly and Ashleigh Raine wow us with some of the best of the best that there is in erotic fiction. I hope to see these authors all in the same book again someday. But for now, set aside an hour or two (you won't be able to put it down once begun), and be MESMERIZED by these awesome stories." - *Tracey West, The Road to Romance*

5 star review from Timeless Tales!
"This anthology is one of the best I have ever read. The stories are all over the spectrum. The uniting factor of hypnosis gives it extra depth and dimension. I thought the writing chemistries between these authors complemented each other in a way I haven't seen before in print or ebook." - *Alexander Taylor, Timeless Tales*

"Three wonderful authors. Three equally wonderful novellas." - *Robin Taylor, In the Library Reviews*

"Don't pass up this mesmerizing collection of stories." - *Patricia McGrew, Timeless Tales*

MESMERIZED

Sir Philip Ashton's Eyes

Sahara Kelly

Magic In the Works

Ashleigh Raine

True Lies

Jaci Burton

SIR PHILIP ASHTON'S EYES

Sahara Kelly

Chapter 1

"No."

"No?"

"*No*. No, absolutely no. Thank you, but no."

The earnest young gentleman on his knees before Miss Abigail Foxworth looked puzzled, and then his face relaxed. "Ah. You mean you'd like some time to consider my proposal."

"No, Lord Reginald. I *mean* thank you for doing me the honor of offering for my hand, but I must refuse."

"But...but..."

Abby sighed. "Reginald, what part of the simple word 'no' do you fail to comprehend?"

Reginald Abernathy wrinkled his brow while he engaged in the challenging exercise of actually thinking about something other than his horses. "Well, Mama said..."

"Hmm. What did your Mama say?" Abby clenched her teeth. Lady Abernathy was the largest, loudest, most self-absorbed woman in London. Who also worshipped her oldest son as unquestionably the "catch" of the Season.

He wasn't.

"Well, Mama said..." He rose from his knees, carefully withdrawing a handkerchief from his perfectly cut coat and wiping away any lingering flecks of carpet. "She said that ladies *must* perforce refuse the first offer, while they consider all the advantages of being married. To me. Then they'll understand why it's such a good idea. And then they'll say yes." He turned his rather vacant blue eyes to her face. "And I'm a nice man, Abby."

Once again, Abby sighed. "Of course you are, Reginald. You'll make some girl a fine husband, I'm sure." *One who has no brains of her own, and doesn't care that her husband has none either.* "But not for me."

Reginald tried to look desolate at her rejection. But the effort was too much, and he simply looked…well…vacant.

"What am I going to tell Mama, then?" he whined.

Abby took a breath. It appeared that, thankfully, she'd not shattered his heart or his dreams, and blighted the rest of his probably long and boring life. Which assumed some other woman didn't kill him first, thus sparing herself from years of horse-talk.

"Just tell your Mama that I was a completely foolish woman, who couldn't recognize the treasure under my nose, and chose not to accept your offer. Then tell her that you rather agreed with me, since it was clear that by refusing you I was demonstrating how very stupid I was."

Reginald took several moments to digest that rather complex instruction.

Abby's hands fidgeted as she fought the urge to punch him and perhaps jolt his brain, whatever there was of it, into some kind of functioning order.

It took a few minutes, but finally a satisfied smile crossed his chubby face and he nodded. "Right. Very good, Abigail, very good."

He looked around, blinking. "Well, I should take myself off then."

Abigail gritted her teeth. "Yes, Reginald, I think that would be best."

"You're still interested in that filly at Tattersall's, though, aren't you? Dodsman's breakdown?"

Now the man's eyes were focused, and for a moment Abigail caught herself wondering if he should just skip the whole wife business and stick with his horses. At least they brought some animation to the poor chap.

"Yes, indeed, Reginald. If you would take a look at her and send me a note? I'd appreciate it."

"Happy to, m'dear," he chortled, bowing to her. He toddled off, grinning like a child who'd been given a treat. No air of the rejected suitor hung over his shoulders—he was now a man with a mission. A horse mission.

Abigail closed her eyes as the door shut behind him and heaved an enormous sigh of relief.

Another man sent off about his business, another proposal rejected and, she knew, *another* round of recriminations from Aunt Eugenia.

And sure enough, within mere moments of Reginald's exit, the door opened again and a daintily rounded woman tip-toed into the room with an air of buoyant expectancy floating around her, along with a large number of tulle ruffles.

"So, my dear, am I to wish you and Reginald happy? I saw him smiling as he left." Eugenia Foxworth fluttered to the couch and sat next to Abigail, eyeing her niece hopefully.

"Sorry to spoil your morning, Aunt Eugenia. Reginald failed to persuade me that marriage to him would be anything other than a complete disaster."

Eugenia permitted herself an unladylike snort. "Well, for heaven's sake, Abigail. What am I going to do with you? You're not getting any younger, you know."

Abigail rose, and commenced her favorite occupation during these sessions with her aunt. She paced. Some bottled-up energy inside her refused to allow her to stay still for long, and she found striding up and down the long salon helped her keep her temper, and her tongue, between her teeth.

"Aunt, you have pointed out my age, my lack of a husband, and my obvious shortcomings often enough. I know them by heart. Can't we just say that I refused Reginald, it's done with, and move on?"

Eugenia sighed dramatically and fluttered her handkerchief. "You know I love you, dear, as if you were my own. I just worry about you so."

Guilt swamped Abigail and she moved to the couch, dropping a light kiss on her aunt's elegantly, if improbably colored, head. "I know, Aunt, I know. And I'm sorry to be such a trial to you."

Eugenia straightened slightly. "You're never that, my dear. I cannot tell you how glad I am your parents allowed you to come to London and ease my loneliness after your dear uncle…" She pressed her handkerchief to her lips.

Abigail wasn't fooled. "Aunt Eugenia, you and I both know that there are any number of eligible gentlemen who'd be happy to 'ease your loneliness'. Why just the other evening, Colonel Dagenham was commenting on your good looks."

"He was?" Eugenia's eyes sparkled and she turned with a smile. Then she recalled the subject under discussion and straightened her face. "Well, that's nice, but neither here nor there at the moment. We're discussing *you*, Abby."

Damnation. Distraction hadn't worked. She was in for it now. "Do we have to?"

"Yes we do." Eugenia settled her ample bottom comfortably between the cushions. "This makes how many now? Five? Five offers you've turned down flat?"

"I don't keep count," answered Abby wryly.

"Well, there was young Fotherby. You said he was too short."

"He was, Aunt, even you must admit that."

Eugenia permitted herself a slight nod. "Well, I do confess that it would be disconcerting to spend one's life talking down to one's husband whose face was exactly level with one's…um…" She trailed off with a blush. "But there was nothing wrong with Charles Marshfield or Sir Roxburgh deHaven."

"Charles is a gambling idiot who lives for the next turn of the cards. Sir Roxburgh is twenty years my senior and wants heirs. I don't want to be someone's brood mare, Aunt."

"Well, good gracious, Abby, what *do* you want?"

Silence fell as Abby paced the floor, struggling with the answer to the question that had plagued her mind from the minute she'd arrived in London and started suffering through this long parade of would-be suitors.

"I want…I want…" She bit her lip, trying to find the words to explain to her aunt. "I want a *man*, Aunt."

"Well, my dear, all of them so far have fit *that* particular qualification," giggled Eugenia.

Abby ignored her, and continued her own train of thought. "I want a man who makes me *feel* things, who challenges me to *think* things. Who makes me want to—"

A new voice broke into Abby's words. "Toss up your skirts and spread your legs for him?"

Eugenia gasped and fell back on the couch, reaching for her ever-present vinaigrette and waving it under her nose.

Abby laughed and turned to see an elderly woman, carefully leaning on her cane and standing in the doorway. "Grandmama, you were eavesdropping."

"Bet your boots, sweetheart. Only way to find out anything interesting. I hope this means you've sent that ass Reginald off with a flea in his ear?"

"Yes, indeed," chuckled Abigail. My, how she loved this cantankerous old woman.

"Good gel. He was as useless as a pile of droppings from those damned horses he goes on about. Tried to talk me into one, for God's sake. At my age. As if I could still ride *anything*, let alone a horse."

Eugenia gasped again. "Mama Wetherford, *please*. Such conversation is not fit for Abby's ears."

"Damnation, Eugenia. Don't be a nitwit. Abigail is telling you precisely what she wants, and you're not listening. What she wants is a man who'll wake up the woman inside her."

Abby's jaw dropped.

"A man who'll make her think about how what's between his legs would feel between hers. A man with some fire to him, and a brain that might even outstretch the length of his cock."

Eugenia looked like she might faint at any moment.

"Well, gel? Am I right?" The Dowager Duchess of Wetherford glared at her granddaughter fiercely. "You're possessed of brains, a handsome dowry, and a body that makes men's mouths water. But as yet, not one man's done the same for you."

Abby stared.

The wrinkled face smiled back at her. "He's out there, Abby. Never fear, the right man's out there. You've too much to offer him to let it all go to waste on some slack-pricked nincompoop."

Eugenia gave up the battle, and tossed her vinaigrette aside. "Good Lord, Mama. You speak as if...as if...*intimate relations*...were the only important thing." She blushed.

"Well, and aren't they? Gel's got to lie in her husband's bed and breed him heirs. Damn well ought to have fun doing it." A wicked grin creased the folds around the Dowager's mouth. "I certainly did."

"I'll wager you did too, you reprobate, Grandmama," smiled Abby.

"'Twas a different age, a different set of values, Abby. None of this go off and marry an idiot for his title, bear him a couple of sons, and *then* start looking for passion. We knew how to do it right the *first* time. Or maybe the second or third..."

Abby laughed. "You mean I should experiment beforehand, Grandmama?" she asked cheekily.

"*NO*," squawked Eugenia. "No, no, a thousand times no."

"Oh cease your frabbling, Eugenia. Don't think we need worry about our Abby here. She'll keep her thighs together. And if she doesn't, well then, she's found the right man."

* * * * *

The right man.

Her grandmother's blunt words rang in Abigail's ears as she dressed for the evening.

Was the "right man" out there waiting for her?

Was there actually a single man in all of England who could make her feel things and need things and...and...

She glanced down at her body. Was there a fire in there that the right man could light?

She closed her eyes for a moment. She was not *totally* inexperienced. She'd been kissed. Quite a few times. Occasionally with her cooperation.

But there'd been no spark, no flutter in her belly.

Young Johnny Mountwell had even shown her his cock. Many years ago, of course. She'd been fascinated at how it had grown larger under her gaze, and when she'd reached out her hand to touch it, it had swelled even more.

But when he'd asked her to actually put her mouth on the damned thing, she'd responded with something like "Eeeeuuuuwww", and it had shriveled before her eyes. Johnny hadn't spoken to her since.

That had been more than six years ago, and here she was with no more than a few kisses and a forbidden glimpse at an aroused youth to keep her company at night.

It was poor companionship, when she knew she yearned for more.

More than the feel of a man's hardness pressing against her in the waltz. More than the fumbled attempts at kisses that had left her unmoved and wiping her mouth surreptitiously afterwards.

She sighed and pulled the bell to summon her maid.

She must dress for the evening to come, and knew that being late wasn't an option.

Tonight they were to attend a demonstration of mesmerism at Lady Rachel Greenhough's home. At least it held slightly more interest for Abby than another endless ball or soiree, and perhaps there might even be some guests interested in something other than who was engaged to who. Or whom. Or whatever.

Her maid arrived, and together they turned Abby into a lady fit for an evening's entertainment.

Her dark red hair was twisted into a sleek coil, with a few long curls placed delicately across her white skin, lying comfortably on her bosom.

A simple emerald pendant and matching earbobs brought out the green sparkle in her eyes, and her plain gold silk gown made her hair glow with rich, deep slashes of fire. She was unfashionable, and she knew it, but cared not one whit.

Men chorused the charms of the latest petite, blue-eyed blonde, and few had time for a statuesque, brazenly red-haired woman past the first flush of youth.

Her breasts were revealed by the low décolletage that barely covered them, a fashion she dared wear thanks to her advanced years. Not that it mattered, of course, because odds were good that she'd end up chatting with some scientifically-minded people, most of whom, she'd found, were settled, married, and past the point of looking down a woman's dress.

Thankfully.

With an appreciative murmur of gratitude to her maid, Abby picked up her Norwich silk shawl with the golden fringe and tugged her long white evening gloves smooth.

Her reticule clinked a little, not because it held a vinaigrette full of smelling salts, but because it contained a small fold of paper and a pencil, along with her small comb and a little vial of perfume. She never knew when the opportunity might arise to jot down an interesting comment or an idea that demanded pursuing.

She made a little moue at herself in the mirror. *Face it, my girl. You're as close to a bluestocking as a woman can get without actually being one.*

It was with that rather depressing thought still in her mind that Abby and her aunt arrived at the Greenhough's town house, their carriage waiting patiently for its turn to disgorge its passengers into the capable hands of the Greenhough's butler.

The home itself was lovely, decided Abby, elegant, fashionable, yet possessing a touch of something indefinable that made it a home.

And after meeting Lady Rachel, it was clear that she herself was the touch.

"Welcome, Lady Foxworth, Miss Foxworth. I'm so glad you could join us this evening. My husband's around here somewhere..." She glanced off distracted. "Drat the man. Never manages to get the idea of where he should be and when."

The happy smile that accompanied these words took the sting out of them and Abby smiled back. "Thank you so much for inviting us this evening. I am looking forward to the lecture."

Lady Rachel grinned. "I'm glad you are, Miss Foxworth. Because unfortunately, no matter how I tried to convince him otherwise, a *lecture* is certainly what it will be."

"Him?" inquired Eugenia politely, giving Abby an unwelcome nudge with her sharp little elbow.

Abby sighed.

Lady Rachel chuckled. "My brother, Ma'am. Philip Ashton. He's our lecturer for this evening. I can only apologize in advance if his discourse should bore you into oblivion. I love him, of course, but such a dull dog. Buries himself in the country all alone with his experiments and that sort of nonsense. I had to verily drag him by his coattails to participate this evening."

"How did you convince him, Lady Rachel?" asked Abby, more from a desire to be polite than a desire to learn the answer.

"I told him I'd come down and personally blow up his laboratory. And since I nearly did once before when we were little, he took my threat *very* seriously."

Abby and Eugenia both laughed at this frank statement.

"But I must greet more guests, and let you ladies take your seats. If you'll follow Matcham?"

Taking their leave of their hostess, Abby and Eugenia dutifully marched behind the stout butler and found themselves seated in a large room, which probably functioned as a ballroom on other, more formal, occasions.

Tonight, however, lines of chairs had been assembled, much as for a musicale, but there were no instruments in sight, just a raised dais.

They allowed Matcham to seat them front and center, and chatted quietly as the rest of the room filled up with whispering, laughing, talking guests.

"I don't think I've ever seen Sir Philip Ashton in town," whispered Eugenia to Abby, under cover of the general conversation. "But I'm almost positive he's single."

Once more, Abby sighed, praying for patience, and she returned some inoffensive comment. Hopefully this wouldn't be one more name added to her aunt's long list of potential husbands for her.

Eventually, the doors were closed and a servant went around the room extinguishing many of the candles, leaving only those that illuminated the dais.

Abby felt a shiver up her spine as the room was plunged into mysterious shadows.

Then a man stepped from those shadows and mounted the dais.

He was uncommonly tall, dressed unfashionably but well, had overlong dark hair tied back behind his neck, and what appeared to be a fine pair of legs beneath smart evening breeches.

Abby looked up from her assessment of him, and met his eyes.

Her world stopped dead.

Chapter 2

The tall man was cursing fluidly at his third attempt to tie his cravat in some sort of acceptable style.

"Here, lad, let me do that for you." The informal comment came from the graying valet folding clothes neatly in the suite in the Greenhough's town house that was presently being occupied by Sir Philip Ashton.

Philip surrendered the chore with relief. "What the hell would I do without you, Fred?" he grinned.

"Like as not you'd have found yourself a wife to take care of this for you," answered the man wryly.

"Oh no, not you too." Philip tipped his head back as Fred's nimble fingers folded, tweaked and tugged on the cravat. "I've had quite enough of that from Rachel, thank you very much."

"And Lady Rachel's in the right of it. You know very well it's time you thought about settling down."

Philip snorted and straightened himself, glancing in the mirror at the now-respectably tied fabric beneath his chin. "We've been through this *ad nauseum*, Fred. I *am* settled. I *am* content. I have Sally in the village to take care of any...needs I may have..."

"Yes. And damn near ruined her for the rest of the lads, you have. All that nonsense about having a woman for pleasure, and then making sure *she* gets her jollies out of it, too."

"Look, I did try to explain it all to them. Don't you remember the time I spent trying to tell those dimwits that there was more to a woman's body than just her...just her..."

"Her cunt? Yes, lad. And damned embarrassing it was, too. I couldn't nip down for a pint for two weeks after that. Shocked the hair clean off half of them, you did."

Philip frowned. "But it was only fair, Fred. And it adds to one's own pleasure too, you know."

"I'll take your word for it. And you haven't even been down to Sally's since I don't remember when. No, it's time for you to find the real thing, Sir Philip."

When Fred assumed his sternest face, Philip knew it was time to throw in the towel and admit himself defeated. The problem with having a valet who'd known him since he was three was that there was no chance at all of winning an argument with him.

"Look," said Fred, obviously taking pity on him. "Go downstairs, put on your show with your mezzy-whatsit, do the pretty with the guests, and then we can go home. Lady Rachel's happy, you're on your way out of town, and your laboratory is still, hopefully, intact and spared a visit from your sister."

Philip sighed.

He loved his home and his scientific experiments almost more than life itself, but deep down inside, he was forced to admit that there *was* something missing. He couldn't share the thrill of a new discovery with anyone, even though Fred tried hard to be supportive.

His bed was cold at night, and although he had his hand for company and Sally, the good-hearted whore, for when his needs got *really* bad, it wasn't enough. There had to be something more, something…someone…

He shrugged and nodded. "You win, Fred. I'll suffer through tonight. Though damn it, if Rachel parades a stream of giggling idiots in front of my face afterwards, I'll hold you responsible and tell them where you're sleeping, instead of me."

Fred chuckled. "Well, now, Sir Philip. I'd not be adverse to that idea…"

"You're a terror, Fred. Don't wait up for me. God knows how long this will take, and I'm sure you've already got an eye on some buxom maid or another."

Fred had the grace to blush.

* * * * *

Philip stood behind the curtains that opened onto the dais in his sister's ballroom and felt decidedly silly.

All these theatrics were sure to deter from the scientific discussion he was about to present. But damn it, he was doing it for Rachel, and she'd decided that the occasion warranted all this hoopla.

He wasn't even an expert mesmerist, for heaven's sake. He'd read Dr. Mesmer's work, even glanced at Father Hell's contributions, and dismissed the cleric's magnetism association completely. Magnetism was an area that fascinated him, but not in connection with mesmerism.

He'd had some small successes, helping a stable boy deal with the pain of a broken leg by just talking to him softly, drawing the crying lad's focus away from his injury and onto himself, as he'd let a small pocket watch swing slowly to and fro in front of the boy's eyes.

It had worked, and he'd had other occasions to practice the same sort of thing. But he doubted that he'd exercised any kind of control over anyone's mind. That was *way* beyond his abilities.

The light behind the curtains was dimming, and that, he knew, was the signal for him to step through and commence his presentation.

Drawing a deep breath and releasing it slowly, he calmed his mind and pushed the curtains aside.

Dazzled for a moment by the remaining candles, he received an impression of thousands of faces staring at him, and his heart missed a beat.

Then his eyesight cleared, and he saw it was merely a few dozen, the jewels of the women glittering as the soft light glanced from their finery. His lip tried very hard not to curl as he acknowledged that this would *not* be a scientifically oriented evening.

Rachel had been right. Theatrics were definitely in order.

With an inner sigh, he moved into the light and casually glanced around. His gaze halted at the front row, and his heart thumped. Once.

Loudly.

A pair of extraordinary green eyes met his.

And the breath left his body.

* * * * *

Abigail stared.

His eyes. His eyes, some kind of odd blend of blue and gold, were devouring her. There was no other word for it.

She forgot where she was, who she was, and every little thought in her brain lay down and went to sleep.

Her mind blanked.

Dear God. *Now* she had flutters in her belly, and the man was three or more feet away from her. What on earth would happen if he touched her?

It seemed like years before he dragged his gaze away and began his presentation, but for Abby, the damage was done.

She wanted him. Wanted, in her grandmother's inappropriate words, to lie down, toss up her skirts and spread her thighs for him.

She shivered.

"Are you chilly, dear?" asked Eugenia, leaning over and whispering softly in her niece's ear.

Cold? She'd never been hotter in her life.

She just shook her head a little at her aunt, anxious not to miss a word of his lecture.

He spoke fluidly and effortlessly, his deep voice casting a spell over his audience, most of whom had come simply out of curiosity. Within a few minutes, however, Abby and the rest of the crowd were hanging on his every word.

He touched on the history of mesmerism, the theories behind it, both pro and con, the confusion that surrounded its practice, and the realistic results of experiments that had been performed using the various techniques involved.

Abby tried hard to focus, to concentrate on the science he was expounding, but for once in her life, failed dismally.

All she could think of was the pounding of her heart and the growing dampness between her thighs as his eyes brushed hers.

And they seemed to do that a *lot*.

As the first part of the lecture concluded, he stepped forward and smiled, and Abby blinked. His smile lightened his harsh features and made her want to smile back. And get very naked, very quickly.

Her nipples were hard against her bodice and she could feel them rubbing the fabric with every breath. She wondered if they'd actually pop out, just so that they could have a look at this man too. She wasn't even sure if she'd mind. Perhaps he'd do something about it if they did.

Like cover them with his hands — or even better, with his mouth. Pulling her softness between those full, sensuous lips of his.

She squirmed, surprised to note that there was now some laughter and conversation around her.

Apparently, Sir Philip was calling for a volunteer to help him in a little "demonstration" of mesmerism.

A gentleman from the back of the room called out. "If you can rid me of this plaguey gout, Sir Philip, I'll be your biggest supporter…"

A general laugh rang across the room and Philip smiled once more, doing increasingly dreadful things to Abby's pulse rate.

"Well, step up, Sir, and let's see what can be done for you," he replied.

A portly gentleman limped and lumbered his way onto the dais, and Philip Ashton arranged a comfortable chair for him, seating him so that he was half-facing the audience.

Silence fell, as Philip produced a fob from his pocket and let it dangle freely from his fingers.

"Now, Sir," he said calmly. "Simply allow your eyes to follow the movement of this fob, and listen to my voice."

Philip spoke smoothly and softly and the man's eyes glazed over slightly as the fob swung in a rhythmic pattern before his face.

Abby found herself watching closely too. Taking in Philip's movements, his quiet tones, the way he relaxed his patient and allowed the man's focus to center on the fob and Philip's voice, nothing else.

It was fascinating, especially to one whose mind was always open to new ideas and thoughts.

So why on earth was she wondering about what hid behind his breeches? She snorted mentally at herself, and followed that with a good swift kick to the brain. She needed to get back into herself, and fast. She *must* stop being some silly ninny who had been struck dumb by a pair of fine eyes.

"You are feeling relaxed, Sir Arthur," murmured Philip, and indeed the man seemed to unroll his erect spine and lean back into the chair. "Any pain you have been experiencing will ease, and your foot will begin to feel warm as the discomfort departs."

He glanced around at the audience, as if asking them to share in this moment. "Do you feel the warmth?"

"I do, lad. 'Tis incredible," answered the man, smiling slightly.

"Excellent." Philip paused for a moment and addressed the crowd. "As you can see, ladies and gentlemen, Sir Arthur is quite conscious, and able to respond to all my questions. I have simply suggested to him that his pain is lessening. I have not cured his condition, but focused his thoughts away from it, and onto my voice."

Abby found herself nodding in agreement. Once more she felt that strange thrill as his eyes glanced over at her.

A small smile crossed his face, then was gone in an instant as he turned back to Sir Arthur.

"Now, Sir, I am going to ask you to promise that you'll forgo your after-dinner port, and stick with wine from now on. In fact, the mere smell of port will make you feel nauseous. In addition, you will feel more like getting out into the fresh air, perhaps a carriage ride at first, and then a stroll, and then maybe a nice ride on some of those fine horses I understand are eating themselves to death in your stables from lack of exercise."

Another laugh rippled through the crowd.

Sir Arthur merely smiled. "What a good idea," he said.

"If Sir Philip can make him do that, it will be a God-given miracle," came a woman's voice from the back of the room. Clearly it was Sir Arthur's long-suffering wife.

Philip merely nodded in her direction and returned his attention once again to his patient. "Now, Sir Arthur, I am going to ask you to count backwards from ten. When you reach one, you will no longer be focused on me, but will feel refreshed, comfortable, and ready to proceed with your life—your *healthier* life, and ready to follow my suggestions."

"If Sir Philip can get him to make it all the way to one, backwards, *that* will be a God-given miracle," called a wag from the crowd, to everyone's enormous amusement.

But sure enough, Sir Arthur made it, hesitating slightly between five and four, but eventually reaching one, and blinking around him, a slow smile spreading across his chubby features.

"Demmed if the pain ain't gone."

He rose and shook Philip's hand boisterously. "Thank you, Sir Philip, thank you," he said effusively, grinning now.

Philip smiled and helped him off the dais.

"How about a glass of port, Sir Arthur?" Someone called out a challenge from the crowd.

Sir Arthur blanched. "For some reason, can't stomach the thought of that right now," he called back.

Applause broke out, and Abby's mind jerked back into itself at the noise.

Sir Philip stood, looking smug, on the dais, and once again running his eyes over her.

Damn him. Couldn't he look at *anyone* else? She was suddenly struck with the unusual urge to slaughter any other woman who might receive that look, and she shook her head at herself.

"Now, ladies and gentlemen, you've seen the serious side of mesmerism, and how it can help overcome some instances of discomfort, and even help people on the road to their recovery from an ailment. Perhaps we should conclude with another small demonstration, but this time, just a simple re-shifting of the thought processes."

He strolled around the stage, stroking his chin, apparently deep in thought.

The audience was still now, waiting for his next move. He snapped his fingers, and at least twelve people jumped.

"I have it. The very thing. But I will require an assistant. A volunteer. Perhaps…perhaps *you*, Ma'am?"

Abby's jaw dropped.

He was holding out his hand and beckoning — *her*.

Chapter 3

Philip had no idea how he kept his hand steady as he held it outstretched to the golden goddess in the front row.

She'd watched him like a hawk the entire time, and yet it had not discomforted him. Well, it had discomforted his cock, true, but her close observation had simply told him that she was interested. *Very* interested.

And so, it seemed, was he. *And* his damn cock, which was thankfully hidden by his rather unstylish jacket.

She rose slowly, after some nudging from the older woman at her side, and extended her hand to his.

Their skin touched, and a flash of awareness shot through Philip like a bolt from one of his electricity machines.

He hid the gasp that the feel of her hand brought to his lungs with difficulty, and helped her step up onto the dais. "Your name, Ma'am?"

She blinked for a second, then answered. "Abigail Foxworth. *Miss* Abigail Foxworth."

Her green eyes were telling him thousands of things, and his body was responding to every single one. She was tall, the perfect height for him. Her head would nestle comfortably onto his shoulder, and his balls would nestle equally comfortably between those long soft thighs of hers that her dress was so softly delineating.

He jerked his mind back into place, stunned anew by his intense reaction to this woman. "Very well. Thank you for agreeing to assist me, Miss Abigail Foxworth. If you'd be seated?"

He helped her to the chair, allowing himself the pleasure of brushing her shoulders with his hand as he led her across the dais, and smiling as he noticed the hard nipples pushing at the soft silk of her bodice.

It was an effort to refocus on what he was supposed to be doing and not her breasts. Very fine breasts though they were.

Just perfect breasts, actually. He allowed himself the brief thought of what they'd look like — taste like…

She was staring at him now, a slight frown wrinkling her brow. "What shall I do, Sir Philip?"

Get naked. Now.

Philip recalled himself and bit down hard on his lip, allowing the small pain to remind him of where he was and what he was supposed to be doing. Lusting after Abigail Foxworth hadn't been part of the evening's scheduled program.

He pulled his shredded wits back into some kind of order.

"Well, Miss Foxworth, please keep your attention focused on my fob here, and my voice. Just as Sir Arthur did."

He produced his fob, and again swung it slowly to and fro.

She seemed to have difficulty removing her gaze from his eyes, but eventually she turned her head to the fob and he launched into his routine that would relax her and allow him entrance into her mind.

And perhaps her body too, whispered an irrepressible urge. He ignored it.

"Now, Miss Foxworth. Are you quite comfortable?"

She smiled a little, bringing beads of sweat to his brow, and nodded. "Yes thank you, Sir Philip," she answered coolly.

"Good. I think for the purposes of our little demonstration, we'll travel back in time a bit."

A mutter traversed the audience which leaned forward, entranced at the sight of the tall man and the lovely golden-clad woman, now apparently under his spell.

"It is the great age of Elizabeth," said Philip, "and *you* are the Virgin Queen herself."

His words dropped into the silence, softly, seductively, bringing a sigh to many of the women present.

"I am Walter Raleigh, your devoted subject, and I have just returned from a successful voyage to lay its spoils at your feet." He risked a quick grin at the crowd. They were nodding and murmuring their approval.

"What say you, Your Majesty?"

Abigail straightened in her chair and quirked an eyebrow at him. "So, Walter Raleigh. We're informed that you bring treasures to your Sovereign."

The crowd sighed, a hushed and fascinated sound.

"I do indeed, Your Majesty. All that I have is yours."

"And England's, of course." Abby's voice firmed in a small reprimand.

"Of course, my Queen."

"Well now, Walter Raleigh. We are most pleased at your tribute, but distressed at your apparent habit of 'finding' such treasures deep in the holds of certain galleons. Ones that belong to our noble friend, King Philip of Spain."

Philip allowed a grin to cross his features. Damn, this woman was good.

"Thoughts of pleasing Your Majesty must outweigh our natural caution," he bowed elegantly. "It was our hope that King Philip might not miss such a paltry sum, especially since he woos our own fair Queen. And our little tribute pales in comparison to *that* particular treasure."

Abigail smiled royally, every inch the willful monarch she was supposed to be. "Well, we must needs take counsel on this matter. My Lord Burleigh..." She beckoned to the space at her side, and bent her head as if listening to an invisible conversation.

Then she snapped her head back up and fixed Philip with a firm look. "Burleigh has the right of it. We cannot reward you for theft and piracy. We *can*, however, reward you for your pretty phrases to our person. Kneel, Walter Raleigh."

And Philip knelt close, swimming in her fragrance and praying he didn't topple over into a pile of screaming lust, as she knighted him with an imaginary sword.

"Rise, Sir Walter Raleigh. Do your best for England. And your Queen, of course."

Applause rang out across the room, as "Sir Walter" rose from his knees and gently raised Abby's hand to his lips in homage.

He could no more have stopped himself from pressing a hot kiss to her skin than he could have stopped breathing. He wondered if his lips were singed.

He recalled himself with difficulty. "Now, Miss Foxworth, please count backwards from ten. When you reach one, you will rise, curtsey to the audience, and feel relaxed and refreshed."

He moved behind her chair, momentarily out of sight of the audience, as he settled her once again.

"And you will find some excuse to stay after this lecture is concluded. Seek me out, Abigail. Come to me."

The instruction was low, whispered so that none but she could hear it.

For once, Philip Ashton found himself praying that he did, in fact, possess the power of mesmerism.

Because *never* had he needed to be alone with a woman more than he did right this second.

✳ ✳ ✳ ✳ ✳

Abigail and Eugenia circulated as the guests chattered amongst themselves and enjoyed the ample refreshments set out by Lady Rachel Greenhough.

A casual word here, a laugh there, a compliment to "Her Majesty", all handled with Abigail's usual grace, elegance and wit.

While her mind boiled.

Philip Ashton. She rolled his name over and over, silently, as she bit into a lobster patty.

His eyes, his body, his height, and above all, his mind, had called to her on some primitive level, and awoken a desire within her that would have made her faint if she'd been the sort of woman who did such a thing.

But she wasn't, and she managed to keep her end of several conversations going even while her agile thoughts darted this way and that, turning over the evening, dissecting it, and coming to the one inevitable conclusion.

She wanted that time alone with him.

Did he know she'd not succumbed to his powers? Had he guessed she'd faked the whole thing, and blessed her lucky stars she was well read enough to carry off the role of Good Queen Bess without a falter?

Part of her hoped so, and another part hoped not. *That* part was about to become a dissembling, dishonest creature and lie through its even white teeth to her aunt. It was a part that was going to use her apparent "trance" as an excuse to seek him out. To be with him.

To see if what she'd felt from a distance was better close up. *Very* close up.

"Abby, you look pale, dear. Should we call for our carriage?" Eugenia came up to her.

God, no.

Abby thought fast. "Actually, Aunt Eugenia, I had promised to have a quick chat with the Rutherfords about their electrical experiments. Would you allow them to take me home afterwards? I know you wanted to drop in at the Morton's soiree, and I also know—" She grinned at her aunt as she leaned closer to the woman. "Colonel Dagenham will be in attendance. He particularly asked if you'd be there this evening."

Eugenia blushed. "Well...if you're sure?"

"I'll see she gets home safely," said a voice behind Abby.

Lady Rachel Greenhough was smiling innocently at the two of them. "If the Rutherfords are unable to drop her off, I'll send her in my own carriage, Lady Foxworth. It's a pleasure to see a young woman interested in the sciences. So few are, these days, don't you agree?"

Abby quirked a brow at her.

"Trust me, Miss Abigail, between my father and my brothers, I grew up in a house full of them. Finding anyone who appreciates science is a miracle in itself. For a lovely young woman to want to talk about it is even more rare. How can I deny you the chance?"

Abby wanted to fall at Lady Rachel's feet and kiss her toes in gratitude. However, she simply smiled.

"I suppose that's all right then, Abby. Just make sure you get home safely, and not too late, mind," nodded Eugenia.

The crowd was thinning now, as many left for other engagements, and the social world that was London during the Season.

Abby looked around. Her eyes found Sir Philip.

As his eyes found her.

He stood next to a small passageway, and with a little smile he turned and allowed the darkness to swallow him up.

The message was clear. She was to follow.

Lady Rachel was elsewhere saying farewell to her guests, and there was no one to see her as she slipped into the shadows and followed Philip.

A door stood ajar, and firelight flickered from within.

Tentatively she placed her hand on the wood and pushed slightly, finding herself in a study, where the lamps were low, and a cheerful fire was blazing.

Sir Philip stood by the mantel, waiting.

Her heart thumped loudly, as she entered, and in response to some strange urge, closed the door behind her.

They were finally alone.

Chapter 4

Philip held his breath as she glided towards him, glowing in the firelight. Her hair flashed brilliant bronze sparks, her gown gleamed as it caressed her lithe body, and her eyes...

Outshining the emerald at her neck, her eyes did incredibly wonderful things to his loins.

With difficulty, Philip suppressed a shudder of lust.

"Greetings, Sir Walter," she said in a low husky voice that also did wonderful things to his loins.

If she did anything more wonderful to his loins, the damn things were going to go off like one of Whinyates's rockets.

But she'd called him Sir Walter. Could it be possible that she was still suffering the delusion that she was Elizabeth?

He decided to find out.

"Kiss me, your Majesty," he asked, hoping that it didn't come out like the needy whine it most certainly was.

Unhesitatingly she crossed the room, reached up and placed her lips on his cheek in a brief embrace.

He winced. "Not like a subject, my Queen. Like a lover."

She looked puzzled. "I have had no lovers, Sir Walter. I am known as the Virgin Queen."

"Then pretend, Lady. Pretend," he growled, sliding his hands around her waist and pulling her body against his.

She thought for a moment, then slipped her hands around his neck.

Her arms tightened and she pulled his face to hers.

With a groan, he lowered his lips, capturing hers with a fierce heat that shattered any preconceived notions he might have had about such a simple thing as a kiss.

He tasted her as she opened her mouth beneath his questing tongue, thrusting it inside and giving way to the rush of desire that flooded him. She tasted of wine and lobster patty and honey, and he couldn't get enough.

And she was kissing him back with all the passion and enthusiasm he could have wanted.

His hands roved freely, encouraged by her body which molded itself to his, dips and valleys meeting and greeting each other like long lost friends.

Within seconds he had her buttocks in his grasp and tugged her hard against his cock, finding her hot mound burning him through their clothes.

They were both gasping for breath when he eased back and gazed at her eyes, unfocused and nearly black with her emotions.

"You taste of magic, my Queen," he whispered, licking his lips and tasting her again.

"Oh Sir, I want…" she said softly.

"What do you want?" he asked.

She rubbed her hips against his in a wanton movement that had him clenching his teeth against another hot rush through his body.

"I don't know what I want," she moaned.

"Show me your breasts, Abigail…" The words were out before he could stop them, coming from some inner place where a fire was blazing and needs overrode everything else.

He stood back and shrugged out of his jacket, ripping off his cravat and popping buttons on his shirt as he bared his own chest. "I want to feel them against me when I kiss you again."

With a little tremor, her hands went to her gown and stayed for a moment at her neckline. Philip Ashton held his breath and prayed.

Slowly, she eased the small sleeves off her shoulders, and lowered her bodice, letting her breasts spring free of their covering. She lowered the gown to her waist and stood there, a goddess with cheeks on fire and the loveliest breasts he'd ever seen bared to his eyes.

He groaned and seized her again, covering them with his own hot flesh.

Her nipples dug into his body, and seared him as his mouth claimed hers once again.

They both moaned at the contact, and the kiss turned savage, a needy and hungry thing that pleased them yet left them wanting.

Philip's hands stroked her bare back, marveling at the hot silky feel of her naked skin beneath his touch.

He couldn't remember ever desiring a woman more.

But he knew that this was only the beginning. His cock was painful now, thrusting against his breeches and screaming at him to do something, anything, to relieve its need.

His mouth roamed over her neck and dotted hot kisses down her throat. He continued on, encouraged by her sighs and the fact that she'd tossed her head back to permit him access to her skin.

He found her breast and unhesitatingly suckled it deeply into his mouth, toying with the rigid bead that topped it and laving it strongly with his tongue.

She groaned and thrust her hips against his, grinding them now, as if her need matched his.

Philip Ashton drowned.

As did Abigail.

This wondrous sensation of having her breasts worshipped by the man she'd desired from the first moment their eyes met was rendering Abby senseless.

It had taken a monumental amount of courage to lower her gown before him, and only the incredible heat burning from his eyes had given her the strength she'd needed.

Now, she was simply ecstatic that she had obeyed his outrageous command and revealed herself to him.

The crush of his flesh against hers was a thing to be wondered at—sometime later when her wits returned. For now, she was just going to relish his attentions, like *that* one, right *there*, and try to remain standing, when all her intuitions were screaming at her to topple him into the fireplace and savage him with her body. Somehow. She was hazy about the details, but the drive was overwhelming.

After long minutes or possibly several eons of being devoured by his wonderful mouth, she felt cold air brush her skin as he pulled away.

Cautiously she opened her eyes and looked at him.

His cheeks were flushed darkly, his hair mussed, and his shirt framed his magnificent chest which was lightly furred with whorls of soft black hair.

"Raise your skirt for me, Abigail," he rasped.

She stared at his eyes, their irises huge, the gold and blue flecks striking sparks within her.

"Raise your skirts," he repeated, his voice hoarse and flooding her with a river of desire.

Oh God. She wanted to. She'd *never* wanted to anything as much as she wanted to lift her hem. Right this second.

A voice of caution rang in her ears, only to be shouted down by the thought of her Grandmother's words. *"And if she does, well then, it's the right man."*

She grasped a handful of fabric and tugged.

Philip was the right man.

The soft stuff slid easily up over her thighs as she bunched her skirts in her hands. She felt her cheeks heat as his gaze dropped to what she was so readily revealing to him.

The brush of the cool air against her skin made her tremble, but she did not stop until her gown was a mere buckled band at her waist.

She found she could not meet his gaze and lowered her eyes.

"Look at me, Abigail," he said, raising her chin with one hand. "Look at me. See how I burn for you. You are so beautiful..."

He claimed her in a kiss once again, but this time he plunged his hand between them, searching her belly, rubbing her thighs and sliding his hand lower until it was between her legs.

She felt him ruffle the triangle of hair he found there and dip lower, seeking, spreading, rubbing her soft wet mound until she was whimpering in his arms.

He slicked her wetness over her skin, and part of her mind wondered at her own body's response to his touch.

Then he suddenly left her lips and dropped to one knee in front of her.

What he did next took every ounce of air from her lungs.

He pressed his hot mouth to her body — *there*.

Her scent, her heat and the fragrance of her juices intoxicated Philip. He wanted to dive headfirst into her cunt and never come out.

Or come, and then come out. Or something.

He had no idea. He just had to get his mouth on her and hopefully drive her to the point of madness that he himself had reached moments ago.

And her moans and cries of pleasure told him he was getting there.

He slid his hands up past her stockings to the back of her naked thighs, and found the smooth curves of her buttocks.

He noted they filled his hands perfectly, and he pulled her slightly, so that his tongue could do what it had apparently been designed to do from the day he was born.

Pleasure Abigail.

He thrust into her softness, again and again, feeling the tremors as they rattled her body.

Then he searched for her little clit, hard and aroused now, and just begging for its share of his attention.

He obliged, noting with satisfaction how she cried out as he stroked and suckled the little bud of flesh into his mouth.

Her hands tugged his hair almost painfully, but he doubted she even realized what she was doing. He certainly didn't care. She could have every strand if she wanted, as long as he could spend his lifetime buried between her thighs.

The thought shocked him, warmed him, and sent a flood of heat to his cock, reminding him that the pain she was inflicting on his scalp was nothing next to the pain emanating from his breeches.

He pulled back, hearing her sob as his face left her cunt.

"Philip, Philip," she moaned.

"I know, Abigail. I know. Yet I cannot take you here, now, much as I would like to."

Her eyes fluttered open in distress.

"Hush, Abby," he said, dropping his hand to his breeches and unfastening their tapes.

His cock sprang free, and if it could have sighed with relief, Philip swore it would have. "There are other ways," he said, his voice choking with his need to claim her.

He pulled their bodies together, and pressed his cock against her heat, sliding it back then raising her body slightly. Pushing himself between the juncture of her thighs, each movement rubbed the already swollen and sensitive tissues he knew were there.

"Let go, Abby. Feel my cock stroking you. I can't be inside you, but this is the next best thing."

Well, almost. Perhaps her mouth on him would be good too. Or then again…

Philip's mind galloped off into a myriad of ways he wanted to take this woman.

But then she moved against his cock and his mind blanked out completely. She rubbed herself along his hardness, hips thrusting, meeting his with a barely controlled movement.

It was ecstasy, exquisite and painful ecstasy, and it wasn't enough.

Philip wanted to be inside her, deep inside her, feeling her cunt tug at him, hold him, pull him further and further until they didn't know where one ended and the other began.

But it could not be. Not in his sister's house. Not in the study. And certainly not while they were standing up.

Well, not this time, anyway.

Philip let her body seduce his, and gently matched her movements, sliding his rigid length across her opening, and tugging on her breasts with his fingers as his lips devoured hers.

Incredibly, it seemed that it was enough for both of them. For now.

He felt her shiver and shudder, and she struggled for breath in his arms. Her whole body tightened, just as he felt his balls harden and lightning dance down his spine.

They exploded together.

Abby shook under the force of her orgasm, held upright only by his strong arms.

His cock throbbed and pulsed as he came, spurting his seed over her inner thighs and mixing his own come with her juices.

Someone cried out, but for the life of him, Philip had no idea which of them it was.

It could well have been both.

Rocked by his orgasm, Philip leaned his forehead against hers, and stroked her damp skin lovingly as their heart rates slowed at last.

Incredibly, they were still standing in front of his sister's fireplace. Weak and panting, but still standing.

It had been the most amazingly erotic experience of his entire life.

He dropped light kisses on the shivering woman in his arms and gently eased her bodice back into place, sighing as her breasts with their now-softened nipples disappeared beneath the gold silk.

He cupped her face, and spoke the first words that came into his mind.

"Marry me, Abby."

Chapter 5

Philip's words acted on Abby like a douche of ice-cold water, and she dropped her rumpled skirts to the floor.

"No. No. A thousand times no."

Her body, of course, screamed *yes, yes, anytime. Right now would be good, in fact.*

She stiffened under his gaze, watching as he refastened his breeches, a look of puzzlement on his face.

"Why not? There is great pleasure to be had for both of us, Abigail," he said gently.

"*That's* why not, Philip. You called me "Abby". Several times in fact. And I called you Philip, and you never batted an eyelash. You knew I wasn't under any kind of mesmeric spell, yet you used it as an excuse to get me in here."

Her conscience rose up and shook a finger at her. Hadn't she done the very same thing?

She blushed. "And yes, I did the same thing." Her conscience nodded approvingly. "I wouldn't have let you…um…all right, *encouraged* you to do those things if I hadn't wanted to. *But…*"

"But?" he asked, crossing the small distance between them.

"But," she said firmly, backing away and holding out a hand to stave him off. She couldn't let him touch her again. That way led to trouble. Very *nice* trouble, but still trouble.

"I'm not looking for a husband. And even if I was, there would need to be more than just a few moments of…intimate contact."

"Oh there is more, Abigail. Much more. Hours, if not days, of intimate contact."

Abby's eyes crossed at his sensual purr, and it took a few moments to get her thoughts back onto their original track.

"Be that as it may. The fact remains that I don't know you, Philip Ashton. The real you. The person behind the hands, and the lips and the…" She waved her hand at his breeches. "I am *not* looking for a husband."

"You repeat yourself. Perhaps you should ask yourself who you're trying to convince."

Abby gritted her teeth. "I would like to go home now."

Philip's expression hardened and he refastened his shirt. "Oh, I see. You've had your fun at the expense of the country bumpkin, and decided the eccentric Philip Ashton is not good enough for Miss Abigail Foxworth?"

"That's not it at all. You misunderstand."

Philip's eyes held hers, fire flashing from their depths. "Really? What am I to think? You come in here of your own accord, let me bring you pleasure, respond wildly, wildly — make no mistake — and then turn down my quite respectable offer of marriage. What the hell am I supposed to think?"

He frowned now, an angry twist to his lips. "Or am I out-of-date in town ways? Is this what you do with any man who catches your interest?"

Abby crossed the room in two strides and swung her arm, landing a solid slap across his face.

She gasped at herself. *Never* had she let go of her emotions like that before.

The imprint of her palm reddened his cheek.

He backed away, a blend of confusion and pain in his eyes.

Abby was horrified at herself, and choked back a sob. "I…I think I'd best leave."

"I'll see you to your carriage."

The words were abrupt and tore at her already-shattered heart.

Before she knew it, she was tucked into Lady Rachel's carriage and looking out the window at Philip, who stood in the doorway watching her depart.

She leaned back against the squabs as the horses picked up their gait and carried her away from him.

From the first man who had ever touched her soul.

The tears gathered in her eyes and fell unchecked down her cheeks as she felt the stickiness between her thighs and the ache around her heart.

She could never marry Philip Ashton. It would be much too easy to fall in love with him.

If she hadn't already.

* * * * *

"You look like you could use a brandy," said an amused voice behind Philip as he slowly shut the door on the night.

His breath whooshed out of his lungs. "I'm not the best company right now, Rach," he growled.

His sister giggled. "My goodness, she made an impression, didn't she?" Her glance took in his disheveled clothing and the fading mark on his face. "Of more than one kind, too."

He glared at her.

Rachel took pity on him. "Come on, big brother. Let's share a drink—if you promise not to tell George on me, I'll have one as well."

She tucked her arm through Philip's and led him firmly into her small parlor, where a book lay open on a desk and a fire burned merrily.

"Were you waiting up for me, Rachel?" he grunted accusingly.

"Of course. I had to make sure that Miss Foxworth got home safely. I did promise her aunt that I would, you know."

Rachel crossed to a sideboard and fussed with the decanter, pouring two healthy glasses of brandy and passing one over to her brother.

His mind rambled as he swirled the amber liquid around in his glass and let the fumes seep up his nose into his muddled brain.

"I asked her to marry me, Rach," he said quietly.

Rachel hissed a breath out through her lips. "You *did*?"

"Yes. She turned me down flat."

Rachel chewed that comment over for a few moments, sipping her drink and settling herself more comfortably into her chair. "Did she tell you why?"

"Some nonsense about not looking for a husband. About not knowing me, as if after what we'd done..." He stopped short, realizing that those things were best not spoken to his sister.

"Philip." Rachel sat up in her chair. "You didn't—you didn't *deflower* her, did you?"

Philip snorted. "I'm starting to wonder if she's got any *flower* left." He gazed moodily into his glass. "She was fire in my arms, Rach. Burning, seething fire. Then suddenly, she's a proper miss, telling me she doesn't know me well enough and turning my honorable proposal of marriage down like it was a load of yesterday's fish."

Rachel suppressed a snicker. "Reeeally." The word drawled from her smiling mouth.

Philip rose and paced the room. "Yes, *really*. I've never touched...um...I've never ki...damn it, Rach, you know what I'm trying to say here. Something special happened between the two of us in your study tonight, and apparently it meant more to me than it did her."

He frowned mightily.

"Oh, I doubt it, brother. I really doubt it."

He glanced up at her. "Why? She allowed me the liberty of taking her in my arms, of—of—kissing her, and—*stuff*, and then she marches out of here when I make the obvious suggestion. What else am I supposed to think?"

He was whining. He knew it, and he couldn't stop himself.

He raised his glass to his lips and caught a hint of the scent of Abby's body that still lingered on his hand.

He shuddered all over again as he recalled her coming apart as she reached her peak.

He let the feelings sweep through him, closing his eyes against the still-aroused fierceness of his desire for the brazen goddess who'd succumbed so willingly to his touch.

And his mouth, and his hands.

He sat down abruptly, as his cock stirred once more at the memory.

Rachel was watching him. "How much do you know about Abigail Foxworth?"

He raised his head. "More than I'd care to share with you, sister mine." His lips curved slightly.

"Not *that* way," snorted Rachel. "I mean, how much do you know about *her*?"

Philip shook his head. "I only met her tonight, you know that. I've never even heard her name before. And yes, before you say it, it's because I'm buried in the country. I know, I know. Consider the nagging discussed and done with, will you? I'm just not in the mood."

Philip glared at his glass, chastising himself for his rudeness. But if one couldn't be rude to one's sister, who could one be rude to?

"Hmm." The sound purred from Rachel, who was looking at him rather smugly over the top of her brandy. "Well, dear brother mine, perhaps you should know a little more about your intended wife."

"Hah."

In spite of his snort, Philip's ears pricked up and he gave in to Rachel's tempting statement. "So what don't I know?"

Rachel grinned. Oh God, he was going to pay for this.

* * * * *

It was a somber and tearstained Abigail that quietly slipped into the Foxworth mansion under cover of the darkness. Fortunately, her aunt had not yet returned from her evening's entertainments, so there was no one to see Abby as she carefully mounted the stairs and sought the sanctuary of her room.

It took but a moment to shed the golden gown and reach for the pitcher of water her maid always left for her.

She'd long ago told her maid not to wait up for her. It was unfair to have the poor woman sit through the dull hours of the night only to rise again at daybreak the next day, and truthfully Abby liked the time alone.

She doused the cloth with the cool water and slipped it over the drying stickiness that still rested between her thighs.

The touch of the cloth against her tissues was heaven and hell. It reminded her of the soft wetness of Philip's mouth as he'd caressed her there, and done such wonderful things to her. She'd never imagined that a man would love her with his mouth like that, or that her whole body would go up in flames when he did.

She sighed, a long shuddering breath, as she rinsed away the last residue of his seed, and her own juices.

Her nightgown was cold and her bed empty.

Her heart, however, was neither.

She slipped between the sheets and lay her head down on her pillow, trying to restore her usual aplomb from the comforting familiarity of her own room, her own belongings, her own *smell*.

But tonight, it was impossible.

She inhaled and could only sense the fragrance of Philip Ashton. Something musky, with a hint of vanilla perhaps, and very male. She closed her eyes, only to have a vision of his wonderful blue and gold irises glittering around inky black pupils, blazing as he'd touched her and brought her to fulfillment.

Without conscious thought, her hand slipped between her thighs and she touched herself *there*, the place he'd found that was so sensitive, so aware, and so damned ready for the touch of his lips.

She shivered once more at the memory.

He'd asked her to marry him. Those words had stunned and terrified her, even as she still shook from the force of the emotions he'd aroused in her.

Her hand moved gently but firmly over her mound, and she pulled her nightgown up and away, freeing her body to the touch of her own hand.

It felt strange, daring, forbidden and yet exciting. Not as good as Philip's mouth, but combined with the memories dancing in her head, enough to once again bring forth a moisture from her body.

Her hand moved of its own volition, seeking out those places that had yielded such an explosive response. Why had she never realized that lovemaking could be so incredibly wonderful?

Her breasts ached, and she turned onto her back, tossing modesty to the winds.

She slid her nightgown all the way up to beneath her chin and brazenly stroked her breasts, finding the nipples hardening again beneath her fingers.

It was lust. Plain and simple lust. It had to be.

She'd been awakened to her body's responses, and she was now exploring them. All it had taken was the touch of a man's body.

So why hadn't it happened before?

Why hadn't any of the men who'd kissed her before made her want to bare herself and plaster herself against them, like a quivering, desperate, lust-filled wanton?

Why had Sir Philip Ashton been the one to rouse the hidden passions inside her?

The thought of Philip made her even wetter, and she found herself panting now, as her hand slid faster and faster over her swollen flesh and her fingers tugged and pinched at her own nipples.

A tingle tightened her buttocks, her muscles trembled and a gasp hovered on her lips.

Once more, an explosion took place inside Abigail Foxworth. She sobbed and moaned with the pleasure of it, body writhing and legs clenching on her own hand as she rode out the waves of orgasm.

Relaxing at last, Abby slid her nightgown back down, and turned over on her side, nestling her face into her pillow and sighing.

It was no good. Her hand was no substitute for his. Her fingers were no substitute for his lips and his tongue.

She had learned a great deal from his lecture and little of it had to do with Mesmerism.

She had learned that she could respond wildly to a touch, desire a man beyond belief, and reach an orgasm without taking his cock inside her.

She trembled.

She'd also learned that she had a heart. And it was aching horribly because she'd *had* to turn him down. She could not conceive of doing anything else.

Hot tears fell into her pillow as Abby tried to hide from her sorrows in sleep.

Chapter 6

The following morning brought rare sunshine, cool breezes and soft scudding clouds over London, and the usual parade of floral tributes to Foxworth House.

Abigail, however, was nowhere near as bright-eyed as the bouquets that arrived in a steady stream. In fact, as her Grandmama acidly remarked, she looked like death-warmed-over.

"Little too much to drink last night, gel?"

Abby raised her head from her teacup and glanced at the old woman across the breakfast table. She managed a rueful grin. "No, just a hard time sleeping. Probably too many lobster patties."

The Dowager's eyes narrowed. "Hmm. Usually when a healthy young woman has a hard time sleeping, there's a man involved."

Abby fought to contain the color she felt sweeping up to her cheeks.

Thankfully, the butler chose that moment to enter, with yet another bouquet of flowers.

Abby glanced at the card and waved him away with a sigh.

"Still a much sought-after young miss, ain't you?"

"Oh Grandmama, it's such a…a…*bloody* nuisance," sighed Abigail.

Grandmama snorted. "Pah, gel. Let them worship you. It's only the ones who'll touch your heart you need be interested in. And it doesn't sound like there's many of those yet, hmm?"

"Only one, Grandmama. Only one." Abby's whisper was almost lost as the long-suffering butler reentered, bearing yet another tissue-wrapped package.

This one, however, was not an enormously colorful arrangement of flowers presented fashionably by some local florist.

With a slight frown, Abby unrolled the tissue, curious now about this unusual offering.

Inside lay a single rose. Brilliant flares of orange and pink dazzled her eyes, and the fragrance was lush and overwhelming. The stem was carefully wrapped and tied with a glittering golden ribbon.

Abby touched it carefully with her finger. "How beautiful," she murmured, entranced by the unusual bloom.

"My," said the Dowager. "*Someone* knows his flowers."

Abby paid no attention, having reached for the sealed letter which accompanied the rose.

She read its contents silently and leaned back, the lace on her gown rising and falling more rapidly than the arrival of a mere rose should warrant.

"Dear Abigail,

Forgive me. I moved too fast last night. Will you give us a chance to get to know each other? To find out more about how we think, what ideas we share? Let me make amends for my behavior?

I do hope so. I shall take the liberty of calling at Foxworth House at eleven, in the hopes that I may persuade you to drive with me today.

Please say yes, Abby. It's my dearest wish to spend time with you, but if the answer is 'no', I shall do my best to respect it. Just send the message back with the delivery boy, and I shall return to the country. Alone. And lonely.

Yrs, Philip

P.S. The rose reminded me of you."

"Well," said the Dowager. "Sounds like this Philip fellow might be an interesting companion."

Abby gasped and snatched the note back from her grandmother, but too late to prevent her from reading it.

"Grandmama. How *could* you? That was private." Abby felt her cheeks color and couldn't quite meet her grandmother's knowing gaze.

"Sweetheart," said the old woman. "Some things are certainly private. But my old eyes tell me that you're far from happy this morning. I want to know why, and this..." she nodded at the note, "gives me a pretty big clue."

Abigail pushed back from the table in the small breakfast salon and did what she always did when uncomfortable. She paced.

"It's from Sir Philip Ashton, Grandmama. I met him last night. He's the one who gave the demonstration and lecture on Mesmerism at Lady Rachel Greenhough's."

"Ah," answered her grandmother, settling in her chair and patiently waiting.

"Ah what?" said Abby, twisting her fingers as she walked.

"*Ah* as in he's the man who's got your corsets in a knot this morning, is he?"

"No. Yes. Perhaps, I don't know."

"Excellent," grinned the Dowager wickedly.

"Excellent? *Excellent*? It's no such thing," retorted Abby. "The man's a dull and boring scientist. He lives permanently in the country messing about with scientific things, according to his sister."

"Ah," said her grandmother again.

"You're repeating yourself, Grandmama," said Abby dryly.

"And I'll do so for as long as I choose, miss, until you say something useful, and stop spouting silliness."

"Silliness? What silliness? What do you want me to say?"

"Oh, let me see. Tell me about him. What he looks like, for example."

Abigail paused, looking out the window but seeing only Philip Ashton. "Well, he's tall. That's one good thing about him."

"The only good thing?" prompted the Dowager.

"Well, no. He does have a fine build to him…"

"That's good. Go on, gel, go on…"

"His hair is dark, Grandmama. Very dark. Like midnight silk. And longer than many wear it these days. It brushes his shoulders. And his skin is a little darker than normal too. As if he spends time outside in the sunshine…"

"I see," mumbled the Dowager softly.

"But the one thing that you can't forget, once you've met him, is his eyes."

"Tell me about them, Abby," said the old woman, leaning back in her chair and watching her granddaughter with an interested gleam.

Abby struggled for words. "They're blue. Well, not exactly blue. More like blue with gold flecks in them. They're like…they're like…sort of like the setting sun as it dances over the waves of a very blue ocean. They're like no eyes I've ever seen…"

Her voice trailed off as a shiver ran over her skin at the memory of those eyes blazing with passion.

The Dowager's harsh cackle interrupted her thoughts. "Well, well, my dear. He sounds like an interesting man."

Abby huffed a wry laugh. "Oh he is that, Grandmama."

"And the problem, then, would be?"

"He's going too fast. Moving too fast. I'm afraid…I'm scared that I'll…"

"Toss up your skirts and spread your thighs for him?"

The quick and inappropriate comment surprised a chuckle out of Abby. "No, not that. I'd rather like *that*, I think."

She blushed. Thankfully, her grandmother didn't. "Well, that's good. So what is it about him that scares you?"

Abby shook her head, unable to answer that question.

"Come here, gel." The Dowager beckoned to Abby who came and knelt by the old woman's chair. "You're not your mother, child."

Abby's face froze. "I…I…"

"Listen to me, Abigail. Women love in different ways, with different amounts of passion, and lust, and desire, and all the mad wildness that goes along with it."

Abby swallowed, hard. A lump had risen in her throat and she found herself incapable of answering.

The Dowager's wrinkled hand caressed Abby's cheek in a loving gesture. "You're a fine and intelligent woman, my girl, your father raised you well."

Abby made as if to speak, but found herself silenced by a cool finger pressed to her lips.

"I'm thinking you'd be wise to give this Philip another chance. For today, lay your memories and worries aside, and just be yourself, the happy, bright, clever woman I know you are. Spend time with him. Learn about him. Put all other thoughts away for the time being. Have some *fun*, Abby."

Abby sighed. Fun. What a novel notion in connection with a man.

"And if he steals a few kisses, so what? Maybe even a touch or two, here or there? Especially *there*…"

A wicked gleam entered the Dowager's eyes, and Abby knew her cheeks were now on fire. "Grandmama, you're outrageous," she giggled, her heart lightening as she realized her decision had been made.

The butler tapped politely on the door. "Will there be any return message, Miss Abigail? The lad's still waiting…"

Abby stood and shook out her skirts. "There will be no return message, Jenkins, thank you. And Sir Philip Ashton will be arriving at eleven to accompany me on a drive. When he gets here, show him into the front parlor, will you?"

"Very good, Miss," said the butler, and withdrew, shutting the door behind him.

"Good girl," said the Dowager, rising slowly from her chair and leaning on her cane. "I'll deal with that ninnyhammer Eugenia. She won't be up until long after you've left, anyway."

She closed the distance between them and dropped a light powdery kiss on her granddaughter's cheek.

"Let the past go, sweetheart. Your present and your future are all that matters now. Find out if Philip is the one you want to share them with. Open your mind and your heart to the possibility. But don't open your legs until you're damned sure."

Abby's laugh rang out, a mixture of shock and amusement. Mostly amusement. "Grandmama, I love you so dearly. I have no idea what I'd do without you."

The old woman smiled. "It's mutual, gel. Now go and pick out your prettiest dress. And make sure it's not too heavily laced, either. Frustration don't look good on a man."

Abby giggled and blushed, and tried to stop her heart from jumping at the visions her grandmother's words had aroused.

She was going driving with Philip Ashton.

And God help her, she couldn't wait.

* * * * *

Philip Ashton's heart thumped loudly as he handed Abigail Foxworth up into his curricle. He hadn't run a mile or carried a heavy load up a long and winding set of stairs, yet he felt just as winded.

The mere sight of her, waiting for him, had been all it took to remove his breath, quicken his pulse, and send a bolt of longing through his breeches.

She wore some filmy gown of cream and green, and her hair was neatly coiled beneath a light bonnet with a broad brim.

He'd have that damned thing off her at the earliest possible moment. He wanted to see her face, her lips, her green eyes laughing at him then turning emerald with desire.

He wanted — he sighed. He wanted Abigail.

And today was a new chance to find out if he could make her want him just as much.

"Thank you," he said to her as he grasped the reins and dismissed his tiger.

"For what, Sir Philip?"

The answer was formal but polite, betraying no hint of what might be going on in this woman's mind.

"For forgiving me. For agreeing to come with me today and enjoy this lovely weather we're having."

He could have kicked himself. The *weather*, for God's sake. He must sound like the veriest idiot.

She chuckled. Well, perhaps she liked idiots. Philip's spirits lifted at the happy sound.

"In truth, Sir Philip, I feel that it is I who owe you an apology."

He risked a glance down beneath the brim of her bonnet to peer at her face. "You do?"

"Indeed I do." She twisted her hands in her lap. Good, she was nervous. She wouldn't be nervous if she didn't feel *anything*.

"I must apologize for losing my temper the way I did. I have never struck a man before, and I do feel quite awful about it," she said quietly.

Philip carefully steered his pair through the traffic and away from the bustle of the city streets as he considered her words. He took a breath. "I forgive *you*."

She turned her head and grinned at him. His guts tightened at the beautiful sight.

"Thank you." Her voice was warm. "Please put it down to the rather confused emotions I was experiencing at the time. I promise it won't happen again."

"Oh, but I'm hoping it will, Abby."

She jerked her face upwards towards him again. "You do? You want me to strike you?"

He laughed. "No, not that. You deliver quite a punch, there. I swear you loosened a few teeth."

She bit her lip against a laugh, obviously not put out by his gentle teasing.

"But I'd like to experience more of those 'confused emotions' you spoke of." He couldn't help his honesty.

She dipped her head, but not before he'd caught a glimpse of the color flying into her cheeks. It would seem that the lady herself might not be averse to the notion of sharing some more experiences. She made no demur, just gazed from the curricle as the city streets turned into country lanes.

"Where are we going?" she finally asked.

"A friend of mine has a small estate not far from here. Augustus James. Ever hear of him?"

Abigail was silent for a moment then nodded. "Yes. He's the man who does some astronomical observations, isn't he?"

Philip smiled. "Indeed he is. It would seem you share my fascination with the sciences, Abby. Not many young women would recognize the name."

Any lingering awkwardness between them rapidly disappeared as their conversation moved into the path of scientific investigation, theories and a lively discussion of the pros and cons of electricity and what it might mean to their futures.

The miles slipped by as the curricle made its way through the sunlit countryside, and Abby seemed surprised when they eased into a small turn off and the horses halted. "Why have we stopped? Are we here?"

"Not quite. There's something I must do first," said Philip.

His hands slipped to her chin and tugged at the ribbon securing her bonnet. He loosened the knot and pulled the offending headgear away from her head, tossing it behind him, where his own hat immediately followed.

"Forgive me, Abigail, but that damned thing hides your face. I want to see you when we talk. Watch your eyes light up, and your smile..."

He leaned closer to her, noticing her green eyes blazing as his grasp pulled her chin to within inches of his. "I can't wait," he breathed.

With the lightest of touches he brushed her lips with his.

The smile he'd been waiting for curved her mouth as he moved back, and a glow began deep in her emerald depths.

"That was...that was most pleasant, Philip," she said, huskily.

"Yes, it was, wasn't it?"

Abby cleared her throat. "But a bit risky, given that we're in a public lane where anyone could see."

Philip's brain snickered. If she wanted to see *risky*, she should take a look inside his mind and peek at some of the visions he was having right about now.

He sighed. "Not much further."

He clicked up his horses, and as he had promised, a tidy little estate came into view less than fifteen minutes later.

They drove up the neat driveway, and found themselves at the foot of a small set of stairs leading to a warm stone mansion.

It was small compared to some other country homes, but had an air of contentment about it, as if it was quite happy the way it was, and so were its residents.

None of whom, apparently, had been notified of their arrival. The front court was empty, and the door closed.

"Is anyone home?" asked Abigail curiously.

"Don't know," answered Philip. "I did send a message, but Augustus is notoriously absent-minded when it comes to visitors. He may be here, he may not. It makes no matter. I have a key."

Abby allowed him to hand her down from the curricle, reaching for her bonnet. His hand stopped her.

"You won't be needing that, Abby. Not here. We scientists are an informal bunch, you know. Protocol and etiquette are not things we care much about at all."

Abigail let her hand fall away from her bonnet and simply nodded.

Philip tethered his team to a convenient hitching post and tugged a bale of hay close. The water trough was full and clean, and the sun warm. Philip left them without a qualm.

Together the couple mounted the steps, and Philip raised his hand to the huge wrought iron doorknocker which he let fall with a massive thud.

Several minutes later a rather harried servant appeared, dressed in shirtsleeves and a large apron.

"Good heavens, Sir Philip. What a shock you gave me. Thought it was the toll of doom, for sure." The man sputtered as he attempted to wipe his hands on his apron.

"Sir Augustus didn't get my message, then?" Philip asked the question quite casually.

"He's not here, Sir. 'Tis just me, today. Sir Augustus took it in his mind to see some planetary alignment from an observatory built by a friend of his. He's gone 'til the weekend." The man looked apologetic.

"I'm sorry we missed him, Mumford. D'you think it would be all right if we visited for a while? I'd like to show Miss Foxworth around."

"Why of course, Sir. You're a welcome guest any time, you know that. And you too, Miss." He bowed politely. "I'm afraid there's little to offer you in the way of refreshments, though. Mrs. Harper's gone off to see her new grandson, so 'tis just me...I could make some tea or something..." Mumford fluttered his hands rather helplessly, as if the thought of making tea was one of the mysteries of life.

Philip chuckled. "Mumford. This is me, remember? I don't need tea. And I've brought a luncheon for Miss Foxworth and myself. You just go off and do whatever you were doing, and don't worry about us. We'll take a peep at Augustus's telescopes and then probably wander off into those orchards of yours and enjoy our lunch. I'll let you know when we're ready to leave. Does that fit in to your schedule?"

Mumford allowed a grin to cross his features. "Indeed it does, Sir. Always the thoughtful visitor, you are. My schedule consists of cleaning the silverware, but I don't mind telling you, I'd rather picnic in the orchard with a lovely lady any day." He colored slightly and bowed to Abby.

She smiled back. "What a lovely compliment. Thank you, Mumford. I can assure you I won't touch anything or get in your way."

"Not at all, Miss. Touch whatever you want. Sir Philip here is about as good as Sir Augustus at this stuff. He can show you everything."

Indeed, thought Philip. That pretty much summed up his plan for the day. He was, without a doubt, going to show Abigail *everything*.

And very little of it had to do with astronomy.

Chapter 7

Abigail felt a shiver of expectancy run through her as Philip slid his hand beneath her arm and brushed her breast as he did so.

It was a genteel gesture, intended to guide her up the stairs to Sir Augustus's observatory, but instead of sending thoughts of science her way, it sent other more wicked thoughts screaming through her brain.

She reprimanded herself. She was here to pursue one of her interests. Astronomy.

Not Philip Ashton.

And she was lying to herself once more.

The rooms Philip showed her were fascinating, and he allowed her a peek through Augustus's telescopes, focusing them for her on the nearby apple orchards.

"That's where we'll have our lunch, I think, Abby. It's quiet and shady, and lovely at this time of year."

His voice was deep, and he was close behind her, under the pretense of adjusting the telescope.

She felt his lips touch her neck. "Although, of course, lunch with you would be lovely *any* time of year."

She shivered, quite noticeably this time. "A nice turn of phrase, Sir Philip." It came out more as a breathy plea than the polite response she'd intended.

She cleared her throat, and turned, finding Philip close. Too close.

His body heat reached her skin through the light muslin of her gown, and her awareness of him grew by leaps and bounds.

She licked her lips.

His eyes lowered to watch her tongue, and she found herself fascinated as the colors within them changed from light blue to a rich, deep hue, shot through with those amazing golden flecks.

"I find I'm getting hungry, my dear. Luncheon calls, don't you think?" Philip's words were quietly seductive, and Abby's thighs trembled.

She nodded. There was a large obstruction in her throat making speech difficult, and she confessed to herself that she didn't want to *talk*, anyway.

She wanted other things.

She blushed.

He dropped a light kiss on her lips and turned away. "I'll grab our basket from the curricle, and meet you on that path there..." He pointed from the window to a lane, which led from the house into the forest beyond which lay the orchards.

With rather shaky steps, Abby descended the staircase and walked out into the sunshine, finding the path he'd shown her with ease.

Her mind, however, was far from easy.

Mere minutes in Philip's company had turned her knees to mush, and her body to a needy ache. She knew if he touched her there'd be no going back, and in truth, she wanted none.

She was almost twenty-three and had found a man who could light her inner fires with just a glance from his eyes or the brush of his hand.

She was a virgin, yet was awakening to all that a man could offer her in the way of passion and desire. The feelings brought a rush of moisture to her thighs, and she knew her nipples were hardening at the notion of sharing "lunch" with him in the quiet privacy of an orchard glade.

Her grandmother had been right. She wanted to toss up her skirts and beg Philip to fill her, to make her whole, to touch that needy place that he'd already roused, and teach her what passion really was.

She was ready.

And judging from the rather nice bulge in Philip's snug breeches that showed clearly as he walked towards her, so was he.

She couldn't help it. She grinned.

* * * * *

Abigail was smiling. Damn. Philip was in trouble now, and he knew it.

He spared a thought for the contents of the basket he'd had the forethought to demand from Rachel's cook, and the blanket he'd tossed over his shoulders.

There was no question in his mind which would get used first.

He moved to her side, letting her pull the blanket from him and place it over her arm. He took her hand, rejoicing as her fingers curled around his, and together they walked silently along the quiet path, listening to the birds as they sang all around them.

A sensual awareness was building between them, and Philip could feel it just as surely as the warm sunshine that beat down on his shoulders.

By the time they reached a leafy glade and she'd spread the blanket tidily on a soft patch of grass, his cock felt ready to explode. He wanted her more than he wanted air to breathe, and he forced himself to remember that she was, as yet, untried.

A tremor of excitement rumbled through his balls.

She would be his. He would be her first. No other man would claim this woman. *His* woman.

He stripped off his jacket and tossed his cravat after it, tugging his shirt loose and making himself as comfortable as a man could be with two tons of eager cock strangling between his thighs.

Abby settled herself in the shade and sighed.

"Such a big sigh, love. Are you tired?"

She shook her head. "No, not at all. It's just so lovely here."

"It is indeed." Philip's eyes never left her face, and she colored slightly as his words and their meaning became clear.

He seated himself close beside her, allowing his thigh to brush hers.

She didn't pull back. She was aware of him too. His balls sent up a little cheer and he grew even harder as her heat warmed his leg.

The birds continued their songs and a small stream rippled nearby, but the sounds of the day were lost to Philip. He could only hear Abby's breaths, coming a little faster now, and the sound of her gown as it slid over her body.

The gown *had* to go.

He leaned close and ran his hand up her spine to her neck. "Abigail, I want to kiss you. I want to touch you. Will you let me?"

The world seemed to stop for long moments before she turned her head and stared at him from green and mysterious eyes.

"Yes."

His heart pounded and his cock jumped as he eased Abby down onto the blanket and slowly covered her mouth with his.

He kept his touch gentle at first, but it was mere moments before her lips parted and she welcomed his tongue inside.

Philip threw up mental hands and surrendered.

Who was seducing whom had become immaterial. He had Abby beneath him, his tongue in her mouth, and her breasts digging their already-hardened nipples into his chest.

He moved his head, tasting her thoroughly now, relishing the sweetness of her lips and the way her tongue dueled frantically with his.

She moaned, and he slid his hand to her bodice, rapidly pulling the ribbons free and releasing her gown so that he could rest his hand against the bare softness within.

His mind whirled as he found what he was seeking.

She filled his hand to perfection. Her soft breast with its rigid nipple seemed to have been made just for his touch.

Her back arched as she thrust herself into his grasp, her body asking for more and his own gladly responding.

Within moments he had her gown stripped from her, and his own shirt and breeches soon followed. His boots had been flung somewhere—he couldn't remember where—all that mattered was getting his naked skin on top of Abby's.

The moment that happened, they both stilled, and blue eyes met green ones.

"Ahhh, Abby," murmured Philip, sliding his body along hers. "So good," he groaned.

"Philip," she sighed, letting her hands dance down his spine. "Oh Philip..."

"I know, love. It's a wonderful feeling, isn't it?" He rubbed himself against her again, sliding his chest firmly over her breasts and loving the brush of her nipples as they tightened beneath the abrasion of his flesh.

He kissed her again then moved his head down to where her luscious breasts were gleaming in the dappled shade.

He suckled her deeply, loving her soft cry of pleasure as he tugged on the peak, rubbing it against the roof of his mouth and letting it go with a damp pop.

"More, more," she whispered, pushing herself closer and twining her hands through his hair.

"Yes..." he murmured. "There's more, Abby. So much more."

He continued loving her breasts until they shone wet from his mouth, the tips dark red now as her heart beat rapidly beneath him.

He licked and sucked her again, but this time slid his hand down over the soft swell of her belly, stroking and smoothing the warmth of her as he moved.

Her legs parted for him, telling him exactly where she wanted to be touched.

But he refused to answer her body's call, simply brushing her woman's hair lightly with his fingers and then moving further still, scraping his nails gently along her inner thighs.

She sighed and moaned and gasped at the sensations his light strokes were creating.

He let his mouth follow the trail his fingers had taken, pausing to explore her navel with his tongue, and avoiding her mound completely. When he reached her knees, he began to lick, long sweeping strokes upwards, towards the softness that was pink and swollen and shining with her juices.

"Philip," she gasped, hips thrusting towards him.

"All in good time, Abby. The best pleasures are enjoyed slowly."

She groaned, and his lips curved in delight.

The scent of her body lured him onwards, and her cunt dripped with sweet honey.

He bent his head to taste her.

Abby's mind spun off into uncharted galaxies.

Once again, his mouth touched her, kissing her, licking her, but this time she had the added sensations of his hands over her nakedness and his heat mere inches away.

She felt wanton, and hungry for him, her whole body aching and trembling inside, as if ready and able to take everything he could give.

And he was giving her so much.

She gasped again as his tongue sought out her swollen folds, learning her, teasing her, and finding that special spot that sent shudders of pleasure up and down her entire body.

Even her earlobes tingled from it.

Her toes curled and her fists clenched the blanket as his tongue slipped inside her. "I can't...I can't..."

"You can't what, Abby?"

His voice was liquid seduction, deep and hoarse, as if he too, was moved by what was happening between them.

"I can't hold back...It's...you're making me..."

"Then don't, love. Let your body go. I'll be here to catch you. Fall, Abby. Fall into me..."

He replaced his mouth over her clit and suckled it, gently and then forcefully as if he could pull her out of herself through that tiny spot of flesh.

And it seemed that he could.

Abby's body thrashed, her buttocks locked, and a shiver spread through her as her legs locked against him.

She screamed and let go.

Wild lights swirled through her mind as her body pulsed and shook and fell apart in Philip's hands and against his mouth.

The sensation of his tongue inside her as she orgasmed was the most incredible thing she'd ever experienced, and as he moved it slightly, she felt herself come all over again.

The spasms seemed to last for an eternity, shocking her with their intensity. She knew her belly was shivering as her womb clenched and released itself in paroxysms of pleasure.

Abby forgot that she was lying naked on a blanket in a quiet orchard. She forgot that she had an equally naked man tucked between her legs. She forgot everything.

Everything but his tongue.

She let herself go completely, surrendering to the joy of physical pleasure with a man who was able to show her the heights of ecstasy. It was incredible, magnificent, and she found herself for the first time in her life unable to think at all.

A chill swept over her as Philip pulled his head from her mound.

She risked a quick glance down at him, only to see his blazing eyes smiling at her. His lips shone from her moisture, and the desire in his eyes overwhelmed her.

"Abby, I have to make you mine, love. I *have* to."

She tried to clear her befuddled thoughts. He was asking her something. Asking her permission to…to take her.

Well, bloody hell. If he thought he was going to get away *without* doing that, he was fair and far off.

Words failed her. She simply opened her arms and held them out to him.

His gaze never left hers as he slid up her body, and finally, *finally*, she felt his cock against her.

Philip wondered if he'd survive this experience.

His pulse was thundering in his ears, his cock had developed a hair trigger, and his balls were hard enough for a quick game of conkers if he'd been so inclined.

He wasn't inclined at all. He was inclined to get inside Abby at the earliest possible moment.

"This may hurt, sweetheart. It's your first time," he breathed, drowning in her eyes.

She smiled. "You won't hurt me, Philip," she said, widening her thighs to settle him even more comfortably.

And he wouldn't. Not if he could help it.

With a shaking hand, he positioned the head of his cock at her wet and slippery entrance and slid forward, clenching his teeth as her hotness closed around him.

She gasped and he stopped. "Am I hurting you?"

"No, it's just so *strange*…" Her eyes were wide, watching him as he claimed her body.

Her words fueled his need to plunge deep into her and seat himself to the hilt, but he held back, reining in his urges and forcing himself to go slowly.

A wry thought crossed his mind that if his cock had been a horse, it would have choked itself to death long before now, so hard was he pulling on the reins.

He let his hips push his cock a little deeper, slowly and easily sinking into her slick cunt. Her juices smoothed his way, and when he felt the light barrier of her maidenhood, he paused.

"I'm touching you, Abby, and I can't stop. Forgive me?"

With a quick move he pushed deeper, parting the delicate tissues that barred his way.

He was finally where he wanted to be. Deep inside Abigail Foxworth.

Chapter 8

For Abby, the taking of her virginity had been a momentary burning thing, quickly replaced by the amazing feel of Philip's hardness sliding into her, filling her and bringing her a sense of completion she'd never have believed possible.

She tightened her thighs around him, holding him right where he was, wanting to explore this new feeling for a few moments.

As if he understood, he stilled, letting her become accustomed to his cock as it stretched and forced her body into new and wonderful shapes.

She opened her eyes and found him gazing down at her, with a mixture of expressions changing the blue and gold irises to pure fire.

She saw desire and need, but she also saw concern and...and...something else. Something that warmed her and made her want to cry.

She saw love.

She closed her eyes against it, and refocused on her body as it accommodated itself to his.

"All right, sweetheart?" he asked softly.

"Oh yes, *more* than all right," she whispered.

His body shuddered against her flesh as he gently withdrew and then moved back again, beginning a slow and gentle rhythm against her inner silk.

"Tell me if this pains you, darling," Philip said hoarsely.

She opened her eyelids a little, and saw him tilt his head. He was watching their bodies as they parted and merged again, in a move as old as time, yet as new to her as tomorrow's sunrise.

His expression sent an erotic shudder through her, and suddenly she found herself responding to his thrusts with movements of her own.

As if finally awakened, her body throbbed and yearned, and she raised her hips a little to encourage him on.

Places inside her swelled and thrummed with pleasure at each stroke of his cock, and as he increased his speed, she began to drown beneath his sensual possession.

His body was touching hers now as he buried himself deeper each time. His hand slipped between them and added a soft stroke to her inflamed clit.

She gazed, spellbound, eyes barely focusing, as he aroused her to new heights, bringing her along with him and letting her feel the pleasure he brought to them both.

She could stand it no more. She closed her eyes and let the moment take her.

She was filled with Philip, surrounded by Philip, being loved by Philip.

Her body was answering his call like a warhorse hearing the trumpet sounding the charge.

Her heart galloped full tilt, her spine rigid, as his cock plundered her very soul.

She stiffened and cried out.

The exquisite shudders ran through her body once more, stealing her breath and this time forcing her cunt to clamp onto the one thing that had been missing from her earlier orgasms.

Philip's cock.

And Philip swore she was going to rip that cock right off.

He felt her begin to climax beneath him, and it took no more than her first rippling spasm to bring him to his own peak.

His neck snapped back, his balls tightened up into a knot, and with a hoarse cry he emptied himself into Abby.

God knew he hadn't intended to. His initial plan had been to withdraw and spurt harmlessly onto the grass before reaching his peak.

But wild horses couldn't have pulled him from her boiling cunt at this moment, and he knew it.

Her soft folds had lured him in and captured him within her as surely as the strongest chains.

He spurted again and again, his orgasm leaving him shuddering and weak, milked dry by her clenching muscles. It was wonderful, incredible, and it took his heart away.

It was as if by claiming her virginity, he had allowed her to claim his soul.

He didn't want to pull out of her.

Ever.

"Abby," breathed Philip, panting, as he lay on top of her. "My God, Abby."

She was silent beneath him, and for a terrible moment he wondered if he'd killed her.

Then she grunted. "I can't catch my breath, Philip," she said, struggling a little.

And no wonder.

He found himself flat on her chest, squashing her lungs and completely covering her with his large body.

He muttered an apology and slid to the side, sighing as his softening cock slipped wetly from between her legs. "Are you all right?"

She turned her eyes to him, lids heavy with passion and perspiration dewing her upper lip. He touched that lip gently with his fingers.

"Define 'all right'," she grinned.

His heart soared. His smile came from his guts somewhere, and his throat clogged. He did the only thing he was capable of at that moment. He leaned over and kissed her.

Slow and gentle, this kiss was a special thing, a pledge, a promise, a warm touch of lips to lips.

She sighed as he withdrew and let him cuddle her against him as the sun danced over their intertwined bodies.

"Philip," she sighed, lazily running her hands over his chest. "That was so…so…"

"Yes. It was, wasn't it?" He couldn't help the note of satisfaction creeping into his voice. He, Philip Ashton, had deflowered Miss Abigail Foxworth, and she'd enjoyed every minute of it. He'd honorably discharged his duties as a man. He'd claimed and pleasured his woman.

For right now, the world was perfect.

"Umm…" She hesitated.

"What, Abby?" His hand traced delicate circles on her hip, gently smoothing and caressing her as his mind purred with satisfaction.

"I know I am—*was*—a virgin. I wasn't experienced at all in this sort of thing. Do…do men *mind*?"

Philip chuckled, feeling Abby's head rise and fall with his low laughter. "Abby, men don't mind. Not when it's a special woman. Our woman. It's a wonderful thing to share that first time with the one woman who turns us into quivering lumps of lustful porridge."

Abby giggled and raised herself up on one elbow. "I do that to you? Turn you into a quivering lump of porridge?"

"Behold. Breakfast trembles." He held out one hand, and sure enough there was still a slight shake to it.

Abby sighed in contentment and settled back onto his chest. "Good. Because you certainly made me quiver. In a lot of interesting places, too."

"Did I hurt you, love?" Philip asked the question again, knowing he was not a small man, and worrying for once that his size might not be an advantage.

"Just a slight pinch. Nothing to worry about. I was so involved in all the other things you were doing, that I barely noticed."

Philip sighed with relief.

"But I must confess something," she added.

Philip paused. "What's that, love?"

"I'm hungry. Does this kind of thing always give one an appetite?"

Philip's shout of laughter scared the birds from the trees. "Only if you've done it right, sweetheart," he grinned. "Time for our picnic, do you think?"

"Oh yes. Yes indeed."

They sat up on the blanket and Abby reached for her gown.

Philip stopped her with his arms. "Forget clothes, Abby. You won't need 'em. Not for a while. The sun is warm, there's no one for miles around, and it's a chance for us to play Adam and Eve. In our own private Eden."

Abby stilled in his embrace as she considered the notion.

She turned slightly and eyed him, a wicked grin on her lips. "Are you sure?"

Philip nodded and kissed her. "As sure as I've ever been about anything, love."

He released her and stood, stretching, and enjoying this newfound feeling of joy, which suffused him from his heels to his eyebrows.

Abby folded her legs beneath her and made to stand, but Philip shook his head. "Wait a few minutes, Abby. There's something I must attend to."

He rummaged in the basket and pulled a napkin out, then disappeared for a moment towards the stream.

When he reappeared, he had a dripping wet napkin in his hand and a huge grin on his face. He couldn't help himself. The grin seemed to be nailed on. It wouldn't go away. Hell, he didn't want it to.

The sight of the smears of Abby's virginal blood on his cock had sent shivers through him as he'd cleaned himself in the stream, and his male possessiveness was choking him with the need to tend his woman.

He approached her as she watched him, a look of curiosity on her face.

"I'm going to take care of you, Abby," he said, deliberately showing her the cloth, and hoping she wouldn't realize that his words meant so much more.

He didn't want to scare her right at this precious moment, but if she had any notions of refusing his offer now, she might as well forget them.

She was his. Irrefutably, permanently, til-death-did-them-part, *his*.

* * * * *

Abby's mouth dried up as she watched Philip stride towards her, his cock and his balls lying softly between his legs, surrounded by a dark frame of hair.

It was a picture she'd never forget.

So strong, so handsome, with those eyes shining at her with tenderness and desire.

Her heart melted, and she gripped on to what little was left of her wits.

She eyed the dripping cloth. "What are you planning on doing with that?" she asked, quirking an eyebrow.

"Simply making you comfortable, sweetheart. Lie back. Trust me."

She snorted. As if he needed to tell her to trust him. She'd just lain with the man, for goodness sake. How much more trust could she possibly place in him?

Obedient to his push, she lay down, and jumped as he swept the cloth between her thighs and across her mound.

"Aaargh, Philip...that's *cold...*" Torn between a laugh and a shriek, she let him cleanse her body of their juices, carefully tending the delicate tissues and turning her skin rosy with his attentions.

"Sore, sweetheart?" His question brushed over her skin as he bent over her.

"Um..." She explored her body's sensations. "A little. Not much. Actually, not much at all."

"Good," he purred, finally finishing his task to his satisfaction. "It will be even better the next time."

"The next time?" Dammit. She'd squawked. She'd intended to be cool and self-possessed about all this, but that resolution had flown out of her mind with the first ripples of her first orgasm.

"Oh yes, Abby. The next time. And there will be many more next times, I can assure you." Philip's eyes blazed. "But not today. You must rest and heal a little before we can move on to other things."

Abby was torn. Part of her wanted to protest his calm assurance that they would do...*this*...again, and another part desperately wanted to find out what those "other things" he was talking about might be.

She sniffed. It seemed like an inadequate response, but it sufficed until she could get her jumbled thoughts in order.

Philip merely grinned. "How about some food?"

Her stomach rumbled loudly in response, and his grin became a laugh. "I'll take that as a definite 'yes'."

Mother Nature seemed to smile on their meal, shedding brilliant rays on their naked bodies and telling her creatures to serenade them. Abby drifted on a sea of contentment as she polished off her second blackberry tart and declared herself full.

Philip tossed back the dregs of his wine and joined her, lying beside her and pulling her into his body. She marveled at how perfectly her curves matched his, and how comfortably her head rested on his shoulder. Replete and sated, their conversation lagged, and they both allowed the beauty of this idyllic moment to creep into their minds, lulling them into a light doze.

Abby jerked awake as a hand gently circled her breast.

"I'm sorry, love. I didn't mean to wake you. It's just that this little bit here was calling for some attention."

She blinked, and looked down to where his hand was stroking her skin. Her nipples were hardening and he hadn't even touched them.

"It's incredible," she breathed, "how your touch affects me so."

"It's mutual, Abby," he answered, moving his hips slightly.

His cock lay on her thigh, a hot and heavy weight, aroused back to its full glory.

Abby's inquisitive mind got the better of her. After all, there were few chances for investigation of this particular phenomenon, and Philip was no Johnny Mountwell. Philip was all man, every inch of him, and she had some questions that cried out for an answer.

"Hmmm." She tugged on her lower lip with her teeth. "Philip, can I touch you?"

She could have sworn that his eyes crossed for a moment, but he obligingly lay flat on his back and smiled at her. "Be my guest."

She noted that his words were followed by a rather large gulp. Inquiring scientific minds noticed that sort of thing and filed it away for future reference.

She slid down his body, letting her hands wander where they would, finding his navel and giggling as he hissed in a breath at her light touch. "My, my. Ticklish there, are we?"

Philip's jaw twitched. "Not in the least."

She snorted, and continued her quest.

The delicate smattering of hairs on his belly thickened out into a full bush as she found her way down to where his manhood rose from between his thighs.

"My goodness," she muttered, seeing the ridges and veins that rumpled its smoothness.

Tentatively, she reached out a hand and ran her fingers lightly up and down.

Philip's gasp and shudder surprised her. "Am I hurting you, Philip?"

"Not at all," he choked. "It's something a man much enjoys. Forgive me if I show my pleasure...just ignore me. Carry on with what you were doing. *Pleeeeease...*"

Swept by a new sense of boldness, Abby did, indeed, carry on.

And to judge from the moans and stifled gasps, Philip was desperately trying to hide a great deal of pleasure.

She ran her fingers around the ridge that circled the head of his cock, and watched, fascinated, as a small bead of moisture oozed from the tiny slit at its tip.

Touching it delicately, she brought it to her lips. He'd tasted her, and she'd practically drowned him. What harm could there be in this tiny drop?

It was salty-sweet, tangy to her taste buds, and she rather liked it.

One thought led to another, and before she realized exactly what she was doing, she had placed her mouth on him, running her tongue up and down his length. There was no "Eeeeeuuuuww" this time. Just a gusty sigh from Philip and a great deal of curiosity on her part.

It was her blend of curiosity and eagerness that would probably kill him, thought Philip.

Never had a woman touched him quite like this. While he'd enjoyed such things in the past, it was *different* with Abby. He

79

grunted to himself as she found a particularly sensitive spot and tickled it with her tongue. *Everything* was different with Abby.

She lit a fire inside him that consumed him, his heart, his soul, and his back teeth. And if she kept up what she was doing, he'd be coming all over *her* back teeth very shortly.

Her questing fingers discovered his balls, and her touch took his breath away.

Gently she fondled them, weighing them, rolling them slightly, seeming fascinated at the way they hardened in her palm as she cradled them.

"So different," she murmured, leaning closer for a good look. Well, hell. Now she was in imminent danger of getting an earful.

Damn it. He had to stop her. Sometime over the next century he was *definitely* going to stop her.

Still keeping a warm hand around his balls, she returned her attention to his cock, sliding the entire head into her mouth, and quite cleverly, if inadvertently, reproducing almost the exact feeling of sliding into her cunt.

Philip clenched his teeth and waited for his jaw to explode. Or his balls. It was a toss-up which would happen first.

He gasped in air to his starving lungs. "Abby, Abby...you must stop, love." *No. Nooooo.*

"Why?"

Philip's mind blanked. He couldn't think of a single reason why at that particular moment, but he knew there had to be one. Just give him a year or two and he'd find it.

"Because," he ground out. "Because I'm going to come any second if you keep that up."

She eased her mouth from his cock, which lost no time in reminding him he was a complete dolt.

"I think I'd like to see that, Philip."

Her quiet words acted like a fuse on gunpowder, and Philip's entire body shuddered with the thought.

She kept her hands around him, stroking him slowly up and down, as if encouraging him. "It's only fair, you know. You watched me as I...when I..." She blushed. "You know. I'd like to see you, watch you as you reach your peak, too."

Philip closed his eyes and offered up a prayer for guidance to his guardian angel. Should he? Shouldn't he? Did he have any choice at all?

She lowered her lips once more, and he gave up the fight.

Within seconds his body tightened beneath her touch, and he felt her draw back as she sensed the changes beneath her mouth.

He couldn't hold it, didn't want to hold it, and he let his iron control go.

With a cry of pleasure, he came, spurting his seed into the sunshine, watched by the eager green eyes of Abigail Foxworth.

His one and only love.

Chapter 9

The drive home to London was accomplished in good time, with the two participants of the curricle exploring the new relationship that now lay between them.

Abby drew great pleasure from the occasional brush of Philip's thigh against hers, and found herself continuously watching his strong hands as they held the reins.

She battled to force away images of what those hands could do when allowed to roam freely on her skin.

"Philip, I…"

"Abigail, we…"

They laughed as they broke the silence at the identical moment.

"Ladies first," chuckled Philip.

"I am trying to find the words to thank you for today," she said quietly. "I don't know if I can. How *do* I thank you for what you showed me today? For the experience you let me share?"

Philip's grin broadened. "By letting me do it again?"

Abby joined his laugh, but shook her head slightly. "I don't see how that could be possible." She knew that her words had a sad overtone to them, but was beyond controlling it. "It was quite acceptable for the eccentric Sir Philip Ashton to escort the equally eccentric Miss Abigail Foxworth to a scientist's house for a short excursion. But we can't continue that sort of trip without becoming noticed. And I *hate* being noticed."

She stared absently over the horses' ears at the road ahead. "Not that I would mind doing it again, Philip. Never think that. But we must accept the reality of our lives. You are who you are and I am who I am. Society has put very well-defined structures around us."

She turned to Philip, letting her eyes show her emotions. "I cannot, and *will* not, devastate Aunt Eugenia or Grandmama by becoming your mistress."

A muscle twitched in Philip's jaw and his eyes narrowed. "I would never ask such a thing of you, Abby. Get that right out of your head."

"Then we must put today from our minds. Treasure it as a precious memory, and move forward with our lives." Abby folded her hands tightly, clenching them against the pain her words sent to her heart.

The muscle twitched again, and Philip was silent for some time. Abby wondered if he had a headache perhaps, since his brows were now drawn together in quite a fierce frown.

They were now approaching the outskirts of town, and would be at Abby's front door in a short time.

Philip took a deep breath. "Abigail."

She jumped at the harsh sound of her name as it gusted from his throat. "Yes?"

His fingers tightened on the leathers. "I have *no* intention of asking you to be my mistress. I shall not *ask* you to be my anything. I am going to *tell* you. For once and for all."

He turned to her, eyes blazing. "You *will* be my wife. You *will* share my bed for however many years God sees fit to grant us. I don't care what bee is in that silly bonnet of yours about marriage, but there is no other acceptable or desirable course for us. So get it through that lovely head. It's a fait accompli."

He negotiated a tight turn onto Abby's street, as she felt the first hot words of denial rising in her throat.

The horses drew to a standstill, and Philip glared at her. "I shall be calling on your aunt at noon tomorrow. At that time, you will agree to accept my proposal of marriage. If you don't, I shall make it quite clear where and how we spent today. I don't care what I have to do to get you by my side, Abby. No price is too great."

Her eyes blazed in their turn. "How *dare* you?" She hissed the words at him. "Just because we've lain together it doesn't give you the right to order my life around like that."

"Yes it does." Philip bit the words off, clenching his teeth. "You're mine, Abby. As sure as the sun rises, and the stars come out at night. You gave me a treasure today, and a memory that will never fade. I want us to make more such memories. I want us to experiment with a variety of scientific equipment and a whole lot of bedroom equipment."

His words made her dizzy and she shut her eyes.

"I want to fill you with our children. Make a life and a home with you. I've never asked another woman to marry me, and I'll be damned if I let the only one I want turn me down." He nodded at the door.

"Now get down and go inside, before I really lose my temper and put you over my knee."

For a blinding second, Abby's heart lurched at the thought, and then she hardened her heart. "I shall refuse to see you."

She clambered down from the curricle unaided.

"No you won't, love."

She risked a look at his face. His dear face with those amazing eyes blazing down at her. "Don't try any of your mesmerism tricks on me, Philip Ashton."

A grin eased the tension around his jaw. "I don't need to. We mesmerize each other, Abby. Think about that. Think about us, tonight, as you slip into that cold bed of yours. And think about a lifetime spent slipping into a hot bed with me."

His gaze gentled, and he passed her the long-forgotten bonnet from the rear of the curricle. "I love you, Abigail Foxworth."

Abby's jaw dropped as he slapped the reins on his horses' back and clattered off down the street.

In a daze, she turned and mounted the steps to her home, nodding absently at the butler as he opened the door to her knock.

"Good afternoon, Miss Abigail."

Abby dredged a polite smile from somewhere, her heart and mind still tumbling around in a far-off emotional vortex.

"I'm glad you're here. Your aunt asked you to attend her in the Salon as soon as you arrived. You have a guest."

Jerking her thoughts back into reality, Abby nodded and tossed her bonnet on the small hall table.

Glancing in the mirror she gasped and did her best to straighten her tousled and windblown hair.

Green eyes gazed back at her. The green eyes of a woman who'd experienced passion, lust and a healthy dose of desire. Confused eyes, scared eyes, and ones that could offer no answer to her dilemma.

Sighing, she entered the Salon.

Three women were inside.

Eugenia was stalking the length of the room in what was, for her, a quite unusual display of agitation.

The Dowager was seated on an upright chair, looking amused, interested, and aloof, all at the same time.

The third woman was standing next to the empty fireplace, one hand resting delicately on the mantel.

She was tall, and very elegantly gowned in a dark green traveling dress. Abby received a quick impression of a bonnet and gloves tossed casually on a side table, but her eyes were drawn back to the graceful stranger.

Abigail looked closely at her.

The woman turned her head and met Abby's gaze for the first time, some unknown emotion flickering in their depths.

Their vivid green depths.

Eyes that were as vivid green as Abby's.

She had a superbly-coiffed head of dark red hair.

Hair that was exactly the same shade as Abby's.

"Who...who...are you?" Abby's voice stuttered in shock.

The woman smiled gently, her full lips curving around perfect white teeth.

"Hello, Abigail. I'm your mother."

Stunned beyond belief, still reeling from her experiences with Philip, and shattered at this final shocking revelation, Abigail Foxworth did something she'd never done in her life.

She fainted.

* * * * *

"Drat it, Angelica. You made the poor girl faint. Why the *devil* couldn't you have stayed in Italy?"

The unusually acerbic tones of her aunt brought Abigail swimming back to consciousness. The foul-smelling stuff that she waved under Abby's nose helped, too.

She coughed and found herself on the floor of the salon with three worried faces bending over her.

She shut her eyes for a moment and waited for the buzzing sensation in her ears to subside.

"Abby, dear, speak to me. Abby?"

"That stuff is *awful*, Aunt..." Abby coughed again and pushed her aunt's hand away from her face. She pulled herself up on her elbows and found a graceful hand extended towards her.

Without a murmur, she accepted it and eased herself back to her feet. It seemed natural to allow herself to be led to a couch and settled against the cushions, the stranger taking a seat at her side.

No, not a stranger. Her *mother*.

Abby's lungs heaved. "I believe you said something about being my mother?"

She amazed herself by not squeaking as she stared at this woman, so much like herself, yet who was not her mother. Could not possibly be her mother.

The only mother she'd ever known was settled in the country, enjoying a quiet industrious life with Abby's father.

The woman smiled. "It seems a bit silly, I know, but I should introduce myself. I'm Angelica diConti, and yes, my dear, you are truly my daughter."

"But you're *dead...*" wailed Abby.

"And she should have bloody well stayed dead, too, if you ask me," grunted Eugenia.

Abby ignored the interruption, spellbound by the youthful face so like hers that was smiling warmly at her.

"I had every intention of staying dead, Eugenia. There is nothing in England for me any more. Nothing but you, my dear..." She raised a hand and gently touched Abby's cheek. "So when I heard that you needed me, I decided to pay a short visit. I hope you'll find it in your heart to forgive me."

"I...I needed you? I don't understand." Abby knew her voice was plaintive, but she was all at sea now, confused and scared and fighting the urge to bury her head beneath the sofa cushions until all this went back into the bad dream it must surely be.

Angelica glanced over at the Dowager who managed to look guilty and defiant at the same time.

Eugenia gasped. "You, Mama Wetherford? *You* invited this...this woman here?"

"Oh cut line, Eugenia. If I'd had my way, this would have come as no surprise at all to Abby here. But nooooo." She thumped her cane crossly on the ground. "You namby-pamby snirps had to string a line of Banbury tales from here to John O'Groats, and let this poor gel think her mama was dead."

Abby placed her cold hands on her hot forehead. "I'm confused." And that had to be the understatement to top all understatements.

Angelica laughed quietly. "Will you let me tell you about it, my dear?"

Abigail raised her head. "It would seem there is much to tell, isn't there? You're alive, you're very lovely, and you look like me. And you're my mother. Back from the dead."

The Dowager guffawed. "Well, I've heard Venice described as heaven a few times, but I think that's going a bit far, gel." Her wrinkled eyes narrowed. "Eugenia."

The abrupt command jerked the woman out of her temper and she turned.

"Get those lazy servants in here with a tea tray. We'll be dust dry long before we've finished thrashing this thing out, and damn it, I'm hungry."

In a matter of moments the Dowager was enjoying more than her fair share of cream cakes, accompanied by that most English of restoratives, a nice cup of tea.

Sipping her own carefully, Abby sighed and turned to her mother. "Now. May I have the full story? The truth?"

Green eyes met green eyes as a moment of honesty passed between them.

"Yes, Abby. The whole truth."

* * * * *

Angelica diConti stared at the beautiful young woman next to her and tried to accept the reality that this was indeed the fruit of her loins. She had given life to this vibrant creature nearly twenty-three years before.

How on earth could she describe her life since then? Would it bring a look of disgust to her daughter's face? A rare shiver of apprehension ran up her spine, as she considered where to start.

She sighed. Starting at the beginning was always best, she supposed. She put her cup back on its saucer and returned both to the tea tray. It was time to tell her daughter the truth.

"I was barely seventeen when I was married to your father, Abby."

Abby's head jerked up. "*Seventeen?* So young?"

Angelica nodded wryly. "Indeed. A mere child. My parents believed that it would be a good match, the settlements were adequate, and he was…presentable, I suppose would be the best way to describe it."

She paused. How much to tell? How far to go when it came to recalling that first year of her marriage?

Angelica watched her daughter, noting her interest, her self-possession, and some sort of awareness that flickered deep in her eyes. With a little pang of pride, she accepted that Abigail was a woman who could understand the truth. No—more than that. A woman who wanted and deserved the truth.

"He was pleasant. Tall, like me, and handsome, I suppose. But I didn't love him. I was told that such a thing was not necessary. It would grow between us in time. I went into my marriage with the best intentions, Abby, and I should say clearly, here and now, that it was not your father's fault that those predictions never came true."

"Did he love you?" Abby's soft question gave Angelica pause.

"No. No, I'm pretty sure he didn't. Oh, he liked me. Liked having me around to do the pretty for his guests and to warm his bed at night. And especially liked it when I found myself pregnant with you. But there was no passion there. No *fire*, Abby. Do you understand?"

To her surprise, Abby nodded. "I do. I do indeed."

A rough snort from the Dowager followed this statement, but she subsided back in her chair, lips folded in an odd grin.

"I gave birth to you, a daughter, and frankly your father was a little disappointed. I suppose, in the way of men, he

89

wanted a son first. He drew away from me then, using my new motherhood as an excuse. It was not long after that I discovered he had a mistress living nearby."

Abby gulped.

"I don't blame him, Abby. Our marriage was pretty much in name only from that point on. He found his pleasure elsewhere, and I can honestly confess that I was glad of it."

Angelica reached out and took a sip of her cold tea. Anything to make the next disclosures easier.

"Then I met someone."

Such a commonplace statement. Angelica's heart still beat faster at the thought of her first glimpse of Antonio diConti.

"He was visiting a nearby estate and had crossed over onto our property without realizing it. I was walking alone near that lake…you know the one…"

Abby nodded, eyes wide, never moving her stare from her mother's face.

"I fell head-over-heels in love with him from the first minute I saw him, my dear. His heart, his mind, his body, and most of all, his eyes. They…it was as if they mesmerized me."

Abby choked and gulped another swallow of her own tea.

"Can you understand that?" Angelica's question was plaintive, so much did she want her daughter to grasp the importance of this man in her life.

"I can truly understand…Mama." Abby laid her hand on top of Angelica's, and Angelica felt an unusual sting of tears at the back of her eyes.

She ignored it, bravely determining to finish the tale. "Well, from then on, we stole every moment we could to be together, but eventually, of course, people talked, and your father found out."

She pressed her napkin to her lips. "It was not pleasant."

Next to her, Abby shivered. "I should imagine not."

"He gave me a choice. I could give up Antonio, and he'd continue to be my husband, providing I remained forever down at Foxworth Chase, never coming to London again. I would also never be allowed to see you, either. Apparently my presence in your life would have been considered a contaminant."

Abby gasped. "What was the other choice?"

"That I could leave his house at that very moment, taking nothing but the clothes on my back. I would, of course, never be allowed to see you again under those conditions, either."

She glanced down at her hands, tightly fisted against the green of her gown. "I made the only choice possible, Abby. Either one took you away from me. I could not live in an empty house without you. I could not imagine surviving without Antonio. I trusted that your father would raise you well—he seemed to care for *you*, at least, and I met Antonio that very night. By the next week we were in Italy, and not six months later word came of the divorce."

Her hands trembled slightly. "It was kept very quiet, of course. No one knew but those involved. But it freed me, and allowed me to wed Antonio. Since then, my life has been full of love and joy, and the only regret I have is that I could not be there to watch you grow into the beautiful young woman you are today."

Abby swallowed past the lump in her throat. She was having difficulty reconciling this story as being part of her own life, and not some romantic novel.

"They told me you were dead. That's all they told me. It wasn't until I was about nine or ten I suppose that I heard..."

"What did you hear, dear?" Angelica's words encouraged Abby to reveal all.

"I heard that you'd run away with a foreigner. That you'd acted like a...like a...whore because of your...your...lustful ways. That your physical needs had driven you to take your pleasures anywhere. The servants...well, they loved to gossip, I suppose."

91

Angelica grinned a little. "And let me guess, young ears loved to eavesdrop?"

Abby spared a quick glance at her grandmother. "*That* particular trait seems to run in the family."

The Dowager snorted, but there was a definite twinkle in her eye.

"What else did they say, Abby?" Angelica urged her on.

"They…they said that it was disgraceful that a woman should be led by her body to desert her family and bring shame on such a nice man. That you were no better than you should be, and that you'd come to a bad end. And they said…" Her voice caught.

Angelica covered Abby's hands with both her own. "What, sweetheart?"

Abby's eyes filled with tears. "They said…" She dropped her head. "They said that I'd be just the same if I wasn't careful. Because I was the spitting image of you. That I'd turn into a wanton trollop who'd end up in trouble because of my…my *urges*. That I'd probably bring pain to some nice man, and desert him, like you did to him."

She swallowed and finished her confession. "Later I heard them say you'd been killed in a carriage accident while fleeing another lover."

She looked up. "My father never told me anything. *Anything*. He simply said you'd died. And with such a look on his face that I never asked again. He made it clear that Louisa was now my Mama and would love me just as much as he did."

"And did she?"

"I don't know." That was the absolute truth, Abby realized.

Her parents had seemed affectionate, but absent with her, preferring to devote their time to their studies. She'd tried so hard to earn their approval, devouring the sciences they talked about, and developing her own enthusiasm at the same time.

Anything, she realized now, to get their attention.

Her mind flew back to her afternoon with Philip. There'd been more love and warmth in a mere touch of his lips than she'd had in years from her parents.

She hadn't realized it until this moment. It was a sobering thought.

"Well, now you know the truth. Do you hate me, Abigail?"

Abby huffed out a little breath. "I don't think so. I honestly don't know what to think. I suppose I need a little time to absorb all this."

She shook her head, trying to sort out her thoughts.

"Of course you do." Angelica rose, shaking out her skirts and reaching for her bonnet. "Antonio and I are staying at The Gryphon Hotel for the next few days. May I hope that you'll call on me when you've had time to think all this through? I'd like you to meet Antonio. And he's very eager to make your acquaintance too."

Abby smiled, not willing to commit herself yet, but warming to the affection that radiated from her mother.

"Perhaps," she replied.

"Excellent. Eugenia, I shall now relieve you of my presence, so you can sink into those cushions and damn me every which way to your heart's content."

Abby chuckled. If nothing else, her mother was every bit as acute as she herself.

The Dowager thumped her cane. "Glad you came, Angelica. And, for the record, I apologize for the great disservice I did by marrying that idiot son of mine to you."

"Water under the bridge, your Grace. It was a long time ago. If I hadn't been where I was I'd never have been blessed with Abby or met Antonio."

With a stunningly beautiful smile, Angelica diConti swept from the room, leaving three blinking women behind her.

"Well," exploded Eugenia.

"Aunt," said Abby firmly. "No more. Not right now. I'm going to my room, and I'm not coming out for the rest of this night. Possibly not even tomorrow, either."

Eugenia opened her mouth to protest.

"Gel's right, Eugenia. Pipe down," snapped the Dowager. "She needs some time to come to terms with all this." She smiled at Abby. "Go to bed, dear. Clear your mind and open your heart. Let the truth blow away those silly worries of yours. Tomorrow will bring a fresh perspective. Everything else can wait."

Abby nodded and left the room, heading for the sanctuary and peace of her own suite.

Closing the door behind her, she leaned against it, blowing a lock of hair off her brow as she exhaled.

So much had happened. So many new facts, new truths, and old ones re-sorted and realigned.

And lurking behind, beneath and around them all, one overriding image.

Philip Ashton's eyes.

Chapter 10

It was past midnight and the house was quiet when Abby gave up all attempts at sleeping and tossed the bedclothes aside.

She strode to the window and flung it open, taking deep breaths and trying to calm her roiling thoughts.

A large hand thumped on the windowsill, and a dark head emerged behind it. "Thank you, darling. I had no idea how I was going to manage that," said a familiar voice.

"*Philip*," screeched Abby.

"Ssssh...I just spent the better part of twenty minutes trying not to scream as your damned roses ripped my breeches to shreds. Don't go and wake the whole household just when I've reached my goal, for heaven's sake."

He eased his legs over the windowsill and smiled at her.

Abby groaned and flung herself into his embrace.

Never had a chest felt so good, or arms felt so warm and comfortable. She hugged him for all she was worth, pressing her face into his dark shirt and running her hands up and down his back feverishly.

She felt him chuckle. "Well. And I'm glad to see you too, love. Are you all right? I couldn't sleep for wondering, thinking about you, worrying that I'd hurt you..."

"Oh, no. No, you didn't hurt me. Well, only by being a stubborn man. But never mind that now. Just hold me, please? It's been a longer day than you know."

Philip enthusiastically obliged.

Abby felt the tensions leave her spine as Philip's warmth spread around her, and a new kind of tension crept into her belly.

Philip was hard and hot, and his breeches were betraying the fact that he liked her in his arms. Very much, apparently.

She couldn't help herself. She rubbed her hips against him.

"Oh love," he breathed, kissing her hair. "I didn't come for that. I really just wanted to know that you were all right."

"Well, as you see, I'm all right. Mostly. And I wish you had come for *that*. I could use some of *that* right now." She sighed.

"Really?" His voice cracked.

"Really," whispered Abby, reaching up and pulling his head to hers.

He needed no encouragement. His kiss was fierce, as if he had waited lifetimes to taste her again.

Within moments she was naked, her nightgown whisked off her by two strong hands, and seconds later he pressed his own nakedness to hers.

"We fit, Abby, feel how we fit," he breathed, letting her body find just the right places to cuddle.

"I know, Philip, I know," she moaned, loving his touch, his scent, and the little prickle of his hairs as they rubbed her sensitive skin.

He swept her off her feet and over to the rumpled bed. "Are you sure, love? Not sore from this afternoon?"

Abby grasped handfuls of his hair and pulled him down on top of her. "I'm sure, dammit. Now what are you going to do about it?"

Something snapped inside her, and she suddenly let it all go. She raised herself and kissed him passionately, letting her legs slide around his body and grasp him, tightening her muscles and holding him close.

Her hands dug into him and she moaned, writhing and squirming in an attempt to get all of him against all of her. There was nothing in her mind or her heart now except her need for this man.

His response thrilled her, sent her soul flying free and purged the last of her worries from her overworked brain.

His fingers aroused her to an almost painful state of readiness, his lips followed right behind and the two lovers found themselves adrift in a whirlwind of desire in the darkness surrounding Abby's bed.

Philip paused. "Turn over, love."

Abby unhesitatingly obeyed. Whatever he asked, she'd do. Wherever he took her, she'd go.

"On your knees, Abby. Trust me. It will be a pleasure for you, I promise." "I'll not hurt you, love."

"I know," said Abby on a sigh.

She raised herself to her hands and knees, uncaring that she presented her very naked buttocks to his gaze. Whatever he wanted from her he could have, for this night. Because his touch brought sweet forgetfulness and comfort.

Philip drew in a breath at the beautiful sight before him.

Shadows caressed her smooth buttocks, deepening the cleft between them, and he could see the soft moisture as it dripped from her willing cunt.

His heart jumped into his throat, and his cock jumped simply from the pleasure it knew awaited it.

He let his hands roam over the soft white mounds, smoothing her already-silk skin, just enjoying their leisurely journey.

Her thighs sparkled with her moisture, and her swollen flesh called him to lose himself within.

He slipped his hand beneath her and found her clit, gently stroking it and encouraging it to harden even more.

She sighed and moaned, moving her hips now, pressing backwards, telling him without words how much she wanted his touch.

Experimentally he ran drenched fingers up her dark cleft, just brushing her tight little arse and smiling as she stilled and then shivered.

"Oh lord," she muttered, burying her face into her pillow to muffle her sounds.

"Feel good, Abby?" he asked, still stroking her there, and moving nearer now.

"God, yes. Oh God yessss..." she hissed, writhing like a wild thing. "Everything you do feels good, Philip."

His body blazed.

With a quick move he positioned his cock at her cunt, rubbing himself through the wetness and coating the hot hard skin with her honey.

She moved against his hand, trembling as her muscles responded to so many mixed signals. Her hips wanted more of his fingers against her clit, but her backside wanted to push back against his warmth.

He brought her to the trembling moment before her peak, feeling her muscles tighten and her breath shudder from her lungs.

Then he slowly eased himself inside, gritting his teeth as he took his time burying himself in her white-hot cunt.

Finally, he was there. His balls touched the back of her thighs, and he closed his eyes with the sheer joy of it.

"Abby," he sighed.

"Philip," she gasped into her pillow. "Dear heavens, *do* something."

He chuckled, and did something.

He withdrew almost to the tip and then sank back in again, loving her sighs of pleasure.

Slowly, easily, he moved, back and forth, slipping smoothly now into her slick body.

His fingers kept time with his thrusts, and he started to lose the battle with his own body as his pace quickened.

The feel of his balls as they slapped against her skin, coupled with the tight heat of her folds as they slid over his cock sent him into whirls of light and pleasure.

He couldn't hold back.

Moving faster now, his fingers stroked and rubbed her clit, robbing her of her breath and sending the first shivers of her orgasm through her body.

He felt each and every little twitch and spasm, and as her inner muscles began to clutch at him, he let go.

He bit back a howl of ecstasy and buried himself as deep as he could go, filling her once more.

Her body shuddered and shook around his, and he vaguely heard her cry out into the depths of her pillow.

It was over far too soon. He could have stayed like this for at least a couple of lifetimes.

But eventually her body slackened beneath his, and his thigh muscles started to cramp.

With a sigh of regret he pulled from her, letting his now-exhausted cock slip from her relaxed and soaking cunt.

He moved up beside her and pulled her into his arms, tugging the cover over the two of them.

This was how he envisioned the rest of his life.

Nestled together with Abby, both of them sweaty, sticky and sated from loving, and snuggled into a lump of boneless delight.

Abby sighed and rubbed her head against his shoulder. "Philip. What am I going to do?"

"About what, love?"

"About...about *everything*."

Philip grinned. "Well, let me see. Napoleon's defeated, so you don't have to worry about that. Um...the Congress in Vienna is taking care of most of the European questions, so that's all right, too...of course the Prince Regent could use some advice about his appalling love life..."

Abby chuckled and bit his chest gently, licking the small marks left by her teeth. "You're a dreadful tease, Philip Ashton."

"Yes. Aren't I, though?" He was too content to protest.

Abby sighed.

"Tell me, love. Tell me what made you throw yourself at me when I clambered, at great personal risk I might add, over your windowsill." Philip eased back a little, trying to see what he could of her face in the shadows.

Abby was silent for a moment and then began to talk.

She told him the story she'd learned that day, and her tale bore out all the information his sister Rachel had given him, over which he'd struggled ever since. He needed to find the key, the right way to help her overcome all her worries and fears and realize that loving him was the only thing she could possibly do.

Philip listened quietly as her words painted all kinds of pictures for him. A picture of a lonely young girl hearing things about her mother that had no business soiling such tender ears.

A picture of a child growing up with a fear rooted deep in her soul that she would turn into a woman capable of deserting her family.

A picture of a daughter struggling to make herself a place within the less-than-affectionate hearts of her parents.

He grimaced, putting the pictures together and finally understanding her fear of such a deep commitment as marriage.

He pulled her closer and dropped a light kiss on her head as her voice trailed off at the end of her sad tale.

Philip let the comfortable silence between them grow as he wondered how best to approach the situation. He knew, more than ever, that Abby was his. That they could share a wonderful life together.

More than their bodies fit. Their minds fit. Their hearts fit. Their very souls were matched like identical peas in a pod.

All he had to do was convince Abby.

And *that* was going to take some careful thought.

Chapter 11

"Abby, how old are you?"

Abby turned her head, surprised at the question. "I'm almost twenty-three. You knew that, didn't you?"

She felt his nod. "Yes. But did *you*?"

She blinked. "I don't understand."

Philip drew a breath, making her head rise a little as his chest expanded. "I'm twenty-nine, sweetheart. We're both adults. Grown-ups. Neither of us is an innocent sheltered seventeen-year-old, going into an arranged marriage. We've lived, Abby."

He stroked her arm and she wanted to purr at the sensation.

"You have a mind that can outthink many of the scientists I've met. I've spent most of my life buried in the country, ignoring my sister's urging to find a bride. We were both looking for something, *someone*, that special person who could make us feel complete in so many more ways than this..."

His leg slid between hers, melding them even closer. "Although *this* is good too," he chuckled.

She opened her mouth to speak, but he stopped her with a quick kiss. "Let me finish, love. Your mother found herself in an impossible situation at an unconscionably young age. Do you think for a moment that if you'd been born after she married her Count whatever-his-name-is, she'd have *ever* given you up?"

Abby thought back to her impressions of the elegant woman who she'd met for the first time that day. She recalled the warmth and pain in her mother's eyes as she'd related her story to her daughter.

"Um. No, I suppose not."

Philip's leg moved upwards, slipping into the notch between her thighs and settling itself comfortably against her tender folds. He sighed again, and she couldn't stop a little smile from crossing her lips at the sound.

"That's the difference, Abby. She ended up in a marriage where there was no love, no sharing, no caring. Not like us."

He smoothed her body once more. He seemed to enjoy stroking her, and God knew she wasn't about to object.

"We have everything your mother didn't. We love each other, Abby." He pulled back slightly. "You do love me, don't you?"

Abby thought about that question.

Her mind was as full of him as her body. Her heart whispered to her that she'd never find another who matched her so perfectly. And then she asked herself what her life would be like if he went back to his country home and she never saw him again.

The bolt of pain that idea sent through her made her shiver with its intensity. "Oh *yes*, Philip. I truly believe that I do love you."

"Well, damn, woman. Don't ever make me wait so long for an answer to that question. I swear I could hear my hair turning gray."

His laughter made her smile.

And *that* was the secret. He could make her laugh. He could make her body sing, her soul fly, and within moments bring the joy of a shared joke to her heart. She wanted to be with him, to share with him, to…yes, to *love* him, for the rest of her life.

"I do love you. I've been so scared to love anyone…"

Philip snorted. "I doubt that, Abby. You've been scared of the idea of marriage. Of bearing a child and then deserting it, the way you thought your mother had deserted you. As far as loving anyone goes, well…" He grunted in disdain. "You just hadn't met the right man. Me."

Abby grinned. He was such a typical male in so many respects, and so unique in others. Perhaps that was why she loved him.

A soft warmth spread through Abby as her fears fled before his words, and a weight lifted from her shoulders. One she never even realized she was carrying.

"I suppose you're right," she agreed quietly. "I was so scared of being caught in a marriage with any one of the endless stream of buffoons Aunt Eugenia encouraged, and then meeting someone who could seduce me with a look, and..." She swallowed, trying to find the words.

His arm tightened, giving her strength to go on. "And then leaving everything and everyone behind. Just like my mother had done to me."

Tears stung her eyelids as she let it out.

"Now you know she had no choice, Abby," said Philip. "No choice at all. And much as I hate to speak ill of your father, it was an untenable situation. He should never have made those stipulations."

Abby swallowed back her emotions, and nodded. "I know. Although it doesn't surprise me now. He has always been...distant, I suppose would be the best way to describe it. Fair, and attentive on occasions when he wasn't involved in some experiment or other. But not really seeing *me*, if you know what I mean?"

"How about your step-mother? Was she kind to you?"

Abby considered the question. "Yes, all things considered, she was. She had no children of her own with Papa, and I think she genuinely cared about me. I was so young when they married, of course, that I knew no other mother. I only learned of these things as I grew old enough to ask questions about what I heard. I was told simply that my mother had died, and that Louisa was my mama now."

Abby thought back to her childhood years, remembering the soft, comfortable woman who had become Lady Foxworth.

"She certainly did all that was appropriate in raising me. I had plenty of governesses, books, clothes, all the things I needed."

"Except for one, sweetheart."

She turned her head again and looked at him through the shadows.

"You were missing out on love."

She wished she could see his eyes in the darkness and read the emotions she heard in his voice. They would flicker with heat and warmth and put her under his spell once more.

She snorted to herself. As if she needed any help on *that* particular feeling.

He cuddled her, stroking, soothing, murmuring how much he loved her and all the wonderful things they could spend the rest of their lives doing.

And it would probably take that long, because the man certainly seemed to have an inexhaustible supply of wickedly wonderful suggestions.

She squirmed as he breathed a particularly delicious thought into her ear. She blushed.

"Philip. Is such a thing truly possible?"

He laughed. "Abby, for us, all things are possible."

She couldn't help an answering grin. "Oh good." She spread her arms and hugged him, taking enormous comfort from the steady beat of his heart as it quietly thumped beneath her head.

"But you'll have to agree to marry me, first, of course."

She stilled.

"Face facts, Abby. You've compromised me quite dreadfully. If you don't make an honest man of me, what the devil will our children think?"

"They'll think…" She smiled. "They'll think that their father is a wicked, wicked man who can't keep his hands off their mother."

Philip's arms tightened. "And they'll be absolutely right."

"Or, they might just believe that I was mesmerized. And I was."

Philip yawned. "I never mesmerized you, darling. You mesmerized *me*."

She smiled and settled herself comfortably. She'd surrendered to love. A new life was starting for her. A life filled with laughter and joy.

She'd been mesmerized all right. One glance had been all it took for her to know, deep in her heart, where her future lay.

In Philip Ashton's eyes.

* * * * *

In the dark corridors of Foxworth house, an elderly figure moved quietly away down the dimly lit passage to her suite of rooms.

The murmur of voices had ceased behind the door to which she quite shamelessly had been pressing her ear. A grin curled her wrinkled lips, and her cane made little sound on the carpeted floor.

The Dowager Countess of Wexford was pleased. Her granddaughter had finally found a man she could love.

The wrongs of the past, for which she felt horribly responsible, were on their way to being righted.

And if they kept *that* sort of behavior up, she might just live to dandle her first great-grandchild on her knee.

Now, the most important question remained.

What the devil was she going to wear to the wedding?

The End

About the author:

Born and raised in England not far from Jane Austen's home, reading historical romances came naturally to Ms. Kelly, followed by writing them under the name of Sarah Fairchilde. Previously published by Zebra/Kensington, Ms. Kelly found a new love - romanticas! Happily married for almost twenty years, Sahara is thrilled to be part of the Ellora's Cave family of talented writers. She notes that her husband and teenage son are a bit stunned at her latest endeavor, but are learning to co-exist with the rather unusual assortment of reference books and sites!

Sahara welcomes mail from readers. You can write to her c/o Ellora's Cave Publishing at P.O. Box 787, Hudson, Ohio 44236-0787.

Also by SAHARA KELLY:

Chapter One

Thursday

The first thing Elaine Ridgley noticed about the man was his ass. Bending down to retrieve his belongings, his dark, expensive looking slacks outlined every luscious detail. While settling her luggage into the cab, she watched as he stood up and turned around, displaying an equally appealing package.

What the hell am I doing? Elaine blushed. Listening to the voice in her head calling her a pervert, she tried to turn away. But her eyes weren't listening. They continued their perusal, mentally exploring the possibilities that body offered. And oh the possibilities...

Finally, her gaze wandered up to his face. Damn. The man was an all over hottie. She sighed. It was just her luck to find perfection in an airport—final destination unknown.

Elaine started to close the door to her cab, ready to leave Mr. Delectable Ass behind, but his words to the clipboard wielding transportation director had her stopping her cabbie before he could speed off. "Hey, wait...I'll share."

He grumbled. "Meter's on, Ma'am."

Elaine opened the door. "You need a ride to the Royal Violet? Get in."

"Thanks." Pleasant surprise crossed his face as he turned toward her. As their gazes met, his hazel eyes sparked appreciation and something else...was that interest? *Damn. This man could so turn me into a drooling idiot.*

"Don't mention it." She slid over to the far side of the bench seat as he tossed his bags in the trunk and hopped in next to her.

She watched him attempt to get comfortable and as he shifted and moved, the temperature in the cab went through the roof. Well at least it did in her cunt. Everything about this man just seemed good enough to eat. He turned to her with a smile, and she cursed herself as she quickly looked away, hoping he hadn't noticed her stare. *Note to self: quit spending your nights working and start spending them learning how to pick up hot men so you don't come off as such a pathetic loser.*

Luckily, he didn't seem to notice her ineptitude. "Long line out there today. I really appreciate you offering to share. I'll get the ride. It's the least I can do."

"You sure?" *What can I offer you in return? My body? A night of reckless passion?*

"I insist." He graced her with another charming smile and then turned away, but she could've sworn he'd checked out her cleavage first. Damn. Why had she buttoned up her shirt so high this morning?

The ride was quick. Too quick.

He paid the cabbie and got out of the car, grabbing his stuff from the trunk. "Have a good evening and thanks again. Maybe I'll see you later." He grinned and nodded. The look in his eyes led her to believe he might have actually meant what he said.

"Yeah. You, too." *I hope.* Her words trailed after him but he was already stepping into the hotel.

Just as quickly as he'd come into her life, he'd left again.

It was probably better that way. She needed to focus on Greenlight and making sure it launched without a hitch. AdLive wasn't sending her to the Creative Solutions trade show to get laid. That's why she'd brought her vibrator. But maybe if she did see the hot man again later...

Thank God for later. Not even a half hour had passed and there was Mr. Fine Ass fumbling with his room key...and his room was right across the hall from hers.

Okay, all the signs were pointing for her to go for it. A casual weekend fling could get her out of her relationship slump. Hell, it wasn't like she had time for more than that anyway. *What the hell. Why not?*

"Here, slide it slower." She drifted up behind him, placed her hand over his and grazed her breasts against his arm as she took his keycard. "You here for Creative Solutions, too?" *Oh my God. Can my nipples get any harder? Slow down. Be seductive, not desperate…*

He turned his head toward her. Their faces were only inches apart. She let her gaze roam over his kissable lips, strong jaw, and up to his deep hazel eyes. *Score! The look of lust. Maybe throwing myself at him just might work.*

"Yeah. It's a pretty big show, huh? Maybe we can…ummm…stop by each other's booths." He cleared his throat as he lowered his arm, brushing his elbow down the curve of her breast as he did it.

Elaine gasped, choking out her response. "I'd like that." Swiping the keycard, she pushed open the door. This weekend suddenly held more than just business possibilities.

He let out a light chuckle. "There it is…the magic green light of entry. This whole show is all about Greenlight for me."

No, please say it isn't so. Her heart sank as all thoughts of stress-relieving nights with this man flew right out the window. "Are you with AdLive?"

"Yeah, how'd you guess?"

"Just a few too many coincidences. I'm Elaine Ridgley." *And I'm going to bang my head against the wall now.*

He shoved a suitcase into his room, then turned back to her with a nervous smile. Swallowing hard, he shook his head, then offered up a handshake. "Oh, umm…yeah. Hi Elaine. I'm Mark Ranzetti. It's great to finally meet you. We'll talk some more later tonight when I meet the rest of the group."

From lust to all business in 2.3 seconds. Dammit!

"Sure. Meet you in the lobby with the rest of the guys in an hour." *Hopefully, with a change of panties, I can get on with my life.*

The last thing she saw was that fine ass of his as the door closed behind it.

She sighed, turned around, and entered her hotel room, cursing the damn green light that had ended things before they could get started.

But it could have been worse. She could have actually fucked her new boss, the Vice-President of AdLive Web Development, and the man who'd been transferred to steal Greenlight away from her.

Dammit. Dammit. Dammit!

* * * * *

Elaine was twenty minutes late.

But she'd needed those twenty minutes. Her vibrator had helped take the edge off, but the knowledge that she was going to spend countless hours working side by side with Mark all weekend had her stopping by the gift shop for more batteries.

It should be illegal to have a boss that hot.

Elaine arrived at the Starlight Lounge and handed over the ticket that had been waiting for her at check-in. An interesting way for a new boss to meet and greet his employees. She could already tell that Mark was going to keep her on her toes. She just shook her head and walked inside, studying the crowd around her before spying her crew already seated at a table, the only available seat right next to Mark.

Of all the damn luck…

Mark didn't even seem to notice as she approached. It looked like he'd already befriended the rest of the team.

Larry's gaze strayed to her partially exposed cleavage as she sat down, but he continued talking. "A hypnotism show? Out of all the shows in Vegas, you got us tickets to a hypnotism show? Who the hell is Bill Brentwood, anyway? Probably learned how to hypnotize from some instructions inside a Cracker Jack box."

"He's supposedly the greatest hypnotist of all time. Somehow, I doubt it." Jack smirked.

Elaine just sighed. Was there anything Jack *ever* liked or believed in? His marketing campaigns were always successful, but the man was insufferable.

She looked at Mark, wondering what his first impressions were of everyone. All he did was smile at her, but there was something else in his stare. Something deeper...more personal. A challenge, maybe? "Glad to see you made it, Elaine."

Had he thought he affected her so badly she wouldn't show up? Well she'd show him. "Of course. I need to make sure the new VP knows what he's doing so Greenlight doesn't fail."

Nothing but very loud silence followed. She could feel the stares from her fellow sales team. Earlier that week they'd all been lamenting the fact that a new face was going to run their campaign. Now they were probably wondering when they'd be saying goodbye to her and her big mouth. She hadn't meant it to sound so accusatory but something about Mark kept her off balance. Oh well, she wasn't known for backing down and she sure as hell wasn't going to stammer her way out of this one.

Besides, Mark needed to know where her loyalties lay.

And then Mark grinned. A grin that stretched from ear to ear and caused those gorgeous eyes of his to sparkle. "Well said, Elaine. Remind me not to get on your bad side. And Greenlight won't fail. Not if I have anything to say about it."

Elaine met his smile and nodded. Maybe Hanson hadn't transferred him to sabotage her creation after all.

"So, did you two already meet or something?" Bryan looked at them both, obviously trying to decide exactly what was going on between the two of them. If anyone could figure it out, it would be Bryan. Married to her best friend Jen, Bryan was the one guy on this team Elaine undoubtedly knew she could trust.

But she had to make light of their meeting, or Bryan would worry about her all weekend. Elaine shrugged. "Oh, yeah, we met in the hallway earlier. No big deal."

Mark narrowed his eyes but grinned. "Yeah. Just a coincidence."

Larry harrumphed then wiped his hands on his belly. "Hey, is there a waitress around here? I need a beer."

"Even *I'm* gonna need a beer just to survive this." Tom sighed as he took in the audience. Poor guy. He was the worst salesman on the team and Elaine swore that the only reason he closed any deals was out of customer pity.

"Ah, c'mon guys, this'll be fun. Promise. And the first round of drinks is on me."

The guys cheered Mark's offer and Elaine sank back into her chair, her thoughts turning to the reason she was in Las Vegas.

Greenlight had been her passion for the last six months, thereby becoming her longest passionate relationship. Before she'd had Greenlight, there had been Ronald Hanson. What a mistake that had been. No one else in the company knew that they'd been involved for eight months, when they'd been co-workers competing for the same VP position. Hanson had spent more time kissing the boss's ass than her own, which should have told her there was a problem much earlier on in their relationship. When he received the promotion she'd worked so hard for, he'd asked her to quit...and marry him as the consolation prize. Instead, she chose her career over a lifetime of disappointing fucks.

Hanson was still doing his best to make sure that Elaine didn't rise any further in the company. Ronald feared a woman who enjoyed being on top...especially one more suited to it then he was. His subtle jabs at her design work, the snide remarks about her abilities, just fueled her fire to make Greenlight the success she knew it could be. Transferring Mark in last minute to run Greenlight's premiere at Creative Solutions was another jab from Hanson. If Greenlight succeeded, Mark would be praised; if it failed, she'd be out of a job. She should be worried, but she wasn't. Greenlight would not fail.

Elaine's gaze casually passed over Mark. He looked so damn good, deep blue dress shirt tucked into well-fitting gray chinos. He was clearly in his element and Elaine knew then how he'd made VP at AdLive. Employees felt comfortable being around him, whether at work or at play. He had that certain honest team player air about him. A boss who was still able to be "just one of the guys." She couldn't keep herself from warming up to him. Sure just looking at him made her hot, but there was also something more…

Thankfully the waitress arrived before Elaine could dissect her thoughts too closely. The scantily clad server showed off her merchandise to each of the guys as she passed out their beers, definitely vying for a large tip. Elaine just rolled her eyes, stood up and leaned over the table toward the waitress, determined to get her beer before it turned room temperature.

That was a mistake, Elaine realized, as her breasts practically made contact with Mark's face.

Yet he acted like he didn't even notice! Not that she had meant to do it, but a little visual response, or an announcement that he liked the freckle on her right breast would have been nice.

And then he raised his arm, brushing along the underside of her breast as he grabbed his beer off the tray.

Alert! Pantyhose reaching critical heat level…melting imminent!

But he never looked at her…did he not realize what he'd done?

Damn she wanted him. Wanted him to peel the melting hose off her body, rip her dress off and fuck her on the table in front of her co-workers, consequences be damned.

Instead she sat down and took a long drink of her beer.

The guys resumed their talking which Elaine ignored as she focused on bringing her body back down to normal temperature levels. This was going to be an interesting weekend.

Suddenly, Mark met her stare across the table and grinned. "So, ya gonna do it with me?"

Elaine blinked. Dear God, was it that obvious what she was thinking? She cursed her mind's ability to wander off at the most inopportune times. Returning Mark's grin with a smirk, she prayed that she was giving him the right answer. "With an invitation like that, how could I refuse?"

Mark's eyes twinkled merrily as he stood up. "Let's do it then."

The guys cheered as she stood up. Larry leaned back in his chair and lifted his second beer in toast. His eyes never lifted above her exposed line of cleavage. Would the man ever understand she was more than a piece of meat and that lechers were never her type anyway? "To Elaine...for suddenly making this party a whole lot more interesting..."

Elaine was halfway to the stage when it became obvious exactly what she'd agreed to. Lights began flashing, the music intensified, and scantily clad dancers began gyrating to the wild beat. Then, Mr. Bill Brentwood, the greatest hypnotist of all time — *yeah right* — made his appearance.

"What the hell did you get me into?" Elaine whispered to Mark as they filed on stage.

"I'm wondering that myself," he replied as they sat down next to each other on a bench.

Elaine glanced around her. About twenty people — or hypno-hopefuls as Bill liked to call them — filled the stage. Elaine was sandwiched between Mark and a cute college boy. Standing behind her was a guy who looked like he should be in the NFL, muscles overflowing his tight black T-shirt.

Mark turned toward her and winked. "This is going to be fun."

Like getting teeth pulled, Elaine thought as Bill began the show. She just hoped she wouldn't end up doing something stupid that she'd never be able to live down.

Elaine only partially listened as Bill gave his hypnotism spiel. It was all the normal stuff about these types of stage shows — everything the audience saw that night was real and no one was paid to be up on stage. Elaine snorted. Hell, she was more than willing to pay to go back to her seat to watch the fun from afar, but Mark was so intent on chumming, she knew she had to stay and make good. She reminded herself that she was doing it for the success of Greenlight. Nothing more, nothing less.

And maybe she'd get to have a little fun with Mark in the process. All for the sake of the show, of course.

Bill gestured at all the hypno-hopefuls. "Aren't you all lucky? We're gonna sleep together tonight right here on stage." He and the audience shared a laugh. "All kidding aside, I'm gonna take real good care of you. One hour of hypno-sleep is as good as eight hours of regular sleep. How's that for a bonus? Now, quiet everyone, let's start breathing deeply and relax."

Elaine's internal devil reared its head and she whispered to Mark, "Sleep together, huh?"

"And just what exactly should we do with our sleepless night ahead of us?" Mark replied with what could only be described as a shit-eatin' grin.

So he knew she was off limits, but he still wanted to flirt, did he? Two could play at that game. She tilted her face and blinked coquettishly. "Oh, the possibilities. Hmmm...I see long hours of Greenlight paperwork in your future." She grinned. "You need the prep time. And I need to use my vibrator."

Mark started laughing then hid it behind a cough as Bill shot them both a glance. Elaine faked innocence, pretending to be fully involved with the show. Ha! Score one for her. Oh yeah, being in a cheesy hypnotism show with her boss would make this a night to remember.

Bill continued. "That's good. Most of you are concentrating perfectly. Now on my count of three, your eyelids will start to feel heavy. At two, they will want to close. At one, they will close..." Bill kept going and Elaine just tried to play along. Hell, the show was only supposed to be about an hour. If all it took to fake being hypnotized was to do a bunch of breathing and keep her eyes closed, tonight would be the easiest part of her weekend.

Bill resumed his speech. "As you relax, keep breathing deeply and imagine your body has become a pile of loose rubber bands. Completely relaxed."

The music in the background was hypnotic in its own right as it soothed and calmed. Even with her eyes closed, Elaine could tell that the stage lights had gone out. She yawned, suddenly very tired. Work had kept her so busy for the last several months, she hadn't been sleeping as much as she should. Hopefully, the hotel bed would be comfortable enough for her to get some much-needed sleep.

Elaine could hear Bill walking around and people being moved at his direction. The college kid next to her moved away and Bill leaned her against Mark while saying something about being safe and feeling protected. His words were starting to mush together as she got more and more tired. She thought about sitting back up, but there was something so soothing about Mark's natural scent and the firmness of his shoulder. Relaxing even further, she slid down a bit and discovered the wonder of his tightly muscled chest. Oh yeah, it felt even better than it looked.

Bill's voice reached through the fog of her thoughts. "Imagine you have balloons tied to your hand. Imagine that those balloons tied to your hand are growing. They're growing so big that your hand wants to rise off your lap and into the air. Rising and lifting. Lifting and rising. You are concentrating perfectly."

Elaine mentally snickered. How hokey was this? Imaginary balloons and floating hands. Was anybody actually falling for this?

Then her hand started to leave her lap. It felt so light and buoyant and there was just no way she could keep it down. Bill kept talking about how strong the balloons were tugging and they were! Her other hand joined the first and Elaine felt like she could float away. What the hell was going on?

The tugging on her hands intensified and she stood up, following the pull. Mark brushed against her as he stood up too. So he was playing along as well...or was he really being hypnotized? But she wasn't, she couldn't be. There had to be a rational reason her hands were trying to float away.

Bill interrupted Elaine as she mentally registered her flight pattern. "Everyone freeze and open your eyes to see where you are and how well you have concentrated."

Elaine slowly blinked open her eyes and tried to shake the sleep from her thoughts. There were a lot of people with their hands in the air. It looked like a church revival. She bit her lip to keep from bursting into a chorus of "Kumbaya".

Mark turned to her and gave her a questioning smile, his hands still high in the air. His shirt was pulled taut across his chest, showcasing those magnificent pectorals she'd been up close and personal with. Then he frowned and looked down, lowering his hands to shift his shirt away from his chest. A small, dark, wet stain was visible.

Oh God, she hadn't! Please tell her she hadn't. But there was no denying the obvious.

Elaine had drooled on her new boss's chest.

* * * * *

"I don't think I've ever had a woman drool on me before," Mark said with a grin. Elaine's face turned a lovely crimson, and as he watched, the blush moved lower, disappearing down into her cleavage. Mark swallowed hard. Since she'd offered them up to him earlier, he'd been unable to think of little else, had been fighting all night to keep from staring at those beauties. From what he could tell, they were pretty damn perfect. His mouth watered just thinking about that little freckle on her right breast he'd noticed earlier. *Just one taste...*

One of Bill's dancer-helpers moved Mark away from Elaine before she could reply. Probably a good idea. Mark needed to get his head back and his other head under control. Damn thing was trying to get out of his pants so it could get up Elaine's dress.

He was placed on a bench on the opposite side of the stage where he could easily watch Elaine as the dancers continued moving everyone around, setting up the next part of the show. Damn, she intrigued the hell out of him. Obviously smart—he'd seen enough of Greenlight to know that she had an award winning idea going. *Hot damn, what a woman.* All woman. And unfortunately far behind the firewall of interoffice bad ideas. Hell, his spidering software must be completely malfunctioning because it wasn't responding to the auto-off command after bouncing. Mark shook his head. Using computer terms to define the way a woman made him feel had to be the beginning of the end. Or maybe he really did have a couple of screws loose when it came to Elaine.

Thankfully, she was across the stage, nowhere near his thoughts or his body. Bill took Elaine's hand and moved her to the chair right next to Mark and he inwardly grimaced. Now if he could just keep his sleepy gaze from wandering down her cleavage.

Still holding her hand, Bill began to speak. "I've got a great group tonight. We're going to have a lot of fun." Bill turned his attention back to Elaine. "What's your name, sweetheart?"

Elaine's eyes seemed to grow wider in her face. "Elaine…"

"Well, Elaine, are you here with someone special tonight? Husband? Boyfriend? Someone who just might be mad at me if I keep calling you beautiful?"

She shook her head, her tongue darting out to nervously lick her lips. "No…I'm in Vegas on business, actually."

"Well, let's have some fun…just the two of us." Bill kissed her hand and turned and wiggled his eyebrows lasciviously at the audience who laughed and cheered their response. "Sit down for me, sweetheart. It's time for the show to begin."

Bill started at the opposite side of the bench and asked where everyone was from and right in the middle of the mini-interviews, he put them each into hypnotic sleep. There was Becky, the librarian from Kansas. The college kid's name was Stanley. There was a dad named Bob. As he put them out, he leaned them on each other like fallen dominoes.

After asking Mark's name, Bill put him under without further fanfare. Mark was mostly aware of what was going on around him, but still felt separate from it, comfortable in his own relaxed world. If this was what hypnotism felt like, the show was going to be a piece of cake.

Vaguely, through his sleep, he thought he heard Bill doing some sort of theatrics with Elaine before her body slowly lowered onto his. But did she realize that her hand had settled right on his cock? *So unfair.* He willed his cock to stay calm, but if she didn't move her hand soon, there would be no hiding anything.

Bill cracked some kind of joke and then Elaine's hand lifted and found rest on Mark's thigh. *Thank God.* This was neither the time nor the place for a hard on.

Bill started rambling on and on about hypnotism and he started giving people suggestions, but Mark's thoughts drifted back to Elaine and how he landed in Vegas for Creative Solutions. Hanson was a dick for transferring him in time to steal the unveiling of Greenlight from her, but in a way, he was also glad it had happened. Greenlight was an excellent project. When he found out she'd designed and built most of it, he wanted to bow down to her because by coming up with Greenlight, she was reviving the Web Development arm of AdLive.

He kept an ear open to Bill. Every now and then, he'd go off on another suggestion. Clearly, the show was about making the audience laugh. It was rife with comedy. And somehow, Mark got the feeling that he'd end up doing something he wouldn't be able to live down.

The librarian was hypnotized to swallow fire. The guy next to her was hypnotized to say, "My name is TwinkleToes and I'm the world's best ballerina."

And then it happened.

Bill tapped Mark's shoulder and said, "Person's whose neck I'm touching now—when you hear me say the words 'Are we having fun,' you will jump up and say 'My name is TwinkleToes and I'm the world's best ballerina.' And when you see Bob doing and saying what you just did at the same time, you'll argue with him because you are indeed the world's best ballerina. And there can only be one Prima Ballerina on this stage."

Mark took special note, very much agreeing with what Bill had told him. Perhaps he could be called TwinkleToes. After all, his sister had dared him to take a few ballet classes with her when he was in high school. Hell, it was entirely possible that he could be the world's best ballerina. And there was just no way that some other guy could be a better ballerina. No way. He concentrated on that while Bill went around making a few more suggestions.

"On my count of three, you will all open your eyes feeling awake and refreshed. One, two, three. Awake." Bill's voice jolted Mark from the nice comfort of his sleep. Elaine shifted back fully into her chair. He didn't remember putting his arm around her when she was leaning against him, but it sure felt nice to hold her close.

Bill continued. "This is great. You folks have to be the best crowd of subjects I've had. I love hypnotism!" Bill grinned and Elaine suddenly got up, walked over to Bill and gave him a big hug. Dammit. Bill must have hypnotized her to hug him. Not that he could blame the man. She looked damn good in that tiny little black dress. Mark wouldn't mind her arms wrapped around him, pressing those amazing breasts into his chest. But it didn't stop him from wanting to put his fist through Bill's face, either.

Bill smirked at the crowd then focused on Elaine. "Elaine? Wide awake? What are you doing?"

She looked at Bill with a confused expression and went back to her chair. Mark just hoped he didn't end up hugging Bill at some point. That would look so wrong for the new boss.

"All right everyone! Are we having fun?"

Mark got up and ignoring a sort of distant conflict between mind and body declared, "My name is TwinkleToes and I'm the world's best ballerina!"

Mark stood there proudly until he realized that Bob had the nerve to say the same damn thing. Well, that just wouldn't do. That guy simply couldn't be a better ballerina. No way. Mark strode over to him. "There's no way you're a better ballerina than I am. I'm the world's best. You're mistaken. And I can prove it." Mark did a fantastic leap in the air and began to show his worth.

* * * * *

Elaine could not believe the sight before her. Bob was doing some clunky pirouette, stumbling around on the stage as though he were drunk.

And then there was Mark. Damn that man knew how to dance. He was so graceful, she felt like she could just run up into his arms and he'd toss her into one of those swan poses above his head or something equally fantastic. His muscles flexed and tightened as he moved, just adding to the beauty of his performance. The man hid quite a body underneath those innocent business casual clothes.

Even Bill was somewhat flabbergasted. "Mark, Bob, wide awake. What on earth were you guys doing?"

Bob's jaw dropped and he started laughing as he went back to his spot on the bench.

Mark just stood there. Elaine smirked. At least they had equally embarrassed themselves on stage. Although she definitely had a new admiration for Mark. A hot hunk of male flesh who could prance about like a ballerina and somehow not look like a flamboyantly gay transvestite. What a man. The audience was roaring, but he simply shook his head and chuckled all the way back to his seat. Although he did cast her a sideways glance and grin—it was definitely a camaraderie moment. She just returned his grin, enjoying the adventure.

Interrupting her thoughts, Bill exclaimed. "I love hypnotism!" and Elaine once again got up and hugged him. What the hell was she doing? "Elaine? Wide awake. Will you go sit back down? You must really like me, huh?"

She nodded and did as he directed, finally realizing that whatever was going to happen would happen, and she might as well enjoy it. As long as Bill didn't turn her into a ballerina. Not after Mark's award winning performance. She didn't want to be out-danced by her boss. Thankfully, Bill put everyone out and gave new suggestions before waking them up again.

"Anyone wanna dance?" Bill called out to his hypno-subjects as slow and sensual music began to play.

Mark stood up and held his hand out to Elaine. Dancing with TwinkleToes was the best thing to happen all night. Every time Bill had put her out, she'd leaned against Mark, his toned body reminding her what she'd lost out on earlier. She melted into his arms and they began to sway to the music. Even though she knew that neither one of them was completely in control of initiating their actions, their bodies responded to each other's nearness. His cock nudged her clitoris and she couldn't help but press herself closer, imagining all the things she wanted to do with him.

"We've got a few couples dancing up here now. Ladies and gentleman of the audience, are you ready to party?" Bill's voice rang in her mind and Elaine responded by reaching down and squeezing Mark's incredibly firm ass. And wow...she needed more time. His ass demanded further exploration.

"Did you see that? She just grabbed his butt!" Bill chuckled. "But what I wanna know is where have all the cowboys gone?"

Elaine found herself being deeply dipped by Mark. His movements were so fluid. And his eyes shone with more than just the haze of trance. Passion and lust glimmered there as well.

At least they'd be mutually uncomfortable this weekend.

* * * * *

Mark leaned over Elaine, still holding her in a deep dip. There were so many things he wanted to do to this woman, starting with removing the dress that was blocking his view.

"Ladies and gentleman! Are we ready to rumble?" Bill's voice coaxed Mark into something he'd wanted to do since he first laid hands on Elaine. Pulling her closer, he kissed her neck. Faintly, he could hear the audience roar with delight. Mark nearly dropped her when he remembered he was on a stage. At least he had only given her a quick kiss on the neck and hadn't lingered like he'd wanted to. "Mark, Elaine, Stanley, Becky. Wide awake. You guys were just having way too much fun. Go sit down before the bachelor party in the back tackles me to teach them how to hypnotize."

As they sat down, Mark leaned over and whispered, "I'm sorry about..."

"I don't think I am. I—" Elaine was interrupted as Bill put everyone back to sleep.

Bill made a few more parting suggestions, the crowd cheered and everyone climbed off the stage, the show over.

Mark watched Elaine walk back to the table, realizing that all his excuses to touch her had been left on stage with the floating balloons and ballerinas.

Shit, this was going to be a long weekend.

* * * * *

"Maybe I should've gone on stage with you two," Larry griped as they walked out of the show. "Then I could've stayed up all night playing blackjack and not missed the sleep. And you goody two shoes are probably just gonna go work all night or something. What a waste." He shook his head. "Although with that last suggestion Bill gave you, maybe you *won't* be working." He wiggled his thick eyebrows. "I'll see you guys bright and early." Larry weaved his way through the crowd toward the casino.

Elaine blinked after Larry, still too foggy-headed to make any quick retorts, or even to ask him what the hell he was talking about. Everywhere Mark had touched her still tingled. Hell, all of her senses seemed to be hyper-aware. Mark stood three feet away from her, chatting with Jack and Tom, and she'd swear she could feel his body heat, smell his cologne, feel his lips against her neck. She stared down at her hands. Had she really grabbed his ass?

Oh yeah she had. And what she wouldn't give for a taste...

Elaine shivered. She needed to get to her room, and quickly, before she did something she'd regret. Thank God for her vibrator. It was going to be a long night.

Jack and Tom both walked away, throwing parting shots over their shoulders. Elaine didn't even pay attention.

"Thanks for the show," Bryan said as he patted Mark on the back. "Great fun. I've got to call the wife and kids and tell them good night."

"Tell Jen I said hello, that lunch is still on for next week, and that I won't let you get into any trouble," Elaine said with a smile.

Bryan smiled back. "She always tells me I'm supposed to keep you from getting into any trouble. Guess I didn't do too well tonight, little miss ass grabber." Bryan laughed as Elaine wrinkled her nose. "I'm sure Jen will want details."

Bryan sauntered away. He and Jen were so damn cute together. Even after eight years and two kids they sparkled enough to outshine the lights on the Las Vegas strip.

"So, see you tomorrow then. Thanks for playing along tonight."

Elaine looked up at Mark as he spoke and almost swallowed her tongue. Hazel-green fire burned through her. *Damn, damn and double damn.* Why did this man have to be her boss? "Yeah, no problem. I had a great time." *And you have the best ass I've ever sunk my fingers into…*

They both turned, walking together to the elevator. Mark laughed. It sounded nervous. "Going to your room, too?" He pressed the up button.

"Yeah."

"Great."

Could this get any more awkward? Elaine breathed a sigh of relief when the elevator opened, depositing a crowd of eager gamblers into the casino. Squeezing through the departing group, she pressed her floor button then settled into the back corner. Mark moved to the other corner and an elderly couple stood together in the center, facing forward, as the doors closed.

Elaine stared at her watch. Two minutes. Two minutes tops she could be in her room, on the bed, taking the edge off her arousal. Reaching into her purse she pulled out her keycard. One minute forty-five seconds. Out of the corner of her eye she peeked at Mark.

He was leaning against the back wall of the elevator, arms crossed over his chest, undressing her with his eyes.

Elaine stopped breathing, her nipples tightening to painful points under his intent perusal. Mark grinned, showing those perfect white teeth of his. He *knew* she'd seen him watching her, and he knew she wanted him, too.

Well, fine. If he wanted to watch, she'd give him a show. Starting at her neck, she traced the keycard down her body, running it between her breasts, across her stomach, then lower, right above her needy clit. Narrowing her eyes, she teased the card back and forth, back and forth, pressing it into her clit. Her head dropped back, eyes closed and she bit her lip to keep from moaning.

A hand covered hers, briefly grinding against her clit. Elaine's eyes shot open as Mark pocketed her card and stepped away.

His pants were stretched tight over his erection.

Elaine's eyes widened. His very large erection.

The elevator dinged and the door opened, the elderly couple making their way out. Mark stepped forward, keeping the door open for them.

The older man smiled, his hand gently holding his wife's arm. His wrinkled face shone amusement as he turned back to Mark. "You two have a good night."

"We will," Mark replied throatily as the elevator door closed.

Elaine shivered. *We will…*

Mark whipped around, his long legs eating up the narrow distance between them.

She met him halfway. His fingers sank into the flesh of her ass, kneading and caressing her cheeks through her dress. She ground against his cock and lifted her face to his.

"Elaine…" he growled painfully. And then he kissed her.

All thought processes stopped as she melted into Mark. Wrapping her arms around his neck, she drowned in the velvet of his tongue dancing with hers. She slid her hands down his body and squeezed his ass again. Oh lord, it was even better then she'd remembered.

The elevator dinged again, jerking her from her sensual stupor. They both jumped apart, like two kids caught with their hands in the cookie jar. The door opened onto an empty vestibule and Elaine quickly exited. She needed some distance to gain clarity. She desperately tried to catch her breath and her mind as it ran away with thoughts of long, passion filled nights…with her boss.

What the hell was she thinking?

Mark followed her out of the elevator and the door closed behind them. Elaine turned to him to tell him good night, to tell him that this couldn't happen, to tell him that he was an amazing kisser…but then she was in his arms again, her mouth against his.

Somehow they made it down the hall, arms and tongues still wrapped around each other. Mark tripped over a room service tray in front of someone's door, but somehow managed to stay erect…er…standing. Then they were in front of her door, Mark using her confiscated keycard to gain entrance. He didn't have any problems opening the door this time. The green light flashed, giving them a go.

Elaine didn't think her feet actually touched the ground as Mark swept her into the room, kicking the door closed with his foot. The room went dark as the light from the hall was shut out.

But they didn't need light to see. Her hands found the front of his shirt, gaining some type of world speed record in unbuttoning it. Then she moved on to his pants, beyond desperate…beyond all rational thought.

Mark's hands slid up her nylon-covered thighs, lifting her dress to her hips, then gripped her hose and thong, ripping them down and off her legs.

Elaine shoved his pants and briefs to his knees, then studied his cock with her fingertips. Oh lord, he was huge. The bulge in his pants hadn't lied. Her pussy creamed some more, ready for all he offered.

Foil ripped and his hands joined hers on his cock, unrolling the condom down his length.

Rational thought came roaring back to her, reminding her that she couldn't do this, no matter how wonderful *this* would be.

Then his lips found her neck, one hand dipped into her dress, palming her nipple. Every touch felt too good. Her mind shouted at her to not make this mistake while her body screamed out for more of what he offered.

"Mark, we shouldn't...I don't fuck co-workers anymore..."

His breathing was rough and staggered. She wished she could see his face. "Tell me no, and I'll walk away. Tell me to go back to my room and we'll forget this almost happened."

She couldn't do it. Her hands circled around his neck and pulled him flush against her. "Don't stop."

"I won't." Then he lifted her, bracing her up against the door and slid his cock into her aching cunt.

Elaine bit back her scream. It had been too long since anything had felt this good.

Hell, nothing had ever felt this good.

He thrust into her, his large cock stretching her, filling her, hitting every aching spot. His lips and tongue created a maelstrom of feeling as they caressed her neck, her face, her jaw. It was sensory overload, and she was spiraling toward orgasm quicker than she ever had before.

When it hit, she thought she would die, or pass out, or melt into a puddle of happy orgasm on the floor of the room.

But there wasn't time. Mark lifted one of her legs, anchoring it around his hip and continued his thrusting.

Every thrust, every press of his cock into her cunt had her moaning, gasping, crying out for more. She ran her hands over his body, relishing the coarse texture of hair smattering his chest, the tight muscles in his arms. The man had a perfect body, a body she wanted to visually explore.

Next time the lights were coming on.

Mark's breathing came faster, his cock seeming to plunge deeper. One hand cradled her breast, fondling her tight nipple. Then his hand lowered to where their bodies were joined. His fingers, now wet with her arousal, ground against her clit.

She screamed and climaxed, even harder than the first time. Mark let out a loud groan and kissed her as he shuddered and came inside of her. The rhythmic pulsing of his cock as he came kept her climaxing, over and over…never ending.

With Mark around, who needed the suggestion of hypnotic balloons to fly?

* * * * *

The woman had been killing him in that tight black dress of hers, but after round one underneath it, Mark decided the torture had been well worth it. Every last ounce of her was astounding. Her breasts filled his hands, the perfect size, perfect shape…just damn perfect.

Never in a million years would he have thought getting involved with a co-worker would be a good idea, but Elaine…. Breaking the rules with her was worth every potential consequence. She matched his arousal and shared it with as much abandon as he did. He wanted to remove that torturous dress of hers with his teeth, suck on her nipples until she couldn't see straight and then take her again, harder and faster until both of their voices were raw from screaming.

As her breathing calmed, she sighed and leaned against his chest. He tried to calm his own breathing and find a way of disentangling her shapely leg from around his hip. Truthfully, he didn't want to separate from her, but he knew he would have to soon before the condom leaked.

She kissed his chest and he took his cue to help her down and away from his cock.

Her hand trailed from his chest and then around to his ass, lightly squeezing before she stepped away, into the darkened room.

Was that an invitation for more?

He slid his feet out of his shoes, stepped out of his pants then walked into the bathroom to deal with the used condom. He only ever had the one condom with him in case of emergency. How the hell was he supposed to know that Elaine might constitute more than one emergency in the same night?

Then again, there were so many other things he could do to her without needing another condom.

He left the bathroom and walked into the main room. She'd turned on the lights, and he stopped dead at the sight in front of him. Elaine had stripped naked, and was bent over, rummaging through her suitcase. Her firm round ass beckoned him to fuck her again. Streaks of wet arousal stained her thighs and he stared in fascination at her pussy lips, still wide open from their recent fuck. He swallowed hard as he watched her perfectly round breasts sway back and forth as her hands sought the contents of some small zippered pouch. His cock set a new personal record for quick erection.

She rose and turned to face him. Seductive eyes scanned him from head to toe, the look of lust on her face assuring him that she liked what she saw. She held up her hand, triumphantly displaying an unopened box of condoms.

Hell, yes!

She ripped open the box and pulled them all out. "Thank God for my emergency kit. Never thought I'd have such a good reason to use it, though."

The condoms spilled onto the bed as he claimed her. His mouth sought her breasts immediately—needing to know the taste of them against his tongue. And then he saw it again. The perfect little freckle that had teased him earlier, gracing the curve of her right breast. Leaning in, he swiped his tongue across it, then nibbled on her flesh. He could dine on her luscious flavor all night.

Elaine's fingers ran through his hair, holding him against her chest. She made sweet little mewling sounds that turned him on even more. He moved his attentions to her nipple and as he sucked and licked one, his hand cupped her other breast and kneaded it. She moaned, arching into his touch. Her breasts alone could fulfill many of his fantasies.

Her hands slid over his shoulders, tugging on his shirt, ripping the fabric down his arms. He liked her aggressive style of disrobing him. The heat between them continued to rise as she wrapped one hand around his shoulder, holding him tight to her breasts. The fingers of her other hand teased across his chest, then sought lower until she grasped his cock. Red-hot need burned through him as she stroked her hand up and down his length. He groaned and she chuckled, ever so slightly tightening her grip. He couldn't help but thrust himself in time with her stroking. Damn. If she kept that up, he was going to come before even getting inside of her.

With lightning speed, his hands rushed down from her amazing breasts and crashed onto her ass. He cupped it firmly in both hands, pulling her closer. His cock brushed against her stomach as she worked his complete length. What an amazing body Elaine had. He could easily fuck her day in and day out.

He gritted his teeth to keep from demanding she take him back in hand as she pulled away to reach for a condom. "I need you now. Inside of me. Now, Mark." She unrolled the condom over his shaft. He lifted her up, then sat down on the corner of the bed, her body now straddling his.

His cock slid inside her as though it knew it was meant to be there, her cunt a tight velvet glove as she rode him hard and furious. Her hands ran through his hair, down his body and to his thighs before she reached one hand for his sac. He almost came as she rolled his testicles in her palm, still not breaking her rhythm. She moaned and screamed out as he tilted his hips to match each downward thrust of her body. Claiming her breasts with his teeth, he bit the swollen nubs, making her scream out even harder. Her pussy clenched even tighter around his cock in response.

His hands smoothed over her ass, sliding between her cheeks, just lightly pressing there, testing her willingness. She screamed out and slammed down even harder on him. She would take whatever he had to give.

Right there on the edge of heaven, he licked his way up to her neck, tasting the salt of her body, wanting to taste all of her completely. Then her lips found his and darting tongues mated. Deep moans combined as their bodies found release in each other.

Chapter Two

Friday

Elaine didn't even need to open her eyes to know that Mark was no longer there. It could have been the fact that his cock was no longer inside of her—which is how he'd spent most of his night—that clued her in to his absence.

But it wasn't just that. Even in her sleep she'd missed his presence.

Elaine opened her eyes, blearily focusing on the alarm clock on the nightstand.

Oh my God no! I can't be late!

Tossing back the covers, she propelled herself out of bed. The phone rang as she landed on one of her fancy heeled shoes from last night, further adding to her discombobulation. She grabbed for the phone, falling back on the bed, cradling her bruised foot.

"Ow! Shit! Hello?"

"Elaine, you okay?" Mark's voice radiated concern through the wires.

Oh lord, just hearing his voice had her panting and ready. After their marathon session last night she'd expected her lust for him to at least partially diminish.

Ha! If he were to come knocking on her door right now she'd tackle him to the ground and...

She shook her head. Not now. There wasn't time right now to even fantasize about Mark, let alone do anything about it.

"I'm fine. Just running late. Why didn't you wake me when you left? I'm barely going to make it down there in time for the show to start. And I'd wanted to get there early to make sure everything was running smoothly." Keeping the phone clamped between shoulder and ear, she dug through the suitcase still on the floor next to her bed. Panties, bra, nylons...

"If I'd woken you, I wouldn't have left." His voice was deep and husky.

Elaine froze in her haphazard search through her suitcase. Had he just said what she thought he'd said? Her body had heard what her mind was still trying to assimilate, her nipples growing tight, an ache beginning low in her belly.

Not now. She couldn't. Greenlight was her only priority.

"Mark, I've got to get in the shower. I'll be downstairs in thirty minutes. I promise, I'm not usually this lackadaisical about my job."

The line was quiet for an instant longer than it should have been. Long enough for Elaine to realize she was coming across as a bitch.

"Elaine—"

"Mark—"

They spoke at the same time and then both quieted. Elaine sighed, sinking to the bed, cradling the phone close. "Mark, thank you. I—I'll see you in a few."

"Greenlight will go like gangbusters, Elaine. See you downstairs."

The line went dead in her hand. Elaine returned it to the cradle and began to get ready. She'd been prepared for the premiere of Greenlight for months, had even looked forward to it.

Now she dreaded it, unsure how she'd handle spending the day with the one man she couldn't resist.

* * * * *

Larry approached her as soon as she stepped onto the carpet of the chaotic booth. "Elaine, nothing's working. How are we supposed to sell this thing if it doesn't work?"

Elaine pushed past Larry, into the booth and toward the computer terminals. Dammit! She should have checked this out last night, or gotten here early or...

"Bryan, check the back on tower two. Is it plugged in? It's still not coming up," Mark called out from where he was bent around one of the stations. His fine ass was on display again in those dress pants like yesterday at the airport when her attention was first stolen by him. She forced her gaze from his ass and focused in on the problem computer.

"Which is it? The terminals aren't coming on or Greenlight won't come up?" Elaine asked as she punched a few keys on the computer, trying to bring up the Greenlight homepage. Frustration filled her. Today was not the day to look like an incompetent buffoon.

"Well, of the four, three are on and the fourth is dead. And the three that are on won't bring up the Greenlight homepage." Mark stood up and moved next to where she was working.

"Not even from the server?" The doors were supposed to open in five minutes. Elaine just shook her head. She shouldn't have messed around...literally. Focus. On Greenlight. That's what she was here for. It was her future, her company's future. And she might just have screwed things up by not being her usual anal self and checking everything in triplicate.

"It'll work from the server, but there's no contact outside."

"Great. And we'll look like jackasses having performance problems. We have to get on the net." Elaine headed straight for the booth's central room.

"You going to recheck connections? When I got here, the server had crashed. It rebooted just fine, but maybe something's up with the router. Could you unplug and replug both the router and the server? Maybe that'll help." Mark followed her into the central room.

Sure enough. The router was plugged in, but the main line to the internet wasn't pushed all the way in. She shoved it in and all the little lights blinked accordingly. Getting closer. She looked over at Mark who'd been watching as she bent over. For a moment they just stared at each other, and she knew they were both thinking about all the times they'd fucked last night. They'd been insatiable. Hell with that, she still wanted him.

He winked and smiled, then turned to holler through the door. "Jack, Bryan…try it now. Are we good yet?"

"Like magic, Mark. Thanks," Bryan called out.

Elaine followed Mark out of the room. "You said the other one wasn't coming on at all." She knew she could eventually figure out this problem on her own, but having Mark's help would speed up the process. Not to mention having him around was high on her list of likes. "When's your first meeting?"

"In a half hour." Mark headed straight for the downed terminal. Bryan, Tom and Larry were each on the three good terminals, making sure all the sales files were in order.

"Doors are open. Let's make this happen." Elaine pulled the tower from underneath the workstation podium and checked the connections. They were all good. "We have to trace it. Do you know where they pulled power from?"

Mark leaned down next to a potted plant by the literature caddy. "Right here." He flipped the power strip switch to the "on" position. "I asked Larry to check if it was plugged in to the power strip. I didn't think I needed to ask if it was turned on. Damn, I feel like such an idiot. I guess maybe when they vacuumed the booth or something, they hit the switch."

"Maybe, but don't take time out to feel stupid yet…we still have a problem. This machine's not even on the network." She shook her head as she clicked the mouse through the appropriate windows.

Mark immediately crawled underneath the podium right next to her leg. Even through the turmoil her mind was in, she flashed back to last night and how good it felt with his body next to hers. She inched her leg toward him just so he'd rub against it a little more when he got up.

He crawled backward, the entire length of his body brushing along her leg before he stood up. A simple touch that had her flesh aching for more of that physical connection.

Mark now stood a hair's breath away from her, his eyes focused on her. She wanted to lean into him, knock him over onto the floor and go for it. She couldn't stop the desire to have him close to her...inside of her. Instead she calmly returned his stare.

He grinned, his eyes lighting up mischievously, making her wonder if he was sharing her deviant thoughts. "Well, it's plugged in nice and tight down there. I guess we'll have to trace it all the way to the server."

"Screw tracing it. Let's just run another wire." Elaine purposely brushed her breasts against his arm as she turned toward the central room. She was a glutton for punishment, or at least sexual torture.

Once in the central room, she dug around the mostly empty boxes. There was promo stuff and literature everywhere, but one box had to have the spare cables.

Mark joined her search and had more luck than she did. "Got it. We're back in the game. Found a good one mixed with the miscellaneous unnecessary miles of USB cables."

They set about running it from the terminal to the server. The only way to run it was up through part of the overhead trussing on the booth. She tossed and twisted the wire, but it just wouldn't stay. He tried the same, but the truss was just too far out of reach.

"Give me a lift." She hated to ask, but there weren't any ladders or chairs close by...and she couldn't help but want his hands on her again. Hell, his fingers had been *in* her just hours ago. And TwinkleToes was a master at lifting women in the air.

With a big grin, he put his hands on her hips and boosted her into the air. Last night, he'd always thrust himself deep inside of her after lifting her. Too bad they weren't alone on the expo floor.

She ignored the continuous heat his touch evoked in her and expertly twisted the cord through the trussing. When he set her down she had to restrain herself from grabbing his tie like a leash and pulling him to her. *Dammit.* Why did he have to be her boss? And why the hell couldn't she just forget about last night and move on?

He quickly routed the cord through a break in the booth panels and into the central room. "I'm going to ummm...go plug it into the server. You see if you can get it to come up now." He walked into the central room.

She vigorously typed, clicking all the necessary commands, then went directly into the central room after him. "Thanks, Mark. It's up and running just fine."

"Are you sure? Go back and check. I hardly got it plugged in and I can't exactly go back out there yet." Mark was turned away from her, shuffling some catalogs back into a box.

Elaine moved behind him. "What? Why? Once you plugged in, it saw the network and was happy again." She stepped up next to him and he spun around to face her. Suddenly the heat in the central room shot off the scale. His amazing non-computer equipment strained his pants, reminding her just how happy she was last night when she saw his umm...network.

He took a deep, ragged breath. "See what you do to me, Elaine? I need to calm down a bit before I go to my first meeting of the day...in about five minutes. Could you just humor me, please and go check? If you stay near me the only way this is going to subside is if I can thrust myself inside of you until I'm sated...and we both know that will take longer than the five minutes I have. There's a lot of advance buzz about Greenlight and I'm booked solid all day with people interested in our capabilities. You've done a damn good job." He paused, taking another deep breath, then locked his intense gaze with hers. "You're an amazing woman, Elaine."

Elaine was stunned, could barely catch her breath. She understood the need, desire and want in his eyes. But it was more than that, more than a basic physical connection. And even in her emotionally jumbled mind, she knew it too. She managed a small smile. "Okay...I'll go check." She felt his gaze hot on her back as she walked out of the room.

Mark came out three minutes later, a look of mild frustration on his face. Elaine couldn't blame him. She was still fighting her body for control as well.

Elaine forced a smile for him. "Everything's good now. Maybe some day the guys will be as good at troubleshooting as they are at selling. If you hear that a booth caught on fire or something, don't worry. Just get back here as soon as you can." He chuckled and shook his head, put on his suit jacket, picked up his briefcase and walked out of the booth.

The day sped by as Elaine did what she'd planned for months, and sold the hell out of her project. But no matter how busy she was, a part of her never stopped thinking about Mark.

* * * * *

Hot water flowed over Elaine's head as she almost violently scrubbed at her scalp, wishing that like Mitzi Gaynor in South Pacific, she could wash a man right out of her hair.

All day long the man had plagued her thoughts. What was going on between them? What should she do about it? Would there ever be anything more?

The only answer she'd come up with for that last question was a resounding no. Relationships with co-workers had too much potential to end badly. No matter what happened between the two of them this weekend, when they returned to Los Angeles, all had to be forgotten.

She'd managed to sell the hell out of Greenlight, surpassing even her best expectations of first day success. But it wasn't difficult to sell a product that with its ease of use could essentially sell itself.

When Mark had returned to the Greenlight booth two hours before the end of the show, they'd gone through the expo guidebook to make sure there weren't any potential clients that Mark didn't have meetings with. He'd shared his successes, but had remained very professional in his attentions toward her.

Then Mark had grabbed his belongings, mumbled something about an appointment that would keep him from returning to the booth that day, and left. Elaine had suffered a pang of regret as he'd walked away, even though she knew it was for the best.

Larry had of course asked her to dinner — which she knew would have led to him trying to have dessert with her in his bed. She'd politely but firmly declined the offer, giving the old headache excuse. Bryan and Tom had said something about catching a movie and Jack had taken off as soon as the expo closed.

So she'd returned alone to her room, determined to have a relaxing, comfortable, Mark-free night. She'd called room service before getting in the shower, ordering a salad, then tacking on multiple desserts just for the hell of it. Tonight was all about pampering herself, and desserts sounded like a good way to start.

With one final scrub, she stepped out of the shower, then toweled off and put on her favorite comfy pjs — a pale pink camisole top with Hot Chick emblazoned across the breasts in red glitter, paired with camouflage boxers. Tonight she was all woman — fashion victim woman — but woman none the less.

A loud knock on her door signaled the arrival of room service, and all the fattening calories that would sooth her sexually hyper nerves. Smiling wide, she opened the door.

"You got here quick..." Her words trailed off as she stared at the man who very much didn't resemble room service. "Mark...um...what...?"

Words would be good now. But what the hell was she supposed to say? She'd spent the better part of an hour pretending she was in a Rodgers and Hammerstein musical trying to forget about him. Now her obsession was standing in front of her, a pizza box in one hand, shopping bags in another, a smile growing wide across his face.

"Hot chick," Mark said with a chuckle.

"What?"

"Your shirt. I like it."

Elaine blushed, the heat burning her cheeks. "Right. My top."

Mark shuffled the bags and pizza box in his arms. "Um...I realize that my arrival was unexpected, but I was hoping that pepperoni pizza would convince you to have dinner with me."

Dinner. With Mark. And she was supposed to resist this how?

Grow a spine! You know nothing can come of this. Tonight's supposed to be Mark-free.

Elaine buried the dissenting voice in her head underneath a pile of Greenlight growth charts and statistical tracking analysis.

"Sorry about that. You just caught me off guard. Come on in."

Elaine opened the door, letting Mark back into her hair again.

* * * * *

Camouflage and pale pink. Mark decided that was his new definition of hot chick as he watched Elaine walk over to the bed and plunk down on it. She'd obviously just gotten out of the shower. Her short dark blonde hair was still wet, and her skin had a rosy pink glow to it. Kind of like the glow she'd had last night as they'd fucked.

He swallowed hard then walked toward her as though he wasn't imagining her lying naked on the bed. "I had a bit of trouble trying to decide what wine would go best with pizza so I got champagne instead. I hope you don't mind." He set the pizza at the foot of the bed and the shopping bags on the floor near the edge. He'd need easy access to those later...he hoped.

Elaine opened the pizza as he set up plastic place settings and napkins. Mark laughed at himself. "Now you see my true colors. My idea of a nice dinner, pizza, plastic ware and these lovely little plastic champagne glasses with the removable bases."

Elaine grinned as she took a small bite of pizza. "These are the best kinds of dinners."

Mark stared at the small spot of tomato sauce at the corner of her mouth, wondering if she'd be receptive to him licking it off. But he didn't want her to think he was here just to seduce her.

Before he could lean in and sample tomato à la Elaine, her tongue peeked out the corner of her mouth, licking it away. His cock twitched and he hid behind the open pizza box lid to avoid her noticing. "I wanted to propose a toast to you for surviving the first day of the success of Greenlight. I was well received all day and I believe I owe it all to you for creating a product that sells itself."

"Thanks. But you really didn't have to do all of this. I've got room service coming." She took another bite of pizza.

Mark watched her closely. He couldn't help but wonder if she was completely okay with him being there. Maybe she really didn't want more than a one-night stand. "I can go back to my room, if you'd like. It's no big deal. I just thought we should share a little celebration. Greenlight will succeed if we survive this show."

Saved by a knock on the door.

Elaine jumped up to get the door and take care of room service. She returned, balancing two trays covered in food.

"Actually, I'm really glad you're here because there's no way I'd be able to eat all of this by myself. I had no idea I was ordering quite this much food."

He took the trays from her and set them on the bed, the dishes sliding around just a bit. Judging by all of the chocolate and sin, she must have been planning a night alone. Chocolate syrup dripped from nearly every plate. He almost felt like he was intruding until she picked up his hand and sucked his index finger into her mouth. His cock responded instantly.

A saucy grin covered her face as she slid his finger back out of her mouth. "I couldn't let a little chocolate go to waste."

Before he could pull her down into the chocolate so he could have an excuse to lick her all over, she leaned over the side of the bed and retrieved a napkin and some plastic spoons. "What else did you bring? There's another bag down there."

"I'll show you later. Right now, let's eat, drink and relax. It's been a long day for both of us, don't you think?" His gaze slipped down to her breasts, the nipples taut under her camisole, teasing him. He wanted to rub chocolate sauce onto her nipples and spend the rest of the night suckling them, feasting on their devilish sweet delight.

"Yeah. It has." She sat cross-legged on the corner of the bed, and Mark just stared at the long mile of leg she was showing off. Those legs belonged around his waist as she fucked him long and hard. He'd thought about last night all day, even during his meetings. He'd never been so fascinated by a woman before. Which was bad, considering the circumstances.

He opened the champagne and poured two glasses, handing one to Elaine before raising his in a toast. "To all of our successes real and imagined…" She quirked an eyebrow at his comment. "Well, the show isn't over yet so I want to cover all the bases."

She chuckled and they drank.

One hour later, half the pizza had disappeared along with the first bottle of champagne. They'd talked about AdLive,

Creative Solutions and Greenlight, and they'd even shared stories about their families. He laughed at the way she'd told the story of the surprise 35th anniversary party she'd thrown for her parents last summer. Although she'd been the one surprised when she'd arrived at her parents' house earlier than expected and caught them having sex on the couch.

Elaine laughed again. "So I'll probably need therapy for the rest of my life after seeing that much of my parents, but at least they're still in love." She was reclined on the far side of the bed now, the tray of desserts between them. "What about your family? You have any brothers or sisters?"

Mark stretched out on his side, watching Elaine. It was nice to see her so carefree. "I have a younger sister and a niece who live in San Francisco, where I grew up. My parents have retired to Napa Valley."

"So tell me something about you that no one else knows," Elaine said as she took a small bite of the melted ice cream.

Personal sharing time. This was good. He could do this. "Okay, well, you probably already figured this out, but when I was younger I took a few ballet classes. It started out as a dare from my sister and then I actually enjoyed myself. Until I made lead in a production. There was just no way I was going to wear tights in front of an audience."

Elaine laughed. "Just a few classes? Are you kidding? You were so graceful and so...so...well, it looked like you'd done it a few times before."

"I swear it. Just a few classes in high school. I've just stayed in shape since then." He shook his head. "I never thought my ballet experience would land me on a stage making an idiot of myself, though. I don't think I've ever done anything that stupid when work was involved."

"Ever dated a co-worker?" The question seemed to stumble out of her lips in a rush, then hung uncomfortably in the air between them. He tried to meet her eyes, but she'd focused in on the dessert tray again, her fork currently dissecting some type of pastry. She was nervous. They had that in common.

He wracked his brain to find just the right words. "No. And I was never even interested...until recently." He took another drink of champagne. God help him, he hoped he wasn't being too forward.

She stopped destroying the pastry and her eyes met his. In that moment he saw the interest in her eyes, then she returned her attention to the dessert, closing herself off again. "Yeah, well, I've dated a co-worker before. It's no fun. In fact, it became the bane of my existence. And still kind of is."

"You dated someone else at AdLive?"

"Yeah." She wiped her mouth with her napkin as though she was trying to wipe away a very foul taste. "I dated Hanson. We were even up for the same job, but he got promoted above me and, well, essentially he had other plans for our relationship. I wasn't where he wanted me to be and actually, I wasn't even in love with him. Once we broke up and he started making my life hell, I realized that what he and I had was just sort of camaraderie because we worked together. There were never any sparks."

She gave him a curious smile. "You know, you're the first person outside of my best friend I've ever told about him." She took a deep breath. "And I have another confession. I thought that Hanson sent you out here to steal Greenlight's glory away from me and maybe to make it fail. I know that's not true, though. You're not that type of person and I'm sorry I ever thought that about you."

So there it was in a nutshell. She'd had a bad time with a dickhead like Hanson. Dammit. Mark had known there was something fishy about his sudden transfer. He'd pulled a few all-nighters to learn all he could about Greenlight in the few days he'd had before the show. He'd been given an almost impossible mission, and before meeting Elaine had assumed he was being sent in as a last ditch effort to rescue a failing project.

Not so, though. It sounded like Hanson had wanted Greenlight to fail and Mark had been the scapegoat. Bastard.

Mark tried to keep himself from snarling. "Yeah. Hanson's an ass. And you can tell him I told you that. He knows Greenlight could pump up AdLive's Web Development division. And you're the best person to be in charge of it because you designed and built it. Damn him. Furthermore, the guy's an asshole for letting a good thing slip away."

Elaine just sighed. Then her eyes met his. "I'm glad you're here though, Mark." She smiled and winked. "I hate going to meetings."

Well, that sure was a dodge if he'd ever heard one.

She took a bite of chocolate cake, closing her eyes blissfully as she moaned. "Mark, you've got to try this cake. It's fantabulous." She leaned over the tray, placing a bite in his mouth. "Good, yes?"

He swallowed the cake, not even tasting it as it went down. He locked his hand around her wrist to stop her from pulling away. With his other hand he removed the fork from her grip. He couldn't wait anymore.

"That's not the type of dessert I want, Elaine. I want you. But if you don't want to do this, I understand. But lord, I don't think I can sit here any longer, just watching you. Your shorts riding up, showing me a mile of sexy leg and I happen to know there's a freckle under your camisole that could use some of my attention. Sure, dinner and dessert have been wonderful, but my mouth hasn't stopped watering since you laid down and it's not because of the chocolate. So it's up to you. You know how I feel. What happens next is your decision."

* * * * *

Her decision.

The words rang in her head like an alarm. Elaine didn't want it to be her decision. If he had initiated sex tonight she could have accepted it as his choice and been a willing partner. But now the crux of their relationship lay in her hands and she knew that no matter what, come Sunday night when they got off the plane in Los Angeles, the only relationship they could acknowledge would be boss and employee.

But that was still two days away.

She wanted this man, and if all she could have was this weekend, then she'd be a damned fool if she didn't make as many memories with him as she could.

Elaine moved the hand he still held to his face, tracing along his strong jaw. She wanted to touch him one last time, not knowing if he'd stay after she laid down her ground rules. His eyes remained locked on hers, waiting for an answer.

"Mark. I want you. I want you more than I've ever wanted anyone else in my life." She paused, then forced herself to continue what she didn't want to say. "But I can't have a relationship with someone I work with. Not again. I can't suffer the repercussion of a work relationship gone sour. I've worked too damn hard to take the chance with my career. I'm sorry."

Mark's jaw tightened under her hand and he turned away. He began to stand up. A sharp pain filled her.

"Wait, Mark. I'm not done."

He stopped, still facing away from her, his whole body tense.

She took another deep breath. "We still have this weekend. But on Monday morning when we see each other in the office, the only relationship we can acknowledge is boss and employee. I know it's selfish but it's all I can offer. What we have can't go past Sunday night. Promise me that."

Elaine held her breath, waiting for his answer. When he turned to face her she froze, stunned by the depth of emotion in his eyes. His hazel eyes burned into her, the desire so intense it was almost painful.

His voice was low, barely more than a growl. "Now it's my turn. Promise me this. Whatever I want, whenever I want it. For the next two days, you won't deny me anything. If you give me this, I promise I will never mention this weekend to you again."

A mixed thrill of fear and excitement lanced through her body. At this point, she would have offered him anything just to keep him from leaving, and what he asked was far from a sacrifice. Her words were little more than a whisper. "I promise."

In one swift movement, Mark slid the remaining dishes from the bed into the pizza box and threw it onto the table. Then he was back on the bed, his hands on her hips, his fingers teasing the flesh underneath her waistband. "You're so fucking hot, Elaine." One hand slid up from her hip, barely skimming her body, his palm coming to rest on her distended nipple.

Elaine let out a quiet whimper as his hand cupped her breast, teasing her nipple between his thumb and forefinger. "So damn beautiful. Do you know that, Elaine? Do you know how beautiful you are?" His other hand moved to her shoulder, and he slid the thin strap of her camisole down. Lips touched the flesh of her neck, his tongue flickering, tasting.

He was killing her. Her shorts were damp with her need, her body shaking with desire. Every touch of his tongue against her flesh pulsed fire. She wanted to move her arms around his neck, but his hands held them down.

Both of her cami straps slid down her arms. Mark pulled down her top, freeing her breasts. He let out a low moan. "God damn, Elaine." Then his mouth covered her nipple, suckling, biting. She couldn't stand it. Anchoring her hands into his hair, she didn't know whether to hold him close or push him away. The pleasure was almost more than she could bear, but she didn't want him to stop either.

"Mark. God, Mark. Please...I want you now...inside me...please..."

But he didn't listen. He continued to love her breasts, if not with his mouth, then with his hands. She'd never known her breasts could be so sensitive, but her clit throbbed, her pussy clenched and she was spinning toward orgasm without him ever touching below her shorts.

Elaine closed her eyes, lost in sensation. His tongue played havoc with her nipples, his teeth marking the curves of her breasts. All focus narrowed down to Mark and the way he made her feel.

Lifting his head from her breast, Mark wrapped an arm around her waist. He surrounded her. But she still needed more, all of him.

His hand slid down from her breast and over her stomach, then continued its downward path until he cupped her aching pussy through her shorts. She whimpered, rocking against his hand.

"Mmmm...Damn, baby. You're so wet." His finger ran along the seam of her shorts, rubbing the soaked fabric against her pussy. Elaine quivered, her knees shaking. She didn't think she could hold herself up any longer but his arm around her kept her upright.

"God, Mark. Please. Take me. I can't handle much more."

She opened her eyes to see the smile cross his face. "Oh baby, sure you can. And I've got so much more to give you, too. I'll show you a paradise you've only ever dreamed about. Over and over, until you feel yourself melting into me as I melt into you. Now stand up and take off your clothes. All I've been thinking about tonight is your sexy body. I need to satisfy my mind with fresh, hot visions of you without any barriers between us."

Elaine watched him as she scooted backward off the bed and stood on quivering legs in front of him. His stare remained intense, reverent. Bending slowly, she began to slide her sopping shorts off her body. She'd just lowered them from her hips when his voice called out.

"Stop. Turn around."

Elaine just stared at him, her eyes widening. She knew what he wanted. His devilish grin had her aching even more as she turned her back to him, and she continued to slowly lower her shorts. She bent at the waist, pulling her shorts off and dropping them to the ground.

"Baby, you're killing me. Your fine ass and that hot pussy wanting me in it. Begging me to come home. Don't move. Not yet."

Hands caressed her ass, running down the slit and over her cunt. Her juices covered his hands as he stroked back and forth, but never delving inside. She was panting, aching...

And then she felt something else, something hot and hard stroking between her thighs. She moaned as his cock slid through her slick cream. But he didn't thrust himself inside. Why wouldn't he take her? She couldn't get any more willing.

One warm hand rested on her lower back, keeping her bent over. She whimpered and moaned at the burning, her need making her mad with lust. But his cock continued its slow torture, never entering, just rubbing back and forth. Juice flowed down her legs, saturating them both.

Through her haze, she realized something. In her position, she could see his cock sliding between her thighs as he stroked her. Her arousal only grew as she watched him thrust, never entering, just adding to the anticipation of what was to come.

"Do you like what you see when I fuck you like this, Elaine? Knowing that at any moment I could thrust my cock inside you, filling you completely." His voice was strong, but his breath shook as though he was reaching the edge of his control.

She let out a moan as he slid his cock back, then deliberately pressed it against her anus. He rubbed the wet head of his cock in slow circles against her hole. "Or is this what you want, baby? Do you want me to fuck you like this? Tell me what you want, Elaine. You know I'll take good care of you. I could never hurt you."

Elaine's heart skipped a beat, nervous at the extent of her arousal. Although far from a virgin, she wasn't a sex goddess either. She'd always wanted to try more, but her previous lovers had lacked the experimental gene. But with Mark she needed more than just his body…and that's what scared her the most.

Subtly shifting, she pressed back against his turgid member. "Does that answer your question, Mark? I'm all yours this weekend. I want…no, I *need* what you want."

She felt a shudder run through his body but he didn't verbally respond. One of his hands caressed her back while the other wrapped around her waist, resting just above her clit. Then one finger barely touched her swollen nub and she gasped as her whole body jerked, exploding with a sharp, sudden orgasm. Nothing like this had ever happened to her before. Her knees gave out, and if Mark hadn't been holding her so tightly, Elaine knew she would have fallen to the floor.

Mark held her until she regained her balance and slowly stood up. He nuzzled her neck, his hands sweeping over her breasts, stomach, hips. His cock pulsed against her ass. His voice was hoarse as he spoke. "Damn, Elaine. I almost came just watching you. You're so hot it's like I'm stroking fire. And you're only going to get hotter. I'm going to fuck you so well you'll never forget." Then he was gone and she heard the sound of the bed creaking behind her.

She turned to follow but her knee had barely touched the bed when he spoke again. "No. Not yet. Take off your top."

She wasn't giving him a show this time, dammit. Ripping the top over her head she threw it behind her and then leapt on the bed toward Mark.

He caught her in his arms and pulled her to him until their bodies touched. But she wanted him inside her and she struggled to get him there. He held her back just enough that she couldn't impale herself on him. "Mark…"

His hands surrounded her face, bringing her mouth to his. His kiss was slow, deliberate, as though he had all night to seduce her. As though she wasn't already so hot for him she was soaking the bed. As though she truly did belong to him.

But he did have all night. She'd promised him that. And she was at his mercy.

Her hands found his cock and she stroked his length. In her haze last night, Elaine hadn't realized that Mark was much longer than any man she'd ever been with. At full erection, he had to be at least ten inches in length. She shivered. Would she be able to take him all the ways he'd promised? She should be scared, but she wasn't. He was the best, most attentive lover she'd ever had. He would never hurt her. A quick ache hit her that they only had two nights, and then she dismissed it, refusing to let those thoughts ruin what she had with him now.

He still kissed her, although the kiss had become deeper, more desperate. Elaine felt the same desperation inside of her, the need for Mark to complete her, merge with her, make her his. How had this man gotten so fully under her skin in such a short time? She wanted to pleasure him, hear his moans, and feel him climax while deeply inside of her. Then his strong hands lifted her hips and in one thrust, his cock was all the way inside.

Their kiss broke as they both let out low moans. "Oh God, Elaine. God. You're so hot. So beautiful." He lifted her hips, then thrust again.

Elaine watched his face as his cock filled her. Drops of sweat fell from his hairline and she leaned forward, licking them away. Then his eyes widened and he started to pull out of her. Elaine tightened her legs around him, not letting go.

"Mark, what?"

He shook his head. "Shit! I forgot. I forgot a condom." His cock jumped inside her at that admission. "I wasn't thinking. You make me lose my mind."

It was her turn to smile as she lifted her hips, rocking back and forth on his cock. He groaned. "Elaine. Stop. I'm going to come."

"I want you to come in me. No condoms. I'm healthy. I'm on the pill. And I know I can trust you. So fuck me. Come in me. All night. Please, Mark. I need you."

He moaned again and kissed her, and they fell back on the bed together. His strokes sped up, almost wild, desperate. His need was clear.

With one final thrust, they both came. Elaine cried as Mark filled her, the rhythmic gush of his come intensifying her orgasm. No part of her untouched by him.

She never wanted it to end.

* * * * *

Elaine woke up sometime later to the warm, wet caresses of a washcloth cleansing her body. Mark was so gentle as he washed her, spreading her legs, bathing her tender skin with slow, caring strokes. She purred, her body humming with arousal.

Mark whispered in her ear. "Wake up, baby. We can sleep later. I have to have you again."

Elaine smiled and turned her face toward him. Before she could say anything, he kissed her, tender and sweet. Within seconds the kiss intensified, their hunger for each other growing.

They both pulled away, Mark's eyes mirror reflections of Elaine's feelings. There was a certain level of fear in wanting someone so badly.

He just shook his head. "Damn, Elaine. There's not near enough time for me to do everything I want to do to you."

She tried to smile past the lump in her throat. "Then we better get started."

Mark grinned and lowered his lips to her flesh. Starting at her shoulder, he alternately nipped and kissed her, creating a fever everywhere he touched. He didn't stay in any one place long, just enough to inflame the skin. Her arms, her neck, breasts, legs and stomach, all received his attention.

When her whole body tingled, he stopped, kneeling over her. "I want your whole body to know my touch. To never forget."

Elaine panted, her hands wrapped in the tangled sheets beneath her. She couldn't ever forget him. He'd already proven that.

He moved on the bed, spreading her legs and lying between them. His hand rested on her upper thigh, his thumb lightly stroking her shaved mound. She watched him as he seemed to study her, his gaze caressing. Then he looked up at her and caught her staring. He winked then lowered his mouth to her cunt.

Elaine trembled as his tongue laved her folds, dipping deeply into her pussy. She could feel the walls of her vagina growing slick again, the red heat of need pulsing through her. With slow, deliberate strokes, Mark loved her, and her arousal continued to heighten. How much could a body take?

More than she'd ever imagined.

He looked up at her with a devilish grin. "Damn I love the way your body responds to me. Now close your eyes. I have a surprise for you."

Elaine followed his directions and closed her eyes. Moments later she heard the sound of a paper bag rustling. Then Mark was back over her again, slowly inserting two fingers into her pussy. She arched her back trying to make him go deeper. He slid his fingers in and out a few times then pulled them away. She whimpered and started to sit up, to pull him back to her.

"No, baby. Lay down. Trust me. And keep your eyes closed."

She lay back, frustrated, but anticipating what he'd do next. Something cool pressed against the lips of her vagina and she gasped as it slipped inside, slowly filling her. It had to be a dildo, almost as long as Mark, but not as thick.

Elaine wanted to watch, to see the look on his face, so she narrowly cracked open her eyelids. Mark fucked her with long sure strokes of the dildo, the pleasure at her willingness and arousal obvious on his face. A layer of sweat coated his body, and his cock stood tall, a drop of fluid leaking from the tip.

Her gaze returned to his face, to see him watching her. He grinned. "You like to watch." It wasn't a question. "Damn, Elaine. You're so responsive. Do you have any idea what you do to me?"

She arched and moaned as he thrust the dildo in deeper, swiping his finger over her clit as he did it. "Probably what you do to me," Elaine whispered throatily.

He let out a sound, somewhere between a groan and a growl. "Give me your hand, Elaine. It's your turn to use the dildo on yourself."

Elaine slid her hand down her sweat slickened body, covering his hand with her own. She'd never masturbated in front of anyone before, but she couldn't wait to see Mark's response.

Taking the base in hand, she thrust slowly. Her free hand roamed her breasts, pinching her erect nipples. And through the pleasure she watched Mark, watched his chest heave, his cock twitch and his body's desire grow. He leaned over the bed again, returning with a small tube of lubrication. Within moments he was stroking his cock, spreading the lube over his entire length. Elaine knew what would happen next.

"Roll over, baby, and get on your knees, but keep the dildo inside your hot cunt. Keep pleasuring yourself."

She did as she was told, ready for what would follow. She knew there would be pain, but there was no fear in that thought. Instead anticipation filled her, a desire so deep her whole body ached with it.

One finger slathered in a cool gel began massaging her hole in a gentle, circular motion. The touch was almost too gentle for her nerves. Elaine eagerly pressed back against his finger and Mark laughed. "Me too, baby. I just want to make this perfect for you."

Then his finger entered her, breaching her ass for the first time. It burned as he stretched her, hurting, but not enough to pull away. The hurt became a need for more—the anticipation for what was to come accelerating her desire. She whimpered as he continued his slow torture, thrusting the dildo in time with the strokes of his finger.

He spent precious minutes continuing to stretch her, adding more lube, inserting a second finger. Elaine was beyond pain, into a realm of indefinable sensation.

Then his fingers were gone and Elaine was bereft. She didn't even realize that she'd called out to him until he stroked her back, calming her. "Shhh...Elaine. I know, honey. I know. Relax, baby." Then a larger warmth pressed against her anus, slowly entering her, stretching, burning.

Elaine lost all concept of reality as Mark breached every last barrier. Her body shook and she couldn't hold herself up on one arm anymore. The dildo dropped from her vagina as both of her hands struggled to hold her body up.

Their moans mingled as Mark slowly thrust deeper. He lowered himself over her back, rubbing his face against her skin. One of his arms circled her waist, and his fingers entered her cunt as the base of his hand ground against her clit.

Elaine knew she was screaming, moaning, whimpering, lost in sensation. One orgasm after another rocketed through her body. Through her haze she heard Mark. "God, Elaine. I—I've never felt this way..." Then his body tensed. "Elaine, I—" and then his words were lost in his moans as he came, his cock pulsing jets of semen into her.

Elaine was crying as they lowered to the bed together. She couldn't do it. She couldn't let Mark go.

Chapter Three

Saturday

Although it had practically killed her to leave Mark, Elaine knew she needed to get to the booth early, not wanting a replay of yesterday where the morning was spent in unexpected chaos.

She was still running later than she would have liked. She'd slipped out of bed while Mark slept, planning on showering and dressing before waking him up. But Mark had other plans. As she'd washed the smell of great sex off her body, Mark had joined her under the cascade of water and gotten her dirty again. He'd brought her to orgasm twice before coming, then proceeded to wash her body, getting her aroused again.

He toweled her off, arousing her even further. His smile seemed to grow as her frustration mounted and before she knew it she was flat on her back on the bed, his head buried between her thighs, as he brought her to another swift orgasm.

Elaine smiled. The man was insatiable...thank God.

Trying to bring her focus back to Greenlight, she powered up the server and all of the workstations. Everything was coming up just fine. On terminal one, she went to start up the browser, but it wasn't there. She had the computer perform a search of its entire system.

No. Not another idiotic morning like yesterday. Did one of the guys accidentally delete the browser from this machine? No big deal. She could copy one from another computer in no time at all.

Searching the whole damn network, she discovered that not one of the machines had any sort of internet browser. Without a fucking browser, no one could show anyone anything about Greenlight. She took a deep breath and imagined taking a sledgehammer to every monitor. Okay, it wouldn't make her problems go away but it sure would make her feel better.

It had been a few years since the last time she surfed the internet without a browser. Text-based, it was a royal pain in the ass. She opened up a DOS window and typed in the IP address of her ftp site.

As she sifted through the numbers, she cursed under her breath. Browser creators seemed to have forgotten that there might be someone out there in need of a base-model browser just to get up and running. It wasn't easy to find what she was looking for without graphics and buttons and icons, but certainly not impossible. Things could have been much worse.

"Trouble again this morning?" Elaine jumped as Mark placed a hand on her shoulder. Then surprise turned to arousal as his touch rocketed heat through her body. She couldn't stop herself from leaning into him.

"Somehow all of the browsers disappeared so I'm trying to download one. No big deal." She continued navigating with arrow keys, spacebar, tab and enter, her frustration mounting. "Y'know, this has to be an inside job, Mark. All these terminals are password protected and I can't see anyone else at this show going this far out of their way to screw us over. I just don't know who would do this to us unless Hanson flew in last night just to fuck with us. I'm almost afraid to check out everything else. Who knows what else has been messed with?"

"Somehow, I doubt it's Hanson. The man's an asshole, but he's a lazy asshole. Did you manage to download a browser? Once we install it on all the computers, we're good to go, right?" Mark caressed her shoulder, then trailed his hand down to her lower back. She knew she should tell him to stop, that the doors were going to open soon and that the rest of the guys would be showing up any moment. But she knew Mark wouldn't take it too far. He was just testing her.

"Yeah, I just downloaded a browser to the server. I'm annoyed that someone is trying to take us down, but we'll be up and running just fine. It takes more than that to screw up

Greenlight. Want to give me a hand?" She turned to face him, his body inches away. His eyes flashed desire and she fought the urge to give him a quick kiss. Instead she gave him a sardonic grin. "Rather than steaming me up by being so close, go over to the other terminals and get the browsers reinstalled." She tore herself away from him and he chuckled the headed over to one of the other workstations.

"I almost wish I had meetings today. That way I could hide myself." His fingers rapidly clicked the keys and mouse. "But Saturday's always the highest traffic day. It's better I'm here. I just have to somehow stay on my best behavior."

"Yeah. And that's tough for any man." She crossed her arms over her chest and raised an eyebrow, but she couldn't stop the grin from growing on her face. "Well, let's take our mind off sex then."

Mark snorted and Elaine held up a hand to stop him from saying anything. "Somebody here is messing with us, causing us problems we shouldn't have to deal with. And they've underestimated me—which points directly back at Hanson. He's the only one I know who doubts my abilities that much. We need to keep a close watch on the guys. I want to know who, other than Hanson, wants me to fail. Bryan is the only one I really one hundred percent trust."

Mark nodded his head. "Whoever's doing it, they won't win. I told you Greenlight would succeed, and it will." He clicked the mouse a few more times. "That should do it. And what timing. The AdLive crew arrives ready for the big day."

Elaine watched as Mark became all business, welcoming his employees and energizing them for the day ahead. Jack, Bryan, Tom and Larry all looked a bit tired, but ready to work nonetheless. She had to smile. Out of the whole crew, she and Mark should be the most tired, having ignored sleep most of the night for other pleasures.

But she was invigorated and ready to rush through this day so she could spend another night in Mark's arms.

The first hour of the expo was always a bit slow so Elaine took the time to talk to each of the guys, scrutinizing their behavior, but trying not to act suspicious in the process. She discovered only one thing though. She was a much better programmer than detective. Nothing seemed out of the ordinary. Jack was no grumblier than usual. Bryan was no happier than usual. Even Tom and Larry were their usual opposite ends of the salesman spectrum.

Just as she was about to dismiss the happenings as a random attack of Murphy's Law, her cell phone rang. Stepping to a corner of the booth, she answered it. Her stomach dropped as the first words were spoken.

"Hello, Elaine, baby." Hanson's smarmy voice reached through the phone, causing her stomach to churn and bile to rise in her throat. When Mark called her baby it was sexy and arousing, taking her to another level of desire and need. When Hanson called her baby it made her want to take a scalding shower to remove any trace of the slime that dripped off him.

What the hell had she ever seen in Hanson? She shuddered, trying to forget that she'd actually slept with the man. Then again, he'd been a lot different before he'd started to fuck her over.

Elaine lowered her voice. She didn't want anyone else to hear this exchange. "You lost the right to call me baby a long time ago, Hanson. What the hell do you want?"

"You didn't check in last night."

Elaine's anger mounted. "I don't 'check-in' with you anymore. You'll receive an email next week with the details of our premiere, just like everyone else."

"You should stop fighting me all the time…"

Or what?

Her voice was a whispered snarl. "Listen up, you bastard. Whatever you're trying, whatever you're doing, it won't work. Leave me and Greenlight alone—"

"You work for *me*, Elaine. Remember that. I can make your life easy or hard. Your choice." His tone of voice changed, going from one of malice to one of simple disapproval. "Don't disappoint me."

Elaine flipped her cell phone closed, wishing for a handset she could slam down, to ease her frustration. Hanson had to be behind what was going on—the threat had been there in every word he spoke.

Elaine looked around the booth. Her project. Her team. Her Greenlight. She smiled. Her Mark.

Hanson would not succeed. It was more important to sell than worry and wonder about what might happen next.

It seemed like everything in her life was a topic worthy of both those actions.

* * * * *

"Elaine, could you give me a hand over here for a second?" Mark pointed toward the central room. She'd taken a phone call an hour earlier, and since then, tension seemed to ooze from her every pore. Someone or something had upset her and he longed to take her stress away.

Elaine gave him a half smile. "Yeah. What do you need?" She surveyed the booth before following. Mark had already done the same. Everyone was occupied with an interested client, but the booth wasn't swamped.

As she followed him inside, he closed the door behind them. The clock in his head was unrelentingly counting down the time they had together. He knew he had to make it as memorable for the both of them as possible.

"Mark, we shouldn't stay in here too long. They'll get suspicious." She approached him, but stopped short of touching him. It didn't matter. He could still feel her warmth. There was just something about her that lit his fire whenever she came into a room.

Mark stepped behind her and placed his hands on the knotted muscles of her shoulders and neck. He massaged her, and she leaned back into him, letting out small gasps of contentment. His body instantly reacted to her quiet moans. Damn, this woman undid him. "I just wanted to make sure you were okay. I saw you on the phone earlier—"

Elaine's muscles tensed underneath his ministrations. "Hanson. Checking in. I swear he's behind our problems, Mark. I just don't know how."

"Relax, Elaine. Don't let him in. I won't let him hurt you. Greenlight will be fine." Mark's hands left her shoulders, sliding down her arms, pinning them against her sides. He stepped closer.

Elaine responded instantly, leaning back into him. "Mark...call me baby. Please. I need to hear you say it. I need to erase the sound of Hanson calling me that."

What an insolent bastard. How dare Hanson lay claim to Elaine? Mark filled with rancor. She belonged to him. Not Hanson. Never again.

Mark nuzzled her ear, then kissed her neck as he whispered, "Elaine...baby." She sighed contentedly and snuggled deeper into his embrace. "Do you know what you do to me, baby? Do you know how hard it is to watch you walk around this booth and not be able to touch you? Tell me we're still on until tomorrow night. I just need to make sure you haven't had any second thoughts about our arrangement."

She turned around to face him, licking her lips nervously as her eyes met his. He could see the desire in the way she stood, the way she watched him. "I don't break promises, Mark."

"Right answer." He pulled her back into his arms, needing to taste her lips, feel her tongue, envelop himself in her heat. She responded with equal verve, sliding her hands down his back and grabbing his ass.

Her response aroused him further, making him nearly forget the other reason he'd called her in there. He pulled the last of his treasures from the adult store out of his pocket. The small, egg shaped item fit into the palm of his hand.

With his free hand he unclasped her pants and slid her zipper down. He couldn't deny himself a touch. Sliding his hand underneath her panties, he thrust two fingers into her wet cunt, making sure her body was ready. She moaned into his mouth and kissed him harder, rocking her hips against his hand. He moved the tiny vibrator into his other hand and carefully slid it inside her hot, wet cunt. Her body easily accepted it.

Elaine pulled away from his kiss and looked up at him, her eyes glazed over with lust. "Hey...wait...what is that?"

"Trust me." He kissed her again as he fastened up her clothing, then grabbed a stack of catalogs from one of the literature boxes. He had to use something to hide his erection.

He lowered his voice as he approached the door. "You might want to stay in here for a few minutes. You look a little hot and bothered." He winked at her and walked out the door.

* * * * *

Hot and bothered, my ass. Mark had started a fire burning inside of her. Then when she thought he was going to fuck her, he'd left her wanting. What a creep.

Elaine walked around the booth, listening in on everyone's sales pitches. Positive energy filled the air. Greenlight had a good buzz going. As she watched her team work, she couldn't imagine any of them doing anything to sabotage her creation. Although Greenlight was her idea, they'd all helped it grow. Maybe Hanson *had* somehow managed to do it from afar. Even though she knew that was unlikely, she just couldn't imagine anyone else out to hurt her.

Her gaze shifted to Mark and she stopped for a minute, enjoying the view. He was definitely something she'd rather focus her attention on. He stood casually with his hands tucked in his pockets in front of one of the literature stands, clearly selling the man in front of him on Greenlight. He stole a glance in her direction, catching her in mid-stare. She smirked, trying to play it off, but he gave her a small knowing grin before turning back to his customer.

Elaine turned away from Mark, hoping to get him off her mind for more than half a second. She paused as a sort of strange sensation overtook her. Emanating from her cunt, tingles rippled through her body. She gasped as her knees got a little weak and she placed a hand on a table to keep herself steady. What had Mark done to her?

Her gaze sought out Mark again, who now leaned against a nearby podium, one ankle crossed over the other, hands still in pockets. It felt like there was a mini vibrator in her pussy and if that were true, the culprit was right there in front of her, a crooked grin on his face, selling Greenlight and stealing glances at her. Oh she was going to make him suffer when she got her hands on him!

She sat down on the nearest chair, not trusting her legs to hold her up. The man was cruel, but damn, the vibration was nice. It wasn't strong enough to launch her into a colossal orgasm, but it sure gave her a nice buzz. She closed her eyes, enjoying the sensation.

Then it was gone. She jerked open her eyes and turned to where Mark had been standing, but he wasn't there anymore.

A warm hand touched her shoulder and she whipped around to look up at Mark. "You're looking a bit flushed. Is something bothering you?" He pretended concern, but she could see the mischief in his eyes. Then he referred down with a quick nod of his head.

Elaine's gaze swept down his magnificent torso while she tried to fan the fire in her cunt. He'd pulled a hand out of his pocket revealing a slim white plastic object with a dial and a switch. He casually flipped the switch and cranked the dial just a bit and her cunt vibrated, firing right back up again. Her eyes widened and she stared at him. "Oh, you are soooooooo mean."

She took a few deep breaths to hide the mini-orgasm ready to burst through her body.

"I don't know if this is meaner for you or for me watching you." His voice was tight.

Elaine stared at the large bulge tenting his pants, then met his eyes and slowly licked her lips. She knew she was playing with fire, but there was no way she'd be the only one affected.

His eyes narrowed and he cranked the dial a bit further. She gripped the armrests of the chair and took deep breaths, refusing to let the pleasure overtake her body. But she wanted to, desperately. They stared at each other as though daring the other to be the first one to offer surrender.

Finally, Mark flipped the switch and her cunt ceased its agitation, but by no means did it calm down. Maybe she'd end up so wet the darn thing would just slide right on out of her. Then again, having it fall down her pant leg in front of a potential client might not be a good thing, either.

Mark slipped his hand back into his pocket, successfully hiding both his arousal and the device that was her personal tormentor. He grinned at her, then stepped away to greet someone he'd obviously met the day before.

Once again, the same question ran through her thoughts. *Why the hell does he have to be my boss?*

"Hey, Elaine, Larry can't remember how to move around the pages again. Can you go rescue him?" Jack broke her concentration and she was thankful for it. Maybe a little working would take her mind off of Mark and the effects he had on her mind and body. She stood up carefully, her body still weak from the recent pleasure, and walked over to where Larry was stationed.

Larry nodded as she approached then turned back to the man he was speaking with. "Ah, here she is. This is Elaine Ridgley. She designed and built Greenlight."

Elaine listened to their questions then stepped into full salesperson mode. "Right here, just keep clicking the arrows up and down until the page is where you want it. If you were in the page creation section, you could just use the drop down menus. I wanted to make sure that Greenlight was one hundred percent versatile for all of your website building needs. From informative marketing to e-commerce. It's all right here at your fingertips. Nice and easy." Elaine smiled her best fake sales smile.

"Yeah, and cheap, too." Larry always cut to the chase. "Here, let me just go over to this page and we can sign you up for your first month. We have complete customer service and you can cancel at any time. We've got a special offer running for anyone who signs up here at the Creative Solutions show. I'll give you a free month if you sign up right now. And we'll even help you build it. Here. How do you spell your last name, Robert?"

Over and above his sleazy used car sales smile Larry was an excellent closer. Elaine left the new client in Larry's capable hands and walked to the other side of the booth to check on Tom.

"And then, um...I think you can just type in whatever you want the page to kinda say after you click on the generic design for it." Tom stammered through his presentation to an attractive woman in an expensive suit. Under the best circumstances, Tom wasn't a great seller. When a woman was the client, Tom tended to freeze.

The potential client shook her head. "But I need full graphics capability. I can't just use one of the templates and upload my logo. My site needs to stand out more than that."

Elaine stepped in to rescue Tom, knowing that if they didn't give her the answer she wanted, this woman would take her business elsewhere. "Well, that's why we have a full creative department backing up Greenlight. We can design and build your entire site, then hand it over to you. Just by logging in on the manager screen, you can make last minute updates or changes from your office, or even remotely. We're always available to update the site, but you will have complete control over your website whenever you need it. All controls and text are just mouse clicks and keyboard strokes away. Tom, take her though the tutorial. Show her what Greenlight is made of."

Tom gave Elaine a meek smile and whispered, "Thanks" before he began the tutorial. Elaine forced herself to walk away. Tom had clearly known he'd needed help, but had been afraid to ask. The poor guy needed a self esteem boost because he really wasn't a bad seller, he just doubted his abilities, which weakened his approach. Now that he was back on track, she assumed he'd do just fine. She made a mental note to watch him closer, but to also praise him when he made a sale.

Then, it happened again, a buzz filling her cunt. Elaine cursed under her breath. She'd almost forgotten about Mark's damn mini-vibrator, but its merciless dull vibration had her on edge within moments.

Then it quickened. Her mind flashed back to last night and all the ways Mark had fucked her, and she nearly bit her hand to hold back a moan. She glanced around the booth. Where the hell was he?

On tingling legs, she sped over to the other side of the booth. Her tormentor stood there in a heated conversation with Jack. Had Mark discovered something about Jack that made him suspicious? Mark's eyebrows were furrowed and he was shaking his head. Jack gestured sharply. Elaine was just far enough away that she couldn't tell what they were saying.

The darn vibrator went up a notch in speed.

Mark had one hand in his pocket. Did he even know he was fucking with the damn remote control?

Speed up, slow down. She couldn't help but shift her hips back and forth a little. Merciless. Absolutely merciless. Her mind continued to conjure memories of last night. The way he watched her. The sound of his voice as he talked dirty to her.

Her eyes practically rolled back in her head and she tried to think about anything but the yearning ripping through her. The spasms jolting through her cunt were ruthless. She wanted to scream out at him to stop fiddling with the remote, but she was getting far too light-headed fighting the pleasure from overtaking her entire being there on the expo floor. One more flashback to last night, his naked body and his incredibly large cock filling her, and she couldn't stand it anymore.

"Mark, I need to talk to you right now. In private. You two can talk later."

Jack threw up his hands and stalked away as Mark followed her into the central room.

* * * * *

"Close the door."

He did as he was told. Watching her arousal grow, knowing he controlled her pleasure even from afar, had nearly caused him to call a meeting with her in the central room as well. He'd been tired of holding a brochure over his cock or having to stand behind a rack or podium all the time.

"Do you have any idea what you were doing to me?" She didn't wait for his answer before unbuttoning his pants, pulling out his shirt and lowering his briefs and pants to his knees. Her lips sought his in a thermonuclear lock.

He picked her up, set her on the table, his hands sliding her pants and panties down her legs as she fought to be free of them. He reached between her legs, sliding two fingers inside her wetness to remove the dully vibrating bullet, then quickly deposited it into one of the pockets of his pants. He'd have to remember to turn it off later.

Wait. It was on? He hadn't even realized he'd turned it on. How long had he left it going? Had she talked to potential clients like that? He pulled away from their kiss. "God, baby, I'm an asshole. I didn't mean to leave it on. I'm so sorry."

She growled up at him. "Don't apologize. Just shut up and fuck me."

All of his thoughts ceased as she wrapped one of her legs around his waist and pulled him close. He was finally able to do what he'd been thinking and dreaming about all day.

Thrusting his cock deep inside her, they both let out quiet gasps and moans. He leaned in and kissed her again, needing to mask the sounds of their passion. His tongue delved deeper as he kissed her harder and his thrusts increased to match the rhythm her hips were grinding out.

The slick walls of her cunt began to spasm around his cock and her hands grabbed his arms tightly as her whole body trembled.

With one final thrust he came in her. She rocked her hips as he came, prolonging his orgasm.

He bent his head to hers, his hands stroking up and down her arms. "I really didn't mean to leave it on. I'm so sorry. That wasn't meant to be a torture."

"That's okay. I'm better now. Much better. Thank you." She raised her lips to his, gracing him with a slow, lingering kiss.

As much as it pained him, he pulled his cock from her warm hiding place. Their gazes locked. He knew she felt the absence, too, but they had to get back out on the floor before anyone suspected anything.

Putting themselves back together, they didn't say a word. Just watched each other. Longing for more, but knowing there was no time.

She walked out of the room first, and he followed with yet another stack of catalogs. Tom had a rather perplexed look on his face as he held a hand out toward Mark. "I, umm...need a catalog. Did you two find everything all right in there?"

"Sure. We're almost out of these catalogs. The show must be going well." Mark handed the catalogs to Tom and walked away, hoping the after-sex glow wasn't bright enough to elicit comment.

The rest of the afternoon, Mark had trouble pulling his eyes away from Elaine. He couldn't go near her for fear he'd drag her back into the central room and go for it again. Of course, if he took her in there again, they'd likely shake down the booth and everyone would find out what was really going on between them.

She cleverly avoided him, with a sultry expression on her face or one of mischief, there always seemed to be a reason for her to go to the other side of the booth from where he was. It was just as well.

And she was far from an angel. Once, when she knew only he was looking, she ran her hand down her breast to her stomach, then over her hips, landing just to the side of her clit. Oh how he wanted to finish that caress for her.

The show slowly wound down. Bryan approached him, a smile on his face, but his eyes seemed to express something else. Concern, maybe? "We're surpassing our sales expectations, Mark. Elaine's done a damn fine job." His voice lowered as he stepped closer, his gaze piercing. "Elaine's an amazing woman, Mark. She deserves these accolades. I don't want to see her hurt."

Mark met Bryan's eyes, ready to deny everything, but he couldn't. Elaine had said Bryan was the one man she could trust. He was also apparently her appointed watcher. And he didn't deserve to be lied to.

Mark stared at Elaine, who was sitting at a table with Larry, going over some paperwork. "I don't want to see her hurt either, Bryan."

Bryan nodded and walked away. Immediately, Jack approached. Mark sighed. Not again. The man was determined to ruin Mark's good mood with his constant bitching about every little thing at the show. Mark listened with only half an ear as he watched Bryan and Tom shut down the computers. Then his gaze strayed to Elaine and Larry. Elaine's face had grown pale and she was worrying her bottom lip between her front teeth. What the hell had happened?

He turned back to Jack. "Just write me up a report or send me an email and I'll go over it when we get back to Los Angeles." Jack seemed surprisingly content with Mark's offer and strolled away.

When Mark turned back, Elaine was nowhere to be seen. Larry sat at the table alone, going over the paperwork.

Mark's concern grew. "Larry, where'd Elaine go?"

Larry just shrugged his shoulders, but a glint in his eye told Mark that Larry wasn't telling him everything.

Mark sat down next to him and pulled his chair close. "Larry, what the hell happened to Elaine?"

Larry's eyes widened. "Look, I was just teasing her okay. I don't know why she took it all personal like. Damn women. They always take things personally."

Mark held back from grabbing Larry by his sweat-stained collar and shaking the shit out of him. "What did you say to her?"

"I was just telling her that she seemed extra flustered today and that maybe Bill's suggestion from the other night was still affecting her." Sweat glistened on his brow.

"What suggestion? What are you talking about?"

"You know. Bill's last suggestion. Sexual insatiability. I told the girl she was probably horny from that suggestion and she took off outta here like a rocket."

Mark stood up so quickly the chair fell to the floor. "You four close up tonight. Make sure everything's locked up." He didn't even look behind him as he left.

Shit! He had to get to Elaine, had to make her understand that what he felt for her went far beyond any hypnotic suggestion. Mark went directly to her room and knocked on the door. He had to set the record straight.

But there was no answer. Either she wasn't there, or she didn't want to talk to him. He leaned against her door, raw emotion filling him. Why had he let it go so far without telling her what she really meant to him? And why had he let her talk him into only a weekend when they deserved so much more together?

To hell with that. She couldn't stay away from him forever...and there was no way he would let her go that easily.

* * * * *

Elaine's heart beat frantically as she raced toward the Starlight Lounge. What Larry had said couldn't be true. How could her feelings for Mark be because of the damn hypnosis? A part of her seemed to remember a vague notion from Bill Brentwood, something about being sexually insatiable. And that was exactly what had happened between her and Mark. She couldn't ignore the possibility, even though the possibility hurt.

Outside the Starlight Lounge she saw a familiar face, one of the dancers from Bill's show. Elaine made a beeline for him before he could get through the backstage entrance.

Elaine tapped on his shoulder and he turned around, a performer's smile bright across his face. "Hey, do you remember me from the show the other night?"

His eyes flashed recognition and he nodded. "Yeah, I sure do. What's up?"

Elaine realized she was probably going to sound like a desperate fan. At least the desperate part was accurate. "I was wondering if I could talk to Bill. I have some real important questions to ask him about hypnotism. Can you get me back there to him? My whole life has changed and I really need to talk to him about it." She felt like she was begging, but she was also at the point where begging wasn't beneath her.

He eyed her up and down, assessing her, then gave her a real grin. "Sure, sweetheart. You're my girlfriend until we get through the door, okay?" He winked. They both knew he was as gay as they came. He wrapped an arm around her as they passed the guard.

She squeezed his arm tight and smiled up at the kind soul. "Thank you so much. I owe you one."

"Don't mention it. Hypnotism changed my life as well. Go talk to Bill, he's in the far dressing room on the left." He waved as he sauntered into a dressing room down the hall.

Elaine froze for a moment, staring at the door. Here it was, the moment of truth. She couldn't go on with her life not knowing if what she had with Mark was real or just some mumbo-jumbo brought on by hypnotism. She knocked just below the star and sign that read "Bill Brentwood" on the door. It hadn't been closed all the way and opened a bit.

"Oh. I'm so sorry." Elaine stepped back. "I didn't know it was open."

"It's always open." Bill greeted her with a reflected smile through his mirror. "Hello. Elaine, isn't it? What brings you here?" He turned away from the mirror and walked over to the couch near the wardrobe rack. "Have a seat." He gestured to the empty side of the couch.

She took a deep breath and sat down. "Bill, I need you to undo whatever you did to me and Mark. It's really causing problems." There it was, out in the open although she somehow felt ridiculous for saying it.

Bill raised an eyebrow. "What suggestion are you talking about? The effects of the show leave you once you walk off the stage. I always give a few parting suggestions, but those wear off by the time you wake up the next morning." Bill traced his jaw line as though lost in thought.

"What parting suggestions?"

Bill smiled at her, the look in his eyes comforting. "Well, first off, you already know that you can't be hypnotized to do something you don't want to do, right?" Elaine nodded. "So, then I take it you don't remember those final suggestions. You were sleeping deeply enough. Good for you."

Elaine sighed and forced a smile. "I have a vague memory, more of a feeling. I need you to tell me, Bill...what were those last suggestions?"

"I always give a parting gift to the people who make my show happen. When you wake up the following morning, you'll be relaxed, but energized, ready to face the challenges of your new day. And if you find yourself in bed with a very special partner, you will have unlimited sexual energy. Just for that night, though."

Elaine quickly hugged Bill, then stood up, the need to find Mark almost desperate. "I don't think Mark and I needed that suggestion, but thanks." Bill gave her a puzzled smile as she turned around and left the room.

Elaine hurried out of the lounge. She and Mark had been sexually energized long before they'd hit the bed after Bill's show. And even from the first time they met, Elaine had felt something stronger than just sexual attraction. She couldn't blame her feelings for Mark on hypnosis. She'd done the one thing she knew she couldn't.

Elaine had fallen completely in love with her boss.

* * * * *

Elaine knocked on Mark's door, hoping he was there, not knowing what she would do if he wasn't. There was so much she needed to tell him, so much she wanted to know. The complexity of their relationship scared her, but being without Mark scared her even more.

When the door opened, Elaine couldn't remember what she'd wanted to say. Mark's normal, all-together look had vanished. His suit jacket and tie were gone, his dress shirt unbuttoned and untucked, the sleeves haphazardly pushed up. His slacks were wrinkled, his feet bare, one hand clasping an almost empty bottle of beer. The dark shadow of stubble covered his tightly clenched jaw. She'd never seen him looking so rough around the edges.

But it was his eyes, the desperate, heart-wrenching need she saw within them that made everything clear again.

Elaine stepped through the doorway and up against Mark, wrapping her arms around him, rubbing her face against the patch of hair on his chest that his shirt couldn't hide. The door shut and the beer bottle clunked to the floor as Mark's arms surrounded her, holding her tight.

God, she loved this man. Loved the way he smelled, the way he moved, the way he talked. She loved everything about him.

How the hell could they make this work?

Everything inside of her screamed for him, needing him, but it was impossible to just throw away what she'd learned in her miserable relationship with Hanson. Yes, Elaine knew that Mark was a better man than Hanson—there was no doubt in her mind about that—but there was no way to know if in six months, or hell, even six weeks, things wouldn't change between them. And although she'd be stupid not to realize that Mark felt something for her, could she bet her future on them lasting forever?

The whole damn situation was impossible.

Elaine lifted her head and met his burning stare. Her mouth went dry and she shivered. All she could do was live for the present, and right now she needed to love him. She took a deep breath. "Mark...let me make love to you tonight."

Something flickered in the depths of Mark's eyes, and he slowly shook his head. A hard, painful knot formed in the pit of her stomach. She lowered her head, unable to meet his gaze anymore. Was this it? Had he made the decision for her?

His hands cupped her cheeks, forcing her to meet his stare. The rough pad of one thumb ran over her lips. "Elaine, baby, I can't let you make love to me tonight. Because I need to make love to you, too. This is about both of us."

Elaine pressed her face more deeply into his hand. "And the future—"

"I think we both know what we want."

Mark lowered his head, placing his lips softly over hers.

Warmth flooded through Elaine, starting at her lips, her face, everywhere Mark touched her. And the heat wasn't just sexual. It was more than that, filling her soul—a deep, all encompassing exhilarant unlike anything she'd ever felt before. It was as if nothing else mattered in her life from this point on…as if being with Mark was the only thing she needed to stay alive.

They kissed slowly, learning each other's lips…mouths. Taking the time they never had before. As they kissed, their hands and fingers removed clothing, offering light caresses, slight touches.

With their bodies bared to each other, Mark's nearness awakened Elaine to the very depths of her being. Completely elevating every last one of her senses and practically taking her breath away with such beauty and heart's wonder. Tonight wasn't about arousal or sex. The experience permeated much deeper—the need to join their bodies not only for pleasure, but because it made them whole.

Mark kept maximum contact with her body as he gently lowered her down. She hadn't realized they'd moved to the bed until she felt the sheets cool against her back. He kissed and caressed and loved Elaine as he eased himself inside her cunt, filling her with slow, smooth, rhythmic strokes. Every part of her came alive. Wanting Mark. Needing Mark.

His hands found hers and moved them above her head, locking their fingers together. Their gazes met and held, completing the circle between them. And at that point they were one.

Elaine knew she was coming, felt the tidal wave rushing through her. But it didn't end. Her body kept going higher, the orgasm growing rather than receding. She grasped Mark's hands tighter, holding on. But she needed more, needed to tell him…

"I love you, Mark."

The words she'd never before spoken to any man broke down her final barrier and she hit the cusp of her climax just as Mark came inside of her. She closed her eyes, overwhelmed, as their bodies soared together.

"I love you, too, Elaine. Don't ask me to let you go. I need you with me..."

Elaine didn't respond. There was nothing left to say.

Chapter Four

Sunday

Mark unlocked the central room and went inside, the memories of last night still deeply etched in his mind. They'd made love all night, greeting sunrise with moans and sighs of pleasure. Then they'd fallen into a brief but necessary sleep.

He'd awakened alone. In a way, he understood. What had happened was so intense and it had already been confirmed that once the show was over, so was their relationship. Elaine had never agreed to more. He'd thought last night would change her mind, but even though she'd shown her love, it obviously wasn't enough.

That was a thought he tried to force to the back of his mind. It hurt too much to think he'd have to let all of his feelings go.

Back to the task at hand—to the things in his life he could control. He pressed the power switch on the server and while the screen came up, the cursor in the upper left corner remained constant. Giving it a second chance to start working, he pushed the power button again, hoping the damn computer was just having as shitty of a morning as he was.

No luck. The power came on again, but the machine wouldn't boot up. It didn't ask for the password. Nothing.

Anger hit him like a heavy fist to the gut. This was his fault. He'd known that someone was out to get them, had even planned on staying late last night to put a new password on the system, to make it more difficult for anyone to take them down.

But he'd forgotten everything else in his haste to find Elaine. He flinched at the memory. He'd practically sprinted out of the booth after her, completely forgetting to do his job, to take care of his company, all in the need to be with Elaine.

Being with her clouded his mind, made everything else less important. If Greenlight couldn't get back on its feet today, there would be no one else to blame but himself.

"Un-fucking-believable."

"What? Good morning to you, too."

Mark glanced up as Elaine stepped into the room. She gave him an almost shy smile, then her eyes drifted over to the table—the very table they'd sated their lust on just yesterday. His cock—which out of sheer physical overuse and exhaustion should have been hiding—shot to attention, always ready for Elaine. Mark forced his recalcitrant thoughts back to the problem at hand before he took her on the table again...and again...and again. He needed distance between them to survive today.

"Go turn on the towers. We might have a very serious problem, Elaine. I think whoever deleted the browsers yesterday has struck again. Just please tell me that the workstations are okay. Please."

Elaine paused in the doorway, nervously tapping the fingers of one hand on her upper thigh. She looked like she desperately wanted to say something, but then she abruptly turned and left the room.

Mark sighed as he turned back to the computer and typed in a few more commands. The server did the same thing...nothing. He gave all the connections a quick once-over—everything was fine.

In disgust, Mark left the central room and met Elaine at one of the workstations. Just the scent of her drove him mad.

Shit! Something had to give. Work was fucked up, Elaine was pulling away from him. There was no way in hell he could handle working in the same office with her and not have her whenever he wanted her. He wasn't a saint and he couldn't deny his desperate need for her. They couldn't be co-workers and lovers, but he'd be damned before he let her go.

He took a deep breath to avoid shouting out his frustrations. His voice still came out sharper than he intended. "Are the stations coming up all right?"

Elaine shot him a surprised look. "Yeah, but they can't find the network." She brushed against his chest seemingly unintentionally as she turned away and he gritted his teeth in abject frustration. It was everything he could do not to slide his hands over her possessively.

"The server is completely down and out. We're going to need a plan B and fast."

"All right. So who do we think is the asshole?"

Hanson. He transferred me into the arms of a beautiful woman I can't have. "No clue. But it doesn't matter right now. We've got to get up and running first. We'll worry about who screwed us over later." He turned away from Elaine's steady gaze. He had to come up with an answer to their problem, even though the only problem he really cared about was standing behind him.

Heat rushed to his groin as she moved to his side and slid her hand down his arm. Their gazes met and her sleepy eyes widened. There was an uncomfortable silence between them as she slowly removed her hand from his arm. She cleared her throat. "Wait a minute. You have the back-up site and everything else on your laptop, right?"

"Yeah, but I have a meeting with Ambient Medium at ten—and I need the laptop. They're too important for me to go in and wing it without a live demonstration. They'd laugh me right out of the meeting."

Elaine raised her eyebrows. "C'mon, Mark. Work with me here. Can we clone your hard drive before you leave? That way the server will have whatever's on your laptop. Do you have any cloning software?"

Unable to forego temptation any longer, Mark trailed the back of his fingers down Elaine's face. She closed her eyes and leaned into his touch, letting out a soft sigh. His voice came out little more than a whisper. "I want to do more than work with you. That's the problem."

Elaine's eyes fluttered open and she peered up at him, her eyes full of the same need he felt inside. "Mark—"

"What's going on?" Bryan walked up with Jack just a few feet behind him.

Mark quickly stepped away from Elaine and looked around the booth. Larry and Tom had just arrived as well. It was time to solve problem number one. He looked at Elaine. He'd work on problem number two for as long as it took to get the outcome he desired.

"Someone took out the server. It's completely wiped and while we *do* have everything we need on my laptop, we *don't* have any cloning software and I need my laptop for one of our most important meetings in about an hour."

"Well this just sucks," Jack said wryly. And for once, everyone was in complete agreement with Jack.

* * * * *

Elaine stayed on the main floor, checking for any other computer issues as everyone else filtered into the central room, ideas flying fast and furiously on how they could get around this problem. She wanted to make sure nothing else would impede them today...not to mention she needed some time alone to think about Mark.

When she'd left him sleeping in his bed early this morning, she'd returned to her room to do some serious thinking. And she'd come to a decision.

Elaine didn't want their relationship to end. No matter how she looked at it, the idea of returning to her normal life next week held no appeal. They'd have to be careful, figure out how to keep their work life and love life separate, but she wanted to try because she couldn't imagine a life without Mark in it.

She sighed and walked over to terminal one to make sure that it had been left untouched. The browser was still intact. It still knew it was networked. She checked the rest of the terminals. They were all intact. It appeared that the only thing the saboteur had done was erase the hard drive of the server.

And keep her from telling Mark how she really felt.

She'd rushed downstairs this morning, desperate to tell him her decision before the show started, but the damn sabotage had gotten in the way. She'd started to tell him again, only to be interrupted by the arrival of the team. A tiny, uncomfortable feeling filled her that she wouldn't get the chance to tell Mark how she really felt. That thought bothered her more than the sabotage did.

With that thought in mind, Elaine looked at her watch. She still had time to talk to Mark before the show started. She rushed toward the central room just as Bryan, Larry, and Jack exited with their hands full of USB cables. "What are you guys doing? Did you come up with a plan?"

Bryan grinned at her. "We got it figured out. Mark set up terminal one as the new gateway, but we have to network manually in order to make it work. It's going to be just fine, Elaine." He gave her a knowing look. "Everything's going to be just fine." The three of them moved over to the computers and began daisy-chaining them together with long runs of USB cable.

She continued toward the central room when Tom appeared at her side, seeming to come out of nowhere. She jumped as he placed a clammy hand on her arm. "Elaine, I need to talk to you."

She peeled his hand off her arm and looked at him. His eyes were full of regret and sorrow…and suddenly Elaine knew who had sabotaged Greenlight.

Her voice was quiet as she spoke. "Just tell me why you did it, Tom, because I can't understand it."

He looked down at his feet. "I didn't know exactly what I was doing."

Elaine couldn't hide her confusion. "How could you not know what you were doing? You sabotaged us everyday. Dammit, Tom! You've worked with me on this project for months! Why would you do this to me? You're as much a part of this team as everyone else."

Tom backed a step away and ran a shaking hand down his face. "I know I'm not an asset here, Elaine. I suck at sales, at graphic design...I shouldn't have lasted so long at Greenlight. I knew my time was numbered so when Hanson—"

"Fucking Hanson," Mark growled as he stepped out of the central room and up next to Elaine. Fury rose from him in potent waves.

Elaine placed a hand on his arm. Mark looked like he was ready to kill.

Tom took another step back, fearfully looking at Mark. "H-Hanson offered me a promotion if I did him a few favors while I was here. It wasn't supposed to go this far. He just wanted you to look incapable so that the project would be scrapped. But then last night when I told him what I'd overheard going on between you two in the central room..." Tom blushed.

Tom wasn't the only one blushing. Elaine felt the heat fill her cheeks. Mark's arm grew tenser under her hand and she pulled away. She couldn't look at Mark, wondering how he felt.

"Finish the story, Tom," Mark said roughly.

Tom's voice warbled. "Hanson went crazy, screaming and cursing. I've never heard him lose it like that before. Then he told me word for word what to type in. God, Elaine, Mark, I'm sorry. I'm really sorry. I didn't know what he was having me do until it was already done."

"You know you can't stay, Tom," Elaine said quietly. She didn't know what else to say.

"I know. And I'll testify against Hanson if you need me to. It's the only good thing left I can do." Tom walked away, his shoulders slumped. He picked up his briefcase and left the booth.

Elaine stood there, watching Tom leave, the betrayal raw and bitter in her soul. She felt Mark leave her side, but still she stood there, needing to be alone.

And there it was. She'd had a relationship with a co-worker, and look where it had gotten her. Somehow she'd survived this fiasco, but what about the next time?

Mark stepped into her line of sight. "Elaine? The guys got the terminals networked and Greenlight's back in business. I'll call New York and inform them about Hanson and Tom before I go see Ambient Medium. I promise, it's all going to be okay now."

His eyes sought hers, full of sincerity and love. She wanted to go to him, to let him make everything better.

Elaine turned away. It would never be okay again.

Chapter Five

The Following Friday

Elaine pushed the pasta around on her plate, not interested in actually taking a bite. She hadn't had an appetite since last weekend. There wasn't room for anything else but the dull ache burning inside of her. Turning her attention to her salad, she speared a cherry tomato on the end of her fork then deposited the whole thing in her mouth. Ha! She would eat something. She punctured the tangy tomato between her teeth, relishing her small victory.

"You're an idiot."

Elaine choked as the tomato seeds shot down her throat, then quickly grabbed her iced tea to wash everything down. She looked at her friend Jen glaring at her from across the table. What had she done now? The only stupid thing Elaine had done lately was walk away from Mark—but she hadn't even told Jen about him. It still hurt too much. So what was Jen in an uproar about? "Well, I look like an idiot now that you made me choke on my tomato."

Jen narrowed her eyes and crossed her arms over her chest. "No. You were an idiot before that."

Elaine sighed, put her iced tea back on the table and picked up her fork. She needed something to keep her hands busy. "So what did I do now? Is Bryan pissed at me because I wasn't careful enough and Hanson screwed up Greenlight's premiere?"

Jen scowled. "You are dense, dense, dense. How stupid do you think we are?"

Elaine felt her eyes widening. "What are you talking about?"

"You fell in love with him, didn't you? It's obvious. And you didn't even tell me about him! I had to hear about Mark from Bryan. Bryan! You're my best friend, Elaine! You're supposed to tell me when you're screwing an incredibly hot guy! I shouldn't hear this stuff from my husband!"

Elaine's jaw dropped as Jen turned and motioned the waiter over. "We're going to need two Saucy, Sinful Chocolate Delights and two coffees. And bring us extra fudge sauce to pour over the top of the cake, please." Jen sat back in her seat and met Elaine's astonished stare dead on. "Talk. Now. And maybe I'll forgive you."

Elaine took a deep breath and gave Jen a half-smile. "I'm an idiot. I know I am. I fell in love with my boss—"

Jen threw up her hands in frustration. "Falling in love with him isn't why you're an idiot." She shook her head. "Walking away from him was your mistake. I always thought you were supposed to be the smart one of the two of us, but I'm beginning to realize that your brain is about the size of the tomato you choked on."

Elaine smirked. "Thanks for the compliment."

"You're welcome. It's true you know." The waiter came and poured their coffee and Jen angrily stirred in her cream and sweetener. Then she inhaled the aroma of her brew. "You know I love you, right? You know I always want you to be happy. And you haven't been really, truly happy for a long time."

"I've been working. And I'm not unhappy...or, well, I wasn't unhappy...I mean, I love my job." Elaine stared down at her plate, flustered.

"Look, sweetie...Bryan told me about last weekend. About you and Mark. About the glow in your eyes when you looked at him. And according to Bryan, Mark never took his eyes off you, as though he was staking his claim."

Elaine looked up miserably. "Was it that obvious? I thought we were pretty sly."

Jen snorted. "Not even. Bryan actually called me last weekend to ask if you'd talked to me about Mark. I was rather miffed that you hadn't."

"I'm sorry, Jen. I—I think I was having a hard time believing it was happening." Elaine let her mind wander back to the wonders she'd experienced with Mark. Her voice grew soft as the memories overtook her. "It was so intense, Jen. I can't even explain it. Mark is...was...no *is* amazing. I've never felt anything like that before." She met Jen's steady gaze, swallowing the tears welling up in her throat. "He really loved me."

Jen reached across the table, placing her hand over Elaine's. "I know he did, hon."

She briskly shook her head to wipe the memories and the haze of unshed tears before they fell from her eyes. "Doesn't matter. I ended it. Mark has barely even glanced my way this week."

Jen shook her head. "You know, every time you start to redeem your stupidity, you delve right back into it again. Mark's not glancing your way because he's trying to respect your decision. He probably just wants to fuck you against the copy machine or something whenever he sees you."

"Or he could just hate me."

"Damn, Elaine. When did you become so pathetic? And why are you letting the mistake of a relationship with Hanson rule your entire life?"

They were interrupted again as the waiter returned with their chocolate dessert that came with its own warning label. Jen dove right in.

Elaine frowned at the chocolate then took a tentative bite. "Well, Hanson did sabotage my whole existence from the moment I told him I wouldn't marry him. He's made my life miserable for the last year."

"Oh, and of course every guy is just like Hanson and is going to fuck you over." Jen rolled her eyes and took another bite. "Look. Love doesn't magically show up on your doorstep, wrapped in a bow when you're ready for it. You have to take it when you find it, no matter how impossible it is. People who wait for the perfect moment die alone."

"So when did you become so damn smart?" Elaine asked as she took another small bite of her dessert.

"When I stopped overanalyzing my life and just started living it," Jen said with a wink.

"I can take a hint. You know, I don't even know if it matters. I may not have a job after I get back to AdLive today."

"What are you talking about? Bryan said Greenlight was an amazing success."

Elaine shrugged. "Seemed like it at the show, even through all the problems. But there have been a lot of closed door meetings this week and no one's clued me in to what's going on. It worries me." She checked her watch. "But I'll know in about 25 minutes. The bosses called a meeting to 'discuss the future of Greenlight' and demanded my attendance." She motioned the waiter over and paid the bill.

"And Mark?"

Elaine turned to Jen. "Unless I'm fired, he's still my boss. Any relationship is forbidden."

"So I should hope you get fired?" Jen asked with a grin.

Elaine grabbed her purse, stood up and gave Jen a hug. "Just hope for a miracle. Because I don't think I can live without Mark."

Jen just smiled as Elaine walked away. "Good. Because you shouldn't have to."

* * * * *

Elaine took a deep breath and tried to calm the nerves bubbling away in her stomach like a boiling teapot. The few bites of lunch she'd managed to swallow earlier were haunting her now. She didn't know what she was more nervous about; finding out if she still had a future with AdLive, or sitting for a prolonged period of time with the man who hadn't left her thoughts since she'd shared a cab with him last week.

Elaine sighed, squared her shoulders, and walked into the boardroom, taking the first available seat. A few more people filtered in, but Elaine kept her gaze lowered, going through her Creative Solutions notes. She mentally added in other non-Greenlight related details to the daily show statistics, figuring the bosses really weren't interested in the number of times she and Mark had reached new heights together.

Someone sat down across from her and she glanced up, right into those familiar hazel eyes she'd been trying all week to get out of her head. Her hands clutched at the table to keep from reaching out to him. God, she missed touching him, being touched by him.

Then came his million-dollar smile as he spoke. "I hope you're ready for this."

Other than a few non-committal phrases and generic hellos and goodbyes this week, Mark hadn't spoken to her. She cocked her head to the side, studying him. Just what, exactly, was he up to? "Ready as I'll ever be, I guess."

His eyes sparkled and he winked. "Me too, Elaine. I don't want to wait anymore."

What did he mean by that? Elaine's stomach clenched again, this time not from nerves, but the desperate need to climb over the table and into Mark's arms. His grin widened, then he slowly turned away as several more people entered the boardroom. It was time for the meeting to begin.

Michael Reynolds and Briana St. James sat down at the head of the table and a tremor of excitement shot through Elaine. This had to be an important meeting if the New York VPs had been flown in for it. She couldn't imagine they would have flown out here if Greenlight had bombed.

The boardroom door was closed and the bi-coastal AdLive meeting began.

Briana smiled, her bright eyes shining with enthusiasm. Last time Elaine had been in contact with her was through email. They'd always had a great camaraderie in the communications they had shared and it was wonderful to finally see her face in person. And even better that the face was beaming with a huge smile. "I'm not going to beat around the bush here. The response we've received from the Creative Solutions show about Greenlight has been phenomenal. So good in fact, AdLive's Board of Directors has decided to launch Greenlight as its own independent division. Greenlight has been given the green light. Owned by AdLive, run by our very own Elaine Ridgley—if she accepts the position of Vice-President that is?"

Elaine was stunned for all of three seconds and then she swallowed back her shout of glee. But she couldn't hide her smile. "Yes. Absolutely yes. Thank you."

She glanced at Mark and he smiled, mouthing, "Congratulations, Elaine." Her heart racing, she returned his smile.

Briana's announcement meant so many things. Not only had she succeeded with Greenlight, which was a dream in and of itself, but if Mark wasn't her direct boss anymore, did that mean they could make a relationship work?

Elaine turned back as Briana continued speaking. "There's also been some other important personnel changes in the company. Ronald Hanson has resigned, and Mark Ranzetti has agreed to take his place as Executive VP AdLive Web Technologies Los Angeles." Her excitement was contagious. The room filled with an odd happiness never before felt when Hanson had been at the head of the table. A few people clapped at the announcements.

Briana held up her hands to quiet everyone down. "I can see this meets with everyone's approval. Good." She smiled again. "Elaine, we'll be meeting next week to see who you'd like to bring over to Greenlight with you."

"Congratulations, Elaine, Mark. You both deserve it." Mike stood up, picking up his notebook. "Okay, that's it, everyone. I mean, if you want me to, I can tack on some of that boring stuff about making AdLive the best it can be, but everyone in this room is already on the same page, so let's just leave it at that. Besides, it's a Friday at the end of a long week. And I, for one, couldn't sit through another long meeting even if you tied me to a chair." The room filled with relieved laughter and the scraping of chairs as everyone pushed back from the table. "Have a great weekend. I'll see you all on Monday to settle the details."

Everyone stood up to leave, including Elaine. Briana approached with that sweet grin of hers. It was nice to see another woman in a place of power. "Just between you and me, I'm glad Hanson is gone. He was always such a jerk. Mark will do a much better job than Hanson ever did." The tone of her voice changed, lowered, becoming almost conspiratorial. "I've worked with Mark in the New York office for years, Elaine...there isn't a better guy out there. I couldn't be happier for the both of you." She smiled and winked then resumed her normal tone of voice. "I think there are going to be a lot more positive changes around here. I'll be spending next week here as we organize the new business structure. See you on Monday."

"Thanks, Briana. Thank you for everything."

Elaine swallowed her shock. Not only did Briana know about Elaine's relationship with Mark, but she approved of it. Elaine's head was spinning, on cloud nine at least, but still spinning nonetheless. They shook hands and there was an understood camaraderie. Women who play with the big dogs need to stick together.

"Don't mention it." Briana quickly glanced over Elaine's shoulder and grinned, then turned and left the room, closing the door behind her with a soft click.

The room was empty. Everyone had left in a rush...except for Mark. Elaine could feel his presence behind her, just inches away, and the need to wrap herself in his arms became too strong to deny.

She turned to face him, her breath catching in her throat. His gorgeous hazel eyes were full of such love and happiness, it almost hurt to look in them. He made the first move, lifting his hand and smoothing a strand of hair from her face. His fingertips just barely brushed her cheek before he lowered his hand back to his side, but her knees grew weak at the small contact. His voice was soft as he spoke. "Do you have any idea how happy I am for you? You did it, baby."

Elaine kept her gaze locked on his. "No. We did it. Together. I couldn't have done it without you." She swallowed deeply, completely opening her heart to him once more, hoping he still felt the same. "I don't want to be without you. I never want to be without you again."

He smiled. "Thank God I'm not your boss anymore. Working with you was one of the hardest things I've ever done." Elaine's heart jumped anxiously and she opened her mouth to ask him what he meant, when he continued. "We'll be on separate floors, doing separate things. When I'm with you, I don't want to work. I can't think about work. All I can think about is getting you naked. This week has been hell, baby. You were everywhere for me." He took her hand in his, his fingers teasing across her wrist. There was that look in his eyes again. The one that conjured images of a hotel room and passion beyond her wildest dreams. The one where she swore he wanted to kiss her.

"And now?"

"Now Greenlight is in your capable hands where it belongs." Mark's grin widened. "And my work productivity should increase because I won't be staring at you all the time."

Elaine wrapped her arms around him, pressing her face against his chest. His arms circled her and she sighed. This was what she'd needed—to be back in Mark's arms again. "I don't think your productivity will increase right away."

His hands ran through her hair and down her body. "What do you mean?"

She pulled her face away from his chest and met his hungry stare. "We've got a week's worth of time to make up for. I doubt we'll be getting much sleep for awhile."

"I don't need sleep."

"Me either."

Mark's lips crashed down on hers, taking her breath away. Their tongues mated, all the desperation and loneliness from the last week disappearing in the frantic need to take everything the other was willing to give.

How had she ever thought she could live without this man? Why had she thought one weekend with him would be enough? He filled her soul, her heart, completed her in ways nothing else ever could.

Mark's hands swept down her body, grabbing her ass, lifting her until she was grinding against his engorged cock. His lips broke from hers and he growled, "Elaine, I need you now. I can't wait."

Elaine shot a quick glance at the closed door. Mark answered her unasked question. "It's locked. I asked Briana to lock it when she left."

"What?" Elaine's eyes widened. "What reason did you give her?"

Mark grinned. "I told her we had to discuss the future and couldn't be interrupted."

Elaine laughed. "Oh...you're good."

She took a step away from him and his eyes narrowed. "Where do you think you're going, Elaine?"

Elaine reached behind her, unzipped her skirt, lowering it plus her nylons and panties to the floor. "Laying down my terms for our future." Her fingers seemed to fly over the buttons of her blouse until it, too, joined her other clothing on the floor. She decided to keep her creamy lace bra on. If the look in Mark's eyes was anything to go by, it wouldn't last long.

"I like your terms, but I have a few of my own." Mark approached her, a wicked gleam in his eyes.

A wanton thrill rocketed through her body and Elaine retreated from Mark's approach until her ass bumped against the oak table. Her voice was low and husky as she spoke. "And just what would your terms be?"

Mark moved forward until he had her pinned against the cool, polished wood, his fingertips hot flames against her hips. He lifted her, setting her on the very edge of the table. "I want you. All the time, everywhere, I want you. Say you'll be mine forever, live with me, marry me. Those are my terms."

Elaine lifted her face and met the eyes of the man she loved more than anything. "Yes."

Mark grinned, lowering his mouth to hers. "Thank God." This time the kiss was sweeter, gentler.

The start of forever.

Elaine kissed him back, her hands making quick work of Mark's pants and briefs. His cock was velvet steel in her hand. She stroked him, marveling in his strength, his size. It had only been one week since she'd been with him, but her body ached from missing him. She angled her hips, ready for his entrance. Pulling her lips from his, she whispered, "Now, Mark. I need you now."

With deliberate intent, the man she loved slowly thrust inside her, filling her the way only he could. Elaine cried out as she wrapped her legs around his hips, fitting him tightly to her. They moved together, finding their matching rhythm.

Mark nuzzled her neck. "Oh, baby, I've missed you. I don't think I can last long."

Elaine moaned, already at the edge. "Mark, that's where you're wrong. This will last forever."

The sounds of moans and sighs filled the boardroom well into the night.

Epilogue

Six months later

Bill Brentwood's voice filled the Starlight lounge with his enthusiasm as the show began.

Elaine smiled up at Mark. "You just couldn't stay away, could you?" She settled herself into their booth in the back corner. "I'm not going on stage this time though. We both know what happens when we're hypnotized."

Mark grinned. "And this is a problem, why?"

"Because I don't want us to get arrested for having sex on stage." Elaine laughed at Mark's disappointed expression. "You know the possibility is there. We couldn't keep our hands off each other last time, and we don't have the same inhibitions anymore."

Mark sighed dramatically, but his eyes sparked mischief. "You've got a point. Although hearing that a Vice-President of AdLive and the Vice-President of its overwhelmingly successful subsidiary company, Greenlight, were arrested in Las Vegas during their honeymoon for fornicating onstage could be interesting advertising."

Elaine smirked. "Probably not the type of advertising we're looking for."

Mark placed his hand on the bare skin of her thigh below where the hem of her skirt fell. "Yes, Madam Vice-President."

Elaine cuddled against her husband's shoulder and watched the antics on stage. She couldn't help but smile at the memories the show brought back. Although hypnotism hadn't technically brought them together, it had sure eased the way for their relationship to begin. Which is why they'd decided to stop in Las Vegas for one night of their honeymoon before they continued on for a two-week stay in Europe.

Elaine stared at the ring that had been placed on her finger only yesterday. Mrs. Elaine Ranzetti, Vice-President of Greenlight. She couldn't imagine a much better title to go by.

They'd gotten married in a small ceremony in Napa Valley at his parents' vineyard. At the heart of the property, hundred-year-old rose vines bloomed up through the gazebo and around the picket fence, filling the air with their sweet perfume. The giant Victorian house his parents were having restored made the perfect backdrop for their wedding photos.

Her parents had flown in from Boston a week before the wedding to help with the final arrangements. Everything turned out perfectly. Jen had agreed to be her Matron of Honor, and Bryan stood in as one of the groomsmen. Mark's sister, Lindsey, made a beautiful bridesmaid, and his niece, Chelsea, an adorable flower girl.

Elaine had fallen in love with the two of them instantly. Lindsey was a gorgeous blue-eyed blonde, a spunky reporter who covered the music and club scene in San Francisco. Chelsea was a precocious seven-year-old who looked nothing like her mother. Dark brown hair with matching deep brown eyes ringed with long black lashes, apparently a dead ringer for the absentee father. Both of them instantly accepted her into their family.

Mark and Elaine even invited Larry, Jack and Tom. But Tom hadn't been able to make it. He'd gone back to school after he'd left Greenlight, and was working on a degree in Anthropology. It was exactly the fresh start he needed.

Surprisingly, Larry and Jack had come and seemed to enjoy themselves…as much as they ever did at least. Larry had even given her a small hug, and then proceeded to tell her that he'd be waiting if Mark ever screwed up.

Thank God Mark would never screw up. The love she felt for him had only continued to grow, completing her in ways she'd never thought possible. He kept her happy, smiling and sated, and she couldn't imagine a life without him in it.

The sound of Bill's voice brought her out of her thoughts. "We're gonna sleep together tonight right here on stage."

Mark slid his hand even higher up Elaine's inner thigh. He nuzzled her neck before whispering into her ear, "Sleep together, huh?"

Elaine smiled, remembering their first night together just as he was. "And just what exactly should we do with our sleepless night ahead of us?" she asked, then answered by spreading her legs a little wider to give Mark better access. Thank God the lights had dimmed over the audience when the show had started.

He slid his hand under her skirt, letting out a sharp exhale when he discovered her surprise—no panties. His fingers stroked the bare flesh of her pussy, already wet with arousal. "I'm going to fuck my new wife all night long, that's what I'm going to do."

"That sounds like a plan I can get on top of," Elaine said through her quiet moans.

"Sweetheart, you will be on top, and underneath, and against the wall..." Mark delved between her folds, slowly thrusting one finger inside her cunt. He fucked her with his finger, pressing the spot that always made her squirm. The walls of her channel spasmed, tightening around his finger. He added a second finger to his thrusting.

Elaine bit her lip to keep from crying out. Her orgasm wracked her body with silent shudders.

Mark kissed her lingeringly as he removed his fingers from her pussy. "I love you, Elaine."

"I love you, Mark. And, you know, I remember how this show ends. So can we just skip the hypnotism and go straight to the fucking?"

Without a word, Mark swiftly helped her out of the booth. In a rush they left the lounge, Elaine prepared with keycard in hand.

About the author:

Sometimes two people meet, become good friends, and share a lot in common. When you're really lucky, you meet someone who understands you, who thinks like you, can finish your sentences and together, the both of you can create whole new worlds.

Ashleigh Raine is the pen name for two best friends, Jennifer and Lisa, who share a passion for strong alpha males that succumb to the women they fall in love with. These two met in junior high where they were band geeks. (But they swear they really were cool...they were percussionists after all!) But love of the arts didn't end with band. By high school, the two had a small following of fans for their stories and the characters they created...characters that would become the inspiration for their Talisman Bay series. They want to thank those fans for their continued support and interest. They couldn't have done it without them!

Both Lisa and Jennifer are married to their soul mates, who are the best support and inspiration. As Ashleigh Raine, this duo has many stories to tell, as their collective mind never stops creating fantasies that must be written down. They write larger than life stories, with adventures, hot sex, peril, hot sex, mystery, and more hot sex...but most assuredly they have a happy ending, usually with hot sex. Watch for many titles coming soon from this duo who are glad to have found their niche in writing erotic romances.

Jennifer and Lisa (and their alter ego, Ashleigh) welcome mail from readers. You can write to them c/o Ellora's Cave Publishing at P.O. Box 787, Hudson, Ohio 44236-0787.

Also by ASHLEIGH RAINE:

- Talisman Bay 1: Lover's Talisman
- Acting On Impulse

Chapter One

"M'Slork ju kusor Soljilskilon m'nor glusun limsok frr!"

UlRic Lor spit out a stream of curses as he approached the watery planet's atmosphere.

"Of all the cluster fucks in the galaxies, this one has to happen on Earth," Ric mumbled again, this time mentally converting from his native M'Loran to English. Might as well acclimate to the correct language mode before he landed. Although humans were polite enough to aliens, M'Lorans weren't their favorites right now with all the rebel warrior K'Mor running loose on their planet.

He maneuvered the craft through Earth's atmosphere, the directionals guiding him toward the west coast of North America. New California, specifically the northern section. At least that was the information they'd passed on when he'd received the message from Earth's Alien Crime Enforcement Unit.

The message he'd received when he was, literally, inches away from getting good and fucked by a prime M'Loran Pleasure Aide. But did he get the relief he so desperately needed? Well, yes, and no, he thought wryly, aligning the craft to dock at the Unit's headquarters. He'd gotten fucked all right, but not in a good way.

So much for his recreation period. The time he'd been looking forward to for months after chasing K'Mor rebels through the galaxies. He hadn't had sex in a very long time, needed it damn badly, and had been just about to get it when the Commander notified him he'd have to return to Earth immediately.

Earth. Where the women were too short and too ugly to even fantasize about. Not like M'Loran women, whose large bodies could accommodate his natural form. He'd fucked Earth women before, and swore he'd never do it again. They bored him.

He stepped out of the craft and into the wide tunnel leading to the enforcement unit, his lungs filling with the atmosphere that was, at times, too oxygen rich for him. But he dealt with it, like everything else in his job.

The unit was busy today. Crime was up in New California, as he'd learned on his last visit. Some of that had to do with M'Lorans, but not all of it. Earth was a prime place for anyone to hide out with its mix of cultures and differing laws. Bad enough M'Lora had two distinct species that barely saw eye to eye. On Earth it was anything goes.

He nodded to the Unit Enforcement Officer on guard near the entrance to the interrogation center. The guard motioned Ric to the DNA testing sphere. A low hum began and within seconds he was cleared to proceed through the protection grid, his identity registered.

He stopped at a counter and reported in.

"They're waiting for you in Room Three," the officer informed him.

Ric nodded, headed down the brightly lit hallway and stepped into the anteroom.

"Sorry you had to come back so soon but the shit has really hit the grid this time." Lou Maxwell rose to greet him. Lou was one of the best enforcement officers with the unit and Ric had worked many cases with this human. More than a Co'Lal older than Ric, Lou still had the balls and guts of Earth's old time detectives, and had long ago earned Ric's respect.

Ric shrugged. "What happened? I thought you had Vad well imprisoned."

"Beats me," Lou explained. "The hypnotist gave us the code, but when the guard tried to use it to subdue him, it didn't work. He killed two of our facility guards before he escaped."

Ric jammed his fingers through his hair. Just what they didn't need—more negative feelings among the human population about M'Lorans. Could this day get any worse?

"I have more bad news," Lou said, motioning Ric to the wide window where he could see a woman interrogating a M'Loran prisoner in another room.

"I can't wait. Tell me."

"You have to take the hypnotist back with you."

"Bullshit. No, I don't." Ric never took human interrogators to M'Lora.

"Yeah, you do. Commander says she's the only one who can control him and demands you take her along."

"*Kusor!*" Ric bit back the string of other curses that hovered on his lips. The worst part of his job as a hunter was having to deal with other cultures' laws. "I can control Vad without anyone's help."

"Sorry." Lou grinned sheepishly. "You know how they get about their goddamn rules around here. If the hypnocode doesn't work, the hypnotist must accompany the hunt for the escapee."

Ric silenced his anger and turned to watch the action in process. Instead of the stark interrogation rooms of Earth's past, this one had brightly colored walls and comfortable, soft furniture. Ric spotted Mal Vor, a M'Loran one of the other hunters had spent months searching for. His friend, Sev, would be glad to know that Mal Vor had been captured.

"Is that the woman who must accompany me?" Ric asked, motioning to the woman seated in the room beyond the mirror.

"Yeah. Mia Logan."

Ric knew that hypnosis was Earth's prime method of subduing both alien and human suspects. Each unit now had expert hypnotists as part of their police force. They were an advanced breed of mental enforcers, with a very high success rate in maintaining control over prisoners, as well as extracting criminal confessions.

This particular hypnotist apparently sucked at her job, because she'd lost control of Vad. And cost Ric a good weeks worth of fucking in the process.

Bad enough he had to deal with an Earth woman in the first place, especially this one, whom he instantly disliked. Earth women were pushy, opinionated, too skinny, lousy at sex and all around disappointments as a female species.

The woman faced away from them, so he couldn't see anything but her back and hair. What hair she had, anyway. Short, black and spiked on top, there was very little to it. Like the woman herself, who looked like she needed a *Siktor* of constant eating. Didn't they feed the women on this planet? M'Loran women were very tall, with full, heavy breasts, wide hips and ample asses, exactly the kind of female he liked to sink into when the need for sex became overwhelming. Like now.

He sighed and leaned forward, intent on giving the audio command to the system monitor next to the mirror.

Lou stopped him. "No problems with your microchip, is there?"

"It's in place," Ric replied. Knowing how hypersuggestible M'Lorans were, hunters were equipped with microchips that blocked any attempts at hypnosis.

He activated the audio system and the woman's voice filled the anteroom.

"Imagine yourself in the place that gives you pleasure," she said to Mal. "Surrounded by still waters, comfortable air and a beautiful M'Loran woman."

Ric snorted. Yeah, he could imagine that all right. Her voice held a husky, seductive edge that sparked his attention.

"Tell me what you want Mal," she urged. "Let me take you there."

She reached for Mal's hands and held them, massaging slowly with her thumbs. Instantly, images of her long fingers wrapping around his cock had Ric's penis springing to life, despite his aversion to human women and this one in particular.

She had a mesmerizing voice that could coax any man into an erection.

Within moments, Mal had closed his eyes, appearing completely relaxed. No small feat for the six-foot-nine giant with a warrior's sense of vengeance and mayhem.

"Tell me your crimes," Mia coaxed, and Mal confessed as easily as if she'd just asked for directions to the nearest *Jolsu* shopping center. If Ric weren't so annoyed, he'd have laughed at her easy expertise in extracting confessions. Too bad her hypnosis hadn't worked that well at keeping Vad imprisoned.

She continued to massage Mal's hands while he spewed forth his list of crimes in great detail. Her fingers lightly trailed up his arms and down again. Ric fought the ache between his legs. He absolutely did not desire this woman. She merely had a seductive voice. And besides, he was horny as hell, which was her fault in the first place.

"When you hear the phrase, *flowers grow in the sunshine*, you will immediately cease all hostilities. Repeat the phrase to me."

Mal recited the phrase like a lovesick poet and Ric rolled his eyes toward the cosmos. Mia stepped out and a guard came in to remove Mal.

Women. He could imagine some guard at the facility shouting that out as a convict made an escape out the doors. He laughed out loud.

"What's so funny?" Lou asked.

"Flowers grow in the sunshine?"

Lou cracked a smile, his full face wrinkling even more. "Yeah, I know, but they let the hypnotists pick their own subdue codes."

"It's moronic."

"Well, thank you very much for that comment."

Ric turned to find her standing at the door, a very annoyed look on her pixie face.

Urksa. *No, English*. Shit. No wonder Mal was mesmerized by her. He'd never seen eyes so vividly blue, so wide and expressive. She had a flawless face, creamy cheeks and lips made to suck a man's cock. For an Earth woman, she wasn't half bad to look at. Still too skinny, though. And where were her breasts? Those small things under her tight shirt couldn't be all she had. They looked like pieces of *Kinsto*, tiny M'Loran fruits.

She lifted a brow and asked, "And who the hell are you?"

"UlRic Lor."

"Am I supposed to kneel or bow or something? Your name doesn't mean squat to me. What's he doing here, Lou?"

Lou's wry smile widened as his gaze flitted between Ric and Mia. "He's here about Vad."

"Oh." She shrugged and entered the room, inching her skinny ass onto the top of the long table. "I don't know what happened with that. They misused the code, I guess."

Ric approached, stopping only inches in front of her, enjoying the way her eyes widened as she assessed his height. He'd guess she was nearly five-foot-eight or so, which made him a foot taller than her. "So, you blame someone else for your failings?"

She straightened her shoulders and lifted her chin, glaring at him. Gone was the mesmerizing hypnotist, replaced by a woman of fire. "Hey, asshole. I didn't fail at anything. I did my job, the facility guards just fucked up."

Ric turned at Lou's quiet chuckle. "UlRic Lor, meet Mia Logan, the unit's number one hypnotist."

Mia crossed her arms at Ric's snort. "What bug crawled up your ass, M'Loran? Have you got some problem with me?"

"I have no problem with you, Logan. Other than I think you're inept and I'd rather not deal with you."

He could tell she held her anger in check, but it simmered on the surface. She may not be considered attractive by M'Loran standards, but her passion excited him. Which added more fuel to his already pissed off state. He didn't want to feel anything for this female. She wasn't his type at all, despite what his cock thought. He mentally counted to ten in M'Loran to dampen the hardening.

"You want to tell me what the hell is going on here, Lou?" Mia asked, turning her back on Ric.

"Vad's escaped and Ric has to track him."

"If I know Vad, he's probably already returned to M'Lora. He'll seek shelter with the other warriors, who will protect him," Ric added.

"So, why did you come back here if he's already there?" Mia asked.

"Because I was ordered to do so by your superiors."

Mia turned to Lou. "This doesn't make any sense, Lou. Explain it to me, would you?"

Lou held up his hands. "Hey, don't get me involved. I was just here to witness Mal's confession. You and Ric will have to deal with this." With a wink in Ric's direction, Lou made his escape.

Mia heaved a sigh and closed her eyes. She really didn't need this today. Or any day, for that matter. Her caseload had gone through the atmosphere, and now one of her M'Loran subjects, Vad, had escaped and left the planet.

She'd never lost a subject before. Something had to have gone wrong with the way the guard gave the subdue code.

And to top off an already miserable day, this giant with hair like midnight and dark eyes to match had insulted her. Not that she cared. She'd been insulted by better than him. It all rolled off her back.

She scooted around on the table and found him standing in the center of the room, legs spread and hands behind his back. He sure as hell was hot to look at. The man screamed sex like a neon sign emblazoned across his crotch. Dressed in black leather pants, a tight black reflective t-shirt of some kind and a full-length leather duster, he looked dark, dangerous and sexy as hell. A throbbing stabbed between her legs and she felt the dampness gathering, but fought to ignore it.

So, she hadn't had sex in a while. A good, long, drought-stricken while. So, this tall hunk of space beefcake set her libido to pumping like a marathon runner's heartbeat. So what? She'd ignore him and he'd go away.

"Apparently you're going to accompany me to M'Lora."

"Huh?" Had she heard him right? She gazed around the room, wanting to be sure he'd been speaking to her. "Not me, buddy. I stay on terra firma."

"Check with your superiors. I've been told you have to go along. And believe me, I don't like the idea any more than you. In fact, I probably hate it much more than you do."

"Gee, thanks a lot." She slipped off the table and approached the monitor, giving the command to bring up Lieutenant Morris, her unit commander. A gruff voice responded.

"Yeah, Mia, what can I do for you?"

"Some space cowboy named..." She turned to Ric and asked, "What is your name again?"

"UlRic Lor."

"Ul...whatever, says I have to go to M'Lora."

"Yeah, you do," Morris replied. "I want you to help Ric track Vad and accompany him back. We don't want the subdue code to get screwed up by anyone else again. You give it, and you monitor him."

Mia ignored the increased pace of her heartbeat. "You know I don't do space travel, Morris."

"Today you do."

Shit. She hated traveling via those body-melting methods. She'd tried it once with a friend of hers who convinced her a quickie trek to Mars would be fun. She'd had space sickness for a month after that and never cared to repeat it.

She sighed, knowing she had no choice but to follow orders. "Fine. I'm on my way out the door." She turned to Ric and crossed her arms. "Looks like I'm your traveling companion."

"It would appear so. Are you ready to go?"

"No. I need to pack."

Ric laughed. "There's nothing to pack. Your Earth clothes won't be acceptable on M'Lora."

"Why the hell not?"

"Because you'll freeze to death. Meet me at the ship in a *sikto* and I'll have preparations made."

"A what?"

Ric inhaled deeply, showcasing his broad chest and flat stomach. "An hour. Tunnel Seven."

Before she could even respond with an *okay* or *kiss my ass*, he'd turned and walked out.

Rude bastard. But damn sexy. Just what she didn't need to endure right now. Then again, she'd been complaining that her life was routine and boring. Next time she thought about bitching about routine, she'd remember this trip to hell and back she was about to take. Already her stomach was doing somersaults at the prospect of the flight.

She stormed into her office, thinking about the massive amount of work that would only grow while she was gone. She had system entries to make, codes to input, and hypno-classes to teach to new recruits.

No wonder she had no time for a personal life. Work had become her life.

How had she ended up in this line of work? Granted, she'd been born with inherent hypnosis abilities, thanks to her parents, and she'd naturally gravitated to investigative work. But lately, what had once seemed like a thrilling adventure into detective work had turned into nothing but a series of ten-minute hypnosis sessions followed by hours of paperwork.

This wasn't fun anymore. And work had always been her passion. God knows she didn't have any others. Other than a handful of colleagues she called friends, she lived a boring, lonely, isolated life with very little time for fun or pleasure.

Pleasure. How long had it been since she'd had decent sex? Or even bad sex? What had happened to her lifelong dreams of adventure and passion? She'd lost focus somewhere along the way, and had allowed herself to be led into this career that consumed her. Now she was approaching thirty, with no prospects of love, marriage or family in the future.

And she was complaining about space travel? Her somber and thoroughly unpleasant traveling companion wasn't her first choice, but how many years had she wanted to see M'Lora? After dealing with the criminals from their mutant clan, she'd learned much about their culture.

The blue planet, they called it. With two moons—one blue, one amber. The stories she heard painted it as a garden of winter pleasures.

She snorted. If Ric's irritating personality was indicative of the natives to that planet, the only pleasure she was going to get was in leaving it.

She wondered, though, if all the M'Lorans were as hot as UlRic Lor. There was some secret about M'Loran males that she'd never been able to uncover.

Maybe this was her chance to find out why Earth women returned from visits to M'Lora with huge smiles on their faces.

She had no sooner grabbed onto a bar at his instruction when the craft lurched to the side, then did a quick dive before it stopped.

Interestingly enough, she felt no nausea from the trip. Maybe Ric was a better pilot than the last one she'd flown with.

"Let's go." The door slid open and Ric stepped out, then offered his hand to help her down the ramp.

A cold blast of air had her shivering on the platform and she lifted the hood of the jacket to cover her head. Then just as quickly as she had chilled, her body warmed. Whatever the clothing was that he'd given her offered some kind of internal heat allowing her to acclimate to their frigid temperatures immediately.

The landing platform sat inside some kind of hangar. When she turned, a wide tunnel of nothing but space greeted her. Noise from craft take-offs and landings drowned out any attempt to hear what Ric was mouthing as he kept hold of her hand and dragged her through an open doorway.

With a quick whoosh, the doors shut behind them. He dropped her hand immediately and pulled off his gloves. "Follow me," he commanded, his voice curt.

Like she had any other options? She strolled behind him, gaping at the gigantic blue people passing them by in the wide hallway. They towered over her—nearly seven feet tall. Although they had human characteristics and were dressed similarly to her and Ric, they were entirely blue, including their eye color, a pale cerulean like nothing she'd seen before.

At her pause Ric stopped and turned to her. "That's the M'Loran natural form."

She gawked at the blue man walking by. "You look like that?"

Ric nodded at the M'Loran, then shook his head and motioned her down the hall. "Of course not. Slu is shorter than me."

Even the women were blue, and nearly as tall as the men. No wonder he thought her skinny. Their females were massive in size, everywhere. Wide shoulders, ample hips and huge breasts. She looked down and clutched her meager chest, feeling flatter than normal and wishing she'd thought to eat lunch today.

This place must be the M'Loran spaceport. Signs in M'Loran had multiple translations, indicating arrival and departure times for craft to and from surrounding planets and galaxies. In many ways their airport resembled New California Inter-Galactic with the mix of cultures and species.

But she'd never seen a M'Loran in their natural state. They typically didn't shift into their natural state while on Earth, their height making it awkward to maneuver around the planet's architecture. She'd been told they preferred to assume the shape of whatever natural species inhabited the planet they visited. Now she wondered what Ric would look like, all tall and blue like that. And damn if the thought wasn't enticing. She wondered if everything about M'Loran males was big, including their cocks.

She'd never had sex with an alien before. Hell, she'd rarely had sex with human males. And why was she thinking about sex, anyway? Ric had already made it quite clear he wasn't interested in her. Maybe if she hypnotized him she could change his mind.

No. No way. No fucking way. She didn't want that any more than he did. He was a rude, thoroughly unpleasant pain in the ass and she'd just as soon screw herself than let him fuck her.

Although she'd done it herself for too long as it was. She simply needed to get laid. Her body must think it was on vacation the way her libido had suddenly fired to life.

And she was suddenly ravenously hungry.

A M'Loran male stopped Ric along the way, speaking to him in what had to be their native language. Mia stood by silently, not really knowing what else to do. The man nodded in her direction. Ric said something in response and both men laughed.

She steamed, imagining what Ric must have said about her. Probably something about skinny, flat-chested, idiotic Earth women. She crossed her arms and waited for their laughs to subside. When Ric walked on she followed, throwing mental daggers at his broad back.

"Put on your gloves," he said, slipping his on when they approached the main doors.

The icy air stole her breath as they stepped outside. Like being up in the mountains, the air was thinner than what she was used to and she struggled to keep up with his long stride. He turned and frowned, then said, "After a few hours you will adjust to our differences in atmosphere. Until then, I'll walk slower."

He did as he promised and she found herself able to keep up. Excitement bubbled inside her at the prospect of getting away from the space station and into a M'Loran town.

"The city we're in is called *Jolsu*," Ric explained. "It is where I grew up."

They entered another building, this one smaller than the main station. Ric selected a vehicle which looked like a hovercraft, only it had four sides and a top and looked much sturdier than something one would use to tool around on the water.

There were doors similar to one of Earth's battery powered vehicles and they slid inside. Straps immediately descended from the roof and locked her into her seat. Ric waved his hand over a glass screen in the center console and the vehicle powered to life, sailing through the opening to the facility and out into the skies.

Ample window space afforded her an opportunity to see the city from above. There seemed to be no differentiation between business and residential areas. All the buildings looked the same, only some were larger than others and they were all different colors, lending the appearance of a ground rainbow.

Greenery and colorful foliage decorated every dwelling, which all seemed to be one-story stone buildings. Snow tipped mountains surrounded every side of the city, their peaks reaching up into the blue-clouded skies.

"It's lovely," she remarked to Ric as they soared in and out of the fluffy clouds, Ric effortlessly dodging other craft in their vicinity. "I've never seen actual blue clouds before."

"There are many things about M'Lora that are different than Earth. And many things are the same. Your planet, now that you've overcome your pollution problem, is beautiful, too and very similar to M'Lora."

He settled the craft in front of a pale stone dwelling. It looked to be one story but very tall. Given the size of M'Lorans, it was no wonder they needed high ceilings.

"This is my home," he said as he walked through a doorway, which slid open as soon as he approached. "We'll stop here, refresh and eat, then plan our hunt for Vad."

He waved his hand over the monitor and lights came on, fire in the stone hearth flaming to life, instantly warming the massive living space. Everything inside was huge, obviously to accommodate M'Loran height and girth. Couches made of a down-like fabric in a rainbow of colors were much larger than what Mia was used to. Even the chairs in the steel and white kitchen were double normal size. Again Mia wondered what Ric would be like in his natural state.

"Why haven't you changed into your M'Loran form?" she asked as he shrugged out of his leather duster, affording her the opportunity to view his body in more detail.

Wow. Broad shouldered was an understatement. His wide chest gave way to a narrow waist and long, muscular legs with bulging thighs. She resisted the urge to drool.

"Easier for you to recognize me this way in case we're separated. Why? Am I repulsive to you in this form?" he teased.

"Your actions will be under my control unless I give you free reign. Do you understand?"

"Yes."

"Raise your left arm above your head."

He lifted his arm.

"Now, lower it."

Mia gave him a few simple commands to be sure he was fully under. He had to be, otherwise he'd be sitting there laughing at her. "You will follow only my commands, no matter what I ask you to do, do you understand? If so, say yes."

"Yes."

"You may speak to me normally, act as you normally would, do or say whatever you like. However, if I tell you to stop you will stop, is that understood?"

"Yes."

Now was her chance to explore him, to touch him. Actually, she could have him do anything she wanted. The thought heightened her senses, her mind awash in visuals of exactly what he could do to her.

Except none of it would be his choice. She'd just taken away his free will.

She pushed aside the niggle of guilt that twinged in her stomach, and said, "Touch me, Ric."

He placed his palm over her hand.

"Good, very good. Now, touch my arm."

He slid his palm over her wrist, slowly gliding up her arm until she shivered.

"Very nice. Do you think it's nice?"

"Yes."

"You can elaborate if you wish."

"Your skin is soft as a *plrksu's* fur."

She hoped that was a good thing since she had no idea what a *plrksu* was.

"You may touch me anywhere you like," she commanded, needing to know whether her appearance completely repulsed him, or whether he might be able to tolerate touching her.

Up until now, Ric was only playing a game with Mia, planning to surprise her in the midst of it all by laughing at her. Then he'd smugly announce that he was right, he couldn't be hypnotized. He'd explain about the blocking chip and that no matter how hard she tried, she'd never spellbind him.

He was wrong. She *had* mesmerized him. With her voice, so lazy and seductive to his senses, and her touch, the lightest flutter of which drove him nearly mad. He longed to jump up and carry her to his bed, but then knew she'd be angry when she discovered he'd lied. And a part of him didn't want her to stop talking to him in her raspy, seductive voice. He didn't want her to stop touching him, to stop rubbing her hands over his arms. *Milok*, if she fired him up so hotly by merely rubbing his arms, what would happen if she touched the intimate parts of his body?

The lure was too much, and in the end he remained silent and let her believe he was hypnotized. Especially when she invited him to touch her anywhere he wanted. How could he resist? Already he ached for her, wanted her more than he'd ever desired an Earth woman before.

"Tell me what you want, Ric," she commanded.

"I want to gather you in my arms and touch your body, Mia."

Her eyes darkened, her lashes fluttering to her cheeks. "I'd like that," she said, her chest rising and falling quickly.

Pleased that she was as excited as he, he stood and stepped toward her, then paused. She was so small, he wondered if he should change his size.

"Would you like me to shift down to a size more compatible with yours?"

"No!" she said quickly, a red tinge appearing on her cheeks. "I mean, I prefer you this way."

Ric resisted the urge to chuckle. So, the little pixie enjoyed large men, did she? Perhaps she might not be affronted by his M'Loran form. But right now he'd remain human. He didn't want to frighten or hurt her in any way. Not when he was so close to getting what he wanted.

Why he wanted her was beyond his ability to understand. She had a magic voice, a hypnotic touch, and he needed to explore her further. Nothing would come of it other than physical release for both of them, so why not?

"Ric?"

"Yes?"

"Are you going to touch me?"

He couldn't help his smile at the impatience in her voice. "Yes." He reached out and gathered her against him, wrapping his arms around her back. Her small breasts brushed against his lower chest.

"Damn, you're big," she mumbled against him.

"Does that bother you?"

"Hell, no. It's impressive. Your size, your strength, your—"

She stopped speaking and her eyes widened, no doubt due to his growing erection.

"Oh, my," she said.

"I will not hurt you if you wish to feel my cock inside you."

She swallowed and he fixated on her slender neck. "How about we start with touching first, and see how it goes?"

"That is acceptable. I'd like to take you onto my bed where we can stretch out fully. I want to see your body."

She frowned, clearly disturbed by his free thinking. He'd have to remind himself he was supposed to be under hypnosis, and temper his desire to control the situation. "Unless you don't wish it, of course."

"Actually, it sounds like a great idea. I'd like to touch you, too."

He burned with her words, his erection elongating to uncomfortable proportions. If she could see him in his natural state, she'd —

No. Best to wait on that. He could have sex just as easily in human form as he could in his M'Loran form. He may not have all the same equipment, but it would be enjoyable nonetheless. Besides, he didn't want to rush her, to shock her. Not until she grew comfortable with him.

Ric led her to his bedroom. She stood next to the bed and waited.

"May I undress you?" he asked.

Her breasts rose with her sharp intake of breath. "Yes."

With slow movements he approached her, then leaned over and reached for her. "I want to kiss you."

"Okay." She shifted as if she were uncomfortable, although he knew her ailment. Passion. Her body was filled with it. It nearly poured from her being like a flash of fire in the dark.

"Are you hesitant?" he teased, wanting to prolong it, thereby making their joining so much sweeter.

"No, I'm not hesitant. Do as I've commanded you. Kiss me, touch me. Now, Ric."

Her irritation showed her desire. Such passion for an Earth woman. So bold in her words. Exactly the way he liked it. She was more similar to M'Loran women than he thought, and so unlike many of the meeker Earth females he'd known.

His first thought was to strip her down quickly and plunge inside her, taking what she so willingly offered. But he didn't want to rush things. This might be his only chance to touch her and he wanted to make it last.

He started with her fully clothed. Bending down, he grasped her ankles, sliding his hands over her calves and knees. Her legs were reed thin — the woman really did need to eat more often.

When he brushed her thighs she shuddered, spreading her legs apart in an unspoken invitation, her gaze focused on his hands.

L'Nons, she made him throb with a pleasurable pain. His hands roamed further up, ignoring the juncture of her thighs, not yet wanting to touch her there, but prolong her pleasure in the process.

She sighed, a note of frustration tingeing her forceful breath, and he fought the urge to smile. He moved his hands over her slender hips, hoping that when the time came for joining he wouldn't hurt her. Her body was so small, so fragile, not built to join sexually with a M'Loran.

Even in his human form he worried he'd be too big for her.

"You won't hurt me," she whispered in answer to his silent musings.

"I worry that I will."

She smiled down at him. "Let me worry about it. Believe me, I won't be shy about telling you if I feel pain. Now quit talking and touch me."

He laughed then, unable to stop himself. Mia was turning out to be much more than he'd thought. Passion lurked, barely leashed inside her, and he planned to tap into her well of desires. Like a hunt for mysterious treasure, she intrigued him like no other woman before.

Kneeling like this afforded him a view of her entire body. He slid his hands under her sweater, the muscles of her stomach rippling under his touch. Lifting the material up, he leaned in and pressed a kiss to her belly. She shivered, her stomach quivering.

"You like that," he said, tilting his head back to see her face.

"Yes," she said, letting out the breath she'd been holding.

"You want me to kiss you in other places."

"Yes, I do."

His cock throbbed against the binding leather, desperate to be free. But first he wanted to see her, touch her, while she would allow it.

He moved his hands downward over her hips, clenching them hard between his fingers, wanting to know if she'd flinch.

She sucked in a breath but she didn't appear to be in pain. He snaked his hands slowly upward again, until his fingertips brushed the underside of her small breasts. She moaned lightly.

Encouraged, he moved further, rubbing his palms lightly over her nipples. They distended against his hand, shooting fiery sparks of pleasure to his throbbing cock.

"Your nipples are very sensitive," he said, lightly twisting the nubs between his fingers. When she threaded her fingers in his hair and held on tight, he knew he had found a woman whose passions matched his own. His balls tightened, filling with the hot come he was desperate to release inside her tight heat. He inhaled deeply and picked up her scent, a sweet musk unique to a heated female. His nostrils flared with the effort to breathe in her essence.

Relax. Take this slowly. But how could he remain calm when the very scent of her fired his blood to boiling? He restrained the urge to rip the clothing from her body and plunge deeply inside her.

He pulled the sweater over her head and cast it aside, his gaze drinking in her small breasts. Rosy peaks strained outward, long and beckoning. Her breath caught when he pulled at her nipples.

Oh, but he wanted more than just his hands on her. His hands roamed her body, lower and lower until they covered her rear, searching for the zipper hidden within the leather pants. He gently slid it down, his hands brushing over her silken flesh. She shuddered.

When he drew the pants over her hips, the leather sliding gently down her legs, she gasped. Ric inhaled, her scent driving him nearly mad with need for her.

But now he had her naked and he leaned back to look at her.

Not his type at all. Tall for an Earth woman, but short by M'Loran standards. Slender legs, narrow hips, hardly a handful of ass and barely-there breasts.

And he desired her more than he'd ever wanted a woman, no matter what species she was. More than just her appearance, it was her passion that stirred him. For a woman so unlike the full M'Loran females he thought ideal, she was beautiful, inside and out. Her fire, her sharp wit and her eagerness to sexually explore excited him beyond measure.

Quite a revelation for a man who typically chose sex mates by their looks. A revelation he didn't want to explore right now, afraid of what he'd discover about himself. Right now, he wanted to concentrate on pleasuring Mia.

He bent his head toward her center, his tongue snaking out to taste her. Drops of moisture slipped onto his tongue. She tasted so much sweeter than he remembered from their trip, perhaps because he'd assumed a more tangible form, allowing her juices to linger on his tongue long after he took the first lick of her essence.

"Oh my God, Ric!" she cried as he delved between the folds of her pussy, licking and nipping at the hidden bud.

Her whimpers and gasps as he stroked her outer folds were nearly more than he could handle. Barely able to restrain his passions for her, he knew he wouldn't last long once he was sheathed within her. It had just been too damn long since he'd had a woman—any woman. But this one, this first time with her, would be magical.

How he knew this was unclear. He just accepted what was and wanted to make this moment special for her. He wanted to watch her climax against his mouth, feel her body shaking under his lips and tongue, and taste her essence until she had no more to give.

Once she was satisfied he would bring her up again, take her near the edge of reason. Then lose himself inside her, and take her again and again until neither of them could move.

Chapter Five

Mia swallowed hard, her throat dry from her heavy panting. She spread her legs wider to give Ric better access to her throbbing, incessant ache. Never before had a guy turned her on like this. His relentless stroking drove her to a height she'd never before reached.

Mindless with her quest for the pinnacle, she urged him on, stroking the soft, dark hair on his head, watching his every movement, unable to tear her eyes away from the rhythmic licking of his long, soft tongue.

"Oh, yes, Ric, like that," she murmured. He held onto her ass and drank of her, licking, teasing and nibbling until she thought her legs would give out.

And still he continued, taking her to the brink time and time again. The contractions would begin and he'd pull back. As soon as she relaxed he'd resume his movements, finding yet another spot he hadn't touched with his magical tongue.

The torture was merciless. Tension built inside her to explosive levels, and she knew that next time he'd be unable to stop her climax. Pleasure spiraled up from her center, shooting through her body in breath stealing fashion.

"Ric, please," she begged, so close it was maddening.

He hummed low in his throat, the vibrations against her already sensitized flesh searing her blood. When he cupped his lips over her clit and sucked, then slipped a finger inside, her climax rushed like a dam bursting.

She bucked against his mouth, intense waves crashing through her. She cried out and grasped his hair, riding out her orgasm until she managed some semblance of coherent thought again.

When she could move, she looked down to find him watching her intently. Normally not a shy person, she could barely meet his heated eyes.

She was completely naked and he kneeled before her fully clothed. Something about the incongruity of the situation struck a chord within her, and she knew she had to right that immediately.

"Was that pleasurable for you?" he asked, reminding her that she'd left him hypnotized.

"Yes, very much so." She should wake him. Truly, she'd taken advantage of him as much as she dared. And yet, she wanted so much more. She hadn't even seen him naked yet. His huge body intrigued her. Maybe she'd order him to undress, ogle his no-doubt hot bod for a few minutes, then wake him up.

Yeah, right.

"Stand up, Ric."

He stood, once again towering over her.

"I'd like to see you naked."

Without a word he yanked the tight shirt off, exposing a nearly bare, holy-shit-impressive chest.

His broad shoulders glistened with perspiration. His body had a natural dark hue, almost as if he tanned naked. But of course that couldn't be. He could simply shapeshift into any form and skin color he wanted to. And the body he'd chosen was damn fine.

Wanting to touch him and yet forcing herself to wait until the complete unveiling, she nodded when he reached for the button on his leather pants. With slow, precise movements he flipped it open, then dragged down the zipper.

No underclothing. In the dimly lit room she caught a glimpse of fine, black hair inside his pants. What she saw was enough, though. The urge to lick that shadowed spot revealed by his half opened pants was nearly unbearable.

But still, she did nothing except watch. And lick her lips.

He reached for the waist of his pants and slid them down his legs. Huge, muscular thighs tapered down to equally impressive calves.

His feet were enormous, more than twice the size of hers. On any other man they'd look ridiculous. On him, they seemed to fit.

And what centered between his legs, that part of him she'd ignored, afraid of what she'd see, now captured her attention. Rock hard and jutting upwards, it was long and thick and bigger than any penis she'd ever seen.

She just might faint.

"Tell me the word for cock in M'Loran," she whispered.

"*Inson*," he replied.

"That's one impressive *inson*, Ric."

"Thank you. Would you like me to fuck you now?"

She *was* going to faint. Just the thought of him sliding his huge shaft inside her had her shuddering with fear and throbbing with anticipation.

"I think right now I'd just like to look at you."

"Be my guest."

"Turn around, Ric. I want to look at your ass." Men hated to be ordered around, especially by a female. And she knew damn well this one wouldn't care one bit for it. Which was a good way to double check her hypnosis. Just to be sure.

He complied instantly. Her heart pummeled her ribs when she caught sight of his well-shaped ass. Was there a part of this man that wasn't perfect? She thought about his size versus hers and wondered again whether peg A would actually fit into slot B.

It sure as hell wasn't going anywhere near slot C.

He'd shifted into one awesome human body. She wondered what else he could change into? And what about his M'Loran form? She was dying to get a peek at that.

But not right now. Right now she wanted to learn this body.

"I'm going to touch you," she said.

"The same way I just touched you?"

Well, she hadn't thought of that. He'd touched her with his mouth. "I'm not sure I can get…that is, you're kinda oversized and…oh hell, I love a challenge. Turn around."

He swiveled and her eyes were drawn to his massive organ. She licked her lips and heard his swift intake of breath.

Definitely more than a mouthful. She dropped to her knees, admiring his taut flesh on the way down. He was so tall his penis could rest on her head. Okay, she needed a boost here. "Got pillows?" she asked.

He quirked a brow. "No. Why?"

"Because your cock's above my eyes. And I'm not going to do squats to suck it. I need a boost."

"Ah, yes, I see the logistical difficulty here."

Mia laughed at how ludicrous the whole situation was. But then Ric sat on what she'd assumed was a mattress-less bed. Except it did have something there. But it was invisible. "What are you sitting on?"

"Air current. This should work."

It did, putting his throbbing shaft just where she wanted it. She reached out and traced the glistening head with her fingers, marveling at its silky feel. She grazed her thumb over the moisture-laden opening, then sucked her finger.

"*Jorhosfil!*" he groaned.

"Translate, please," she said, smiling.

"Sonofabitch. Suck me, *J'Mun*."

Grasping his thighs, she pulled herself forward, snaking her tongue around the swollen head. He tasted both tangy and sweet.

"You have a full, beautiful mouth, *J'Mun*," he murmured. She lifted her gaze to his and her heart pounded. He watched her like a man who hungered.

Never taking her eyes off his face, she slid her mouth over him, capturing his shaft between her teeth, lightly scraping as she took him in as far as she could. His chest rose sharply with his indrawn breath, and he muttered a string of M'Loran phrases which she hoped meant *damn, you're good at that*.

When she pulled her mouth away, his cock glistened, and she took him in again, deeper this time, as far as she could go. His heavy groan coupled with his throbbing penis told her she gave him pleasure. For someone who'd never given a whole lot of thought to pleasing a man, Mia found Ric's obvious enjoyment exciting.

The throbbing between her legs intensified and she instinctively threaded her fingers into the thatch of down, searching for her clit. Rubbing it gently elicited sparks of agonizing delight. She groaned, taking Ric's shaft deeper into her mouth.

"Enough," he said, his voice low and husky. "I need to be inside you, *J'Mun*."

He stood, pulling her up and gathering her into his arms. She felt so small against his huge body, something she'd never experienced before when with a man. Ric gently laid her on the invisible bed, which felt like lying on an undulating cloud. She reached for something solid and yet when she pushed down her hand could not penetrate the invisible barrier.

How odd, and yet so light, so comfortable, it was like flying. When he settled in next to her on the bed, she hardly felt the movements.

Ric gathered her in his arms and pulled her close. His breath sailed across her face and she focused on his lips. Sensuous, full and inviting.

"Ric?"

"Yes."

"Kiss me."

His lips curved into a devilish smile. He grasped the back of her head and lightly licked her bottom lip. She shuddered at the wet warmth of his tongue. His lips touched hers fully, and she sighed into his open mouth. He moved slowly, seductively, increasing her ardor with every swipe of his tongue against hers until she reached for his hair and pulled him toward her. She ached for him, wanting him inside her with a need she'd never possessed before.

His hands moved over her body, reaching for her breasts, his thumbs making lazy circles over her distended nipples. She arched her back, spreading her legs for him, showing him what she wanted.

He laughed, then, a dark, seductive chuckle that sent shivers through her soul. He palmed the damp curls between her legs, then slipped his fingers inside her.

Too gentle. She needed more.

"Harder," she commanded.

With a half sigh, half groan, he thrust deeper. The fierce plunging of his fingers only increased her passionate need to have him drive his shaft deep within her.

"Now, Ric, please," she moaned, but his relentless assault continued until she was drenched and whimpering. "Fuck me now, dammit!"

With a growl he shifted her underneath him, spreading her legs wide with his knee. He braced his hands on either side of her and slowly, inch by incredible inch, sheathed his cock inside her.

"If it hurts, tell me to stop."

It didn't hurt, it felt fabulous. He filled her completely, stretching her, touching her in places she'd never been touched before, eliciting shockwaves of sensation that nearly toppled her over the edge.

Then he moved within her, capturing her mouth in a heated kiss as he thrust and withdrew over and over again. She lifted her hips to take more of him in, amazed at her body's ability to adapt to his size.

"You're so wet, *J'Mun*," he whispered against her ear, lightly nibbling her lobe with his teeth. "Like a slide through the sweet stars."

When he thrust again she cried out, her nails digging into his shoulders. He increased his rhythm in answer to her unspoken urging. Faster now, he was relentless, his intense gaze capturing and holding hers. She stilled at his movements, the first waves of her orgasm approaching. He seemed to sense she was close because he shifted just enough to brush against her clit.

The force of her climax made her scream his name. He held her close, slipping his hands under her buttocks and plunging repeatedly inside her. Their sweat-slickened bodies meshed together, her nipples tingling against the hard planes of his chest.

Ric never gave her time to catch her breath. He continued to move within her, his pace easy and light, which only served to fire up her desires again. Her juices poured over them both as he pulled partially away, only to plunge deep inside her again and again until she was incapable of speech. Her only thoughts were of him, of their bodies joined together, and the magic he wove upon her senses.

"Now, *J'Mun*," he groaned, lifting up and roaring with the ferocity of his orgasm. She wrapped her legs around his back, digging her heels into his buttocks as he thrust hard against her one more time, then collapsed.

Immediately he shifted to the side, pulling her along with him so that she remained cradled in his arms. She watched his face. His eyes were closed, long, dark lashes resting against his cheeks. She reached up and traced the outline of his nose, and he opened his eyes and smiled at her.

She waited for him to speak, but he didn't.

Realizing she still had him under hypnosis, her joy diminished. He hadn't taken her of his own free will, she had mesmerized him into it. Guilt stabbed at her, but she refused to listen to the voices in her head that told her what she'd just done went against everything she'd been taught.

"Ric, listen to me," she said, fixing her voice in the soft, melodic tones she'd used to put him under. "I want you to close your eyes now and sleep. When you wake tomorrow, you will remember nothing of what happened. Do you understand?"

"Yes." His eyes closed and his body loosened its hold on her.

Mia chewed her bottom lip and contemplated adding one more command to Ric. Would he ever want her of his own volition? What they'd just shared was indescribable. How could she ever go back to having sex with another man when she'd just gotten the best she'd ever had?

And he had indicated he'd been due for some sexual relaxation. Surely she could help him out a little.

"Ric, can you hear me?"

"Yes."

"When you hear me ask, *Ric, do you think I'm beautiful*, you will immediately fall into a deep hypnotic state again, and will remain so until I tell you to wake. Is that understood?"

He paused for a moment, and she wondered if he'd take the post-hypnotic suggestion. Being a M'Loran it should work on him, as it did for so many others when she gave them the subdue code. Ric was no different than any of them.

She asked him again. "Ric, did you understand the phrase I gave you?"

"Yes."

"When you hear that phrase, you will fall into a deep sleep. You will respond only to my commands. Is that clear?"

"Yes."

"Go to sleep now. You will wake naturally, feel refreshed and remember nothing."

She watched as his breathing slowed and his body relaxed. Once she was certain he was in a natural sleep, she slid off the bed and grabbed her things, not wanting to be found in his room when he woke up.

Picking a comfortable chair in his living area, she closed her eyes and tried to rest. But guilt haunted her, prevented her from sleeping.

What had she done? Never in her professional life had she hypnotized a subject for her own personal gain. So why now, and why with Ric? And just because she'd done it once didn't mean she had to do it again.

She simply wouldn't use the suggestion she'd given him, that's all. Once was bad enough. She'd never do it again.

No matter how much she wanted a repeat performance of tonight. Already her body ached for him, wanting him inside her again, needing to feel his strong arms around her, his cock pounding away until she had no memory of any man before him.

That's what she wanted, but she wasn't going to have it again. She'd already had her thrill, at the cost of her integrity.

Chapter Six

Ric stood over Mia and watched her sleep, innocence and beauty bathing her small face. She had surprised him last night, in more ways than one. Sex with her had been not only a physical release, but an emotional joining that he'd never experienced before.

And when she gave him that phrase to remember, he wondered if she'd be using it to repeat their intimate encounter. No. That wasn't going to happen. They had work to do and sex only complicated their relationship.

Then again...he was long overdue for relief. What the hell? She started this sex-by-hypnosis game. He might as well play along.

"I was right about not being able to be hypnotized," he said, trying to keep a straight face.

Mia cracked one eye open, groaned and turned over. She'd been sprawled on his resting chair, her body open and inviting. It took all the restraint he had to keep from picking her up and carrying her back to his bed. But he wasn't supposed to remember what they'd done. Hopefully he wouldn't trip himself up by saying something.

Lying had distinct disadvantages. Which was why he didn't do it very often.

"It's time to wake, Mia."

"Go away. I'm tired."

"You had plenty of opportunity for sleep. I recall retiring very early last eve. Now get up."

"Maybe you got sleep, but I didn't," she grumbled, her face buried in the cushions.

She made quite a sight this morning. She'd dragged a coverlet from the top of the lounger and pulled it over her. Right now she was face down, nearly on her knees, her ass pointed directly at him.

His cock saw that as an invitation and sprang up to pounce. No, not now. Not until he figured things out. Bad enough he'd had to lie his way through last night and pretend to be hypnotized.

Not that it had detracted from his enjoyment. Instead, it only added to her allure. He couldn't quite put his finger on what attracted him, considering her body type wasn't at all what he preferred.

He finally came to the realization that she was an innocent. Oh, she hid behind a false bravado of the tough police officer, but he already knew better. She might be good at her job and show no fear to prisoners, but when it came to relationships and intimacy, Mia Logan was frightened.

That fear made her unique to him. M'Loran women were not vulnerable. They didn't have the innocence that Mia did. A M'Loran woman could easily survive without a man, without children, without anything but their weapons or their minds. They needed nothing, craved nothing and possessed very little warmth.

Pleasure Aides spent years learning to feign passion for the men they serviced, and they were trained damn well in the seductive arts. But deep down, every M'Loran male knew that fucking a M'Loran Pleasure Aide was for purely physical release. They may be trained in how to please a man, but none of the pleasure they gave was emotional.

Until now it hadn't mattered to Ric.

And wasn't that a dilemma? He was stuck with an unattractive Earth woman, a woman he'd fucked, lied to and decided he cared about in one night? And now he had to put her life in danger by dragging her into K'Mor country where she'd be surrounded by warriors who would rather kill her than greet her.

"Get up." His voice was rough with the frustration boiling inside him. "We leave today."

Mia sat up and threw off the covers. She yawned, dragging her hand through her spiky hair. "I'm starving. Let's eat."

They fixed breakfast and Ric smiled at the amount of food Mia ate, considering it was all foreign to her.

"This…what is this stuff again?" she asked, lifting up a spoonful.

"*Mok*."

"Whatever. It's like what we call oatmeal on Earth. And these eggs are fabulous."

"Those are from the *Orsk* you ate last night. They lay eggs similar to your chickens."

She finished two platefuls of food, then leaned back in the chair and let out a loud belch. "Sorry. I'm stuffed. I can't believe I have such an appetite."

"You will find your desire for food as well as other things will increase while you are on M'Lora."

She arched a brow. "Other things?"

"Yes."

"Care to elaborate?"

"No. We need to leave."

She blew out a breath. "I need a shower, first. You do shower or bathe here, right?"

He rolled his eyes at her. "Yes, we bathe. I'll show you how the cleanser works." He beckoned her into the cleaning room.

"Nice," she said, her eyes widening with what he assumed was appreciation. He supposed he had a decent sized cleaning room, with a wide shelf for women to do…whatever it was women did to themselves. Since he'd never lived with one, he couldn't say. And Pleasure Aides never cleaned up in front of him after sexual recreation.

It never occurred to him before that women were more than a bit of a mystery. But based on Mia's smile, he assumed whatever was in this room appealed to her. And it pleased him to see her happy for reasons he wouldn't even attempt to delve into.

"The large chamber contains cleaning agents. Step inside, press the button in front of you, and the chamber will do the rest. As far as your private eliminations, the shelf in the corner there—"

"I think I get the idea, thanks." She began to undress and he stood there, waiting to see if she'd stop herself. After unzipping her pants, her fingers stilled and she turned to him, her cheeks reddening. "Get out."

Ric turned around to hide his smirk and left the room.

While Mia was cleaning, he made a list of supplies they'd need for the trek across the planet. Not only weaponry, but sleeping apparatus, appropriate clothing and food. He scanned the market's wares on his visual screen, recited his orders and advised when he'd be by to pick them up. By the time Mia surfaced, he was ready to go.

"That was fabulous," she said, her skin sparkling and pink from the cleansing. Her hair spiked up and curled on the ends and she pulled her fingers through it in what he assumed was some sort of combing ritual.

"Glad you enjoyed it."

"Oh, I more than enjoyed it. I stood there and this warm air blew over me, then this jelly like substance covered me, which was really weird but not unpleasant. And the jets! Oh my God, Ric, the jets shot out from all over the chamber and the scrubbing and cleansing and oh, wow it was like a million fingers massaging my body. Damn, it was good for me," she finished with a wink.

His cock answered with a resounding twitch, remembering just how good it had been for him last night. "Are you ready to go? We have to pick up supplies first."

She nodded and followed him through the entry door. "I assume we're going to discuss the game plan on the way?"

"Game plan?"

"Yeah. You know, where we're going, what the plan is to capture Vad. I need to know what kind of weaponry we're going to use. Will there be time to give me a quick training on how to use the weapons?"

"You won't be using weaponry."

She halted in front of his vehicle. "Wait a minute. I'm not going in there unarmed."

"You won't be. I'll be armed. Let's get going."

"No way," she said, her feet planted firmly on the ground, her arms crossed and her chin lifted. "I'm not entering hostile land without a weapon."

"You can't use our firearms."

"Is it forbidden?"

"No. You just don't know how to use them."

"I know that, you moron. That's why I asked for training. I'm skilled in most of Earth's tactical weaponry. I just need to know how to use M'Loran stuff."

"No."

"What is your problem, M'Loran? I'm a police officer, trained in all the unit's weaponry, both simple and advanced. I'm perfectly capable of handling any type of weapon your planet uses, so what's the big deal?"

"It's complicated. I'll explain when we get to the Enforcement Office."

He was beginning to think she was going to stand there all day and argue with him, but she finally let out a huff and stepped toward the craft. He heaved a sigh of relief.

"Where are we going?" she asked.

"We'll load up with necessities for travel, stop off at Enforcement to obtain weapons, then head east toward K'Mor territory."

"Why don't you keep your weapons with you?"

"M'Loran law. No weapons in homes. There are scanners to check for that. Even the police officers and hunters, unless on duty, don't keep their weapons on hand."

"How long will it take to get to K'Mor?"

"We're close to the border between the two lands right now. Within two cycles of the blue moon we will cross into the amber moon area."

"And that's K'Mor land?"

"Yes."

"Do you travel there often?" she asked.

"No. Only a handful of times to capture a Molkor, and even then, quickly in and out.

"Molkor are the rebel mutants...half K'Mor, half J'Sol, right?"

"Yes."

"Why are they considered mutants and not simply of mixed races?"

"M'Loran races are pure. There are K'Mor, and there are J'Sol. Our two races were not meant to breed together. Too much potential for volatile results, and as you can see my people were correct. Hence, any child of K'Mor and J'Sol mating are considered mutant."

"And that's what Vad is."

"Yes."

Mia glanced at Ric. He clenched the wheel of the hovercraft, his gaze focused straight ahead. A slight tic formed at the right side of his mouth. The man was tense. But why? "Something wrong?"

He stared straight ahead. "No."

Yes, there was. She could read his body language and it told her he held something inside—something that bothered him. What was it? And why did she care? So he'd been fantastic in bed last night. It certainly hadn't changed his disposition. He was still grumpy and unpleasant.

They arrived at a large, stone building that was rectangular in shape. It looked very similar to a shopping center on Earth. When they stepped inside, M'Lorans were everywhere. So were humans and many other interplanetary species she didn't recognize.

Ric led her into what looked like a clothing store, barked orders in M'Loran to the female standing behind a high counter. Everything was so big on this planet, Mia felt like a midget. The woman presented Mia with a wrapped package, then they proceeded to what she assumed was a check-out counter.

"What am I holding?" she asked Ric, struggling to keep up with his long stride.

"Clothing for you. You will need other things to wear."

"A M'Loran woman's clothing won't fit me."

"They've been adjusted to fit your body."

"Oh. Thank you."

"You're welcome."

"UlRic Lor!"

Ric stopped and turned, as did Mia. Two M'Loran women approached and spoke to him in his language. The women stared at Ric, wide-eyed, although Mia couldn't figure out why for a few seconds. Then it dawned on her. Of course they'd be surprised to see him in human form.

The women smiled, even giggled and shot curiously interested looks in Mia's direction.

"Speak English so my partner here knows what you're saying," Ric said to the women. "It's impolite to speak in our native language in front of other planet's visitors."

The women nodded.

"When will you be visiting us, UlRic?" one woman asked, licking her full, painted lips.

"Yes, when? I was very distressed when you did not make your sex appointment with me," the other said, eyeing Ric as hungrily as Mia had eyed her breakfast this morning.

These were Pleasure Aides. Mia fought the jealousy surging through her. Just because she'd fucked Ric once didn't mean she owned him.

"I'm sorry I missed the recreation," Ric answered politely. "I had been looking forward to it and was disappointed we couldn't have sex."

Mia felt like crawling under one of the shelves. Nothing like discussing sex in the middle of a crowded shopping center.

"You know you are one of our favorites," one woman said, sliding the tip of one very long fingernail across Ric's chest. "Your fucking abilities are legendary."

Ric threw his head back and laughed. "You're good, M'Konu. I will anticipate our next sex together."

Mia looked around for some kind of weapon to knock Ric over the head with. How could he treat her like this after what they'd shared together last night? Granted, she didn't have anything exclusive with him, but—

Oh. Right. He didn't remember last night. Shit. Right now she wanted to scream at him and the two women lusting after him that he'd been fucked quite well last night and wouldn't be needing their services.

What was wrong with her, anyway? She'd gotten what she wanted, and should be satisfied that she'd gotten that much. And it would never happen again, so she might as well forget about being jealous. Ric wasn't hers and never would be.

"I must go. We are on a hunt."

The women nodded and turned to leave, but one said, "When you and the boy there are finished with the hunt, come see me."

Boy? The woman thought she was a boy? "Now wait just one damn minute!" Mia started, but Ric grabbed her arm and dragged her toward the exit.

Mia steamed. *Boy*, indeed. She glanced at the leather jacket compressing her barely-there breasts, then further on down at her skinny legs and small height. Then she looked up at the woman scanning Ric's items. The M'Loran female had to be a good six foot five or so, with wide shoulders, ample hips and legs nearly the height of Mia's entire body.

No wonder they thought her a small boy. She couldn't compare to the M'Loran women's Amazon stature if she tried. But the Pleasure Aide's comment still stung, dammit. She'd never felt inferior before. In fact, on Earth she was considered attractive. Here, she felt ugly.

She might be a good foot smaller than those women, but she bet she could still kick their asses.

She steamed silently while they finished shopping and put their supplies in the vehicle. They flew a few seconds only, then Ric sailed toward a rectangular opening and into a parking area of sorts. He barked orders to a M'Loran guard, who nodded and began retrieving their supplies from Ric's craft.

Ric motioned her into a tunnel near the parking area. They stepped downstairs into darkness and he grabbed her hand.

"My eyes are more accustomed to seeing in the dark than human eyes are. Just hold on to me and you'll be fine."

The warmth of his hand in hers set her on fire, remembering how those hands had caressed her last night. Why did she have to think about that now? This whole hypnosis thing had been a nightmare from the beginning. How could she let her libido overtake her common sense?

Now she'd had a taste of something wonderful, and she wanted more. Problem was, she wasn't going to get more. And it was a certainty that Ric wouldn't be suggesting they have sex any time soon since he wasn't the least bit interested in her that way.

In less than a minute a door slid open into a basement structure, bustling with activity.

"This is the Enforcement Unit," he explained, letting go of her hand.

She chilled at the loss of his body's warmth. They walked through a long hallway and Mia caught sight of technology the likes of which she'd never seen. Holograms centered one room, multiple planets and galaxies hovering in the air as if suspended on invisible wire.

Despite Earth's many technological advances, M'Lorans were centuries ahead of them. At least this side of the planet was.

She stopped and stared at a window through which an entire wall was lit up with images of various M'Loran cities.

"Here we monitor daily activities. If crime occurs, we generally know about it immediately," Ric explained. "These officers are responsible for inhabitants' safety."

"But you can't catch every criminal in the process of committing a crime, right?"

"No, but sometimes we get lucky and we can catch them on the monitor. Other times we can pinpoint it within seconds of it occurring, but our technologists are working on ways to view the entire planet and its inhabitants without sacrificing privacy. We're not there yet, but we will be soon."

"Amazing. Kind of like Big Brother, huh?"

Ric arched a brow. "Big Brother?"

"Never mind. George Orwell was a writer in the twentieth century who predicted a society where every movement was watched. No one had any freedoms. It was frightening."

He nodded. "Yes, it can be. On M'Lora that will not happen. With the massive improvements in artificial intelligence, we're devising a way to have our field police units become aware of impending crime without actually violating privacy."

Mia followed Ric toward the end of the hall where a thick, steel-like door stood. Without a word the door opened and they stepped through.

"How'd you do that?" she asked.

"The doorway possesses the knowledge that it was me standing there, and instinctively knows I am allowed through."

He made it sound so simple, and yet she was in awe. *Hello, door, it's me, Ric.* She snickered.

The room had shelf upon shelf of containers that seemed to be some kind of rugged metal about the size of a vehicle trunk. Ric stepped to the middle of the room and stood in front of one for a few seconds when it suddenly opened.

Peering around his shoulder, she frowned. "What are those?"

"My weaponry."

She watched as he lifted out two dark objects. One was long, about two feet, and thick. The other was only half a foot long, but thinner. "They're sticks," she said, turning her gaze to his. "Your weapons are sticks?"

Chapter Seven

Ric frowned. "They're not sticks. This is advanced weaponry."

Mia found it hard to believe that black batons could defeat any enemy. "What do you do with these? Beat criminals over the head?"

"No. Let me show you." He motioned her to an inner doorway that led to a classroom filled with large chairs and desks. Sliding his hand over a sensor on the wall, a video shimmered to life. "We use these for training purposes."

Mia watched the images on the wall. A M'Loran held the longer stick, pointing it toward what she assumed was a criminal. A lightning-like flash flew out of the end of the stick, paralyzing the criminal.

"Magnetic electroshock. Can drop someone instantly, paralyzing their nerve endings and rendering them immobile for several minutes while the officer applies restraints or administers a sleeping shock.

"Okay, those are familiar to me. What's the little stick for?" she asked.

"They are not sticks. The larger one is similar to your tasers. We call it a *tolk*. The smaller object is a *plikor*. Watch its capabilities."

Mia turned her attention back to the wall. An officer held the small stick in his hand, the object almost dwarfed by the size of the M'Loran's palm. The suspect was fleeing down a long street populated with people, but the officer was not giving chase. Surely the danger of hitting others would prevent the officer from discharging the weapon. Besides, the subject was nearly thirty meters away.

However, a sudden flash of red shot out the end of the *plikor*, skirting around objects and people on the street and striking the suspect in the back. The suspect froze and fell to the ground. The subject appeared to be either dead or out cold.

"Amazing. How could that blast not hit all those people?" she asked, turning to Ric.

He smiled at her. "The *plikor* is the latest advance in artificial intelligence. It travels the owners line of sight, knowing instinctively which suspect should be hit with the laser."

"You mean it's alive?"

"Not really. It's connected to the owner's brainwaves. Kind of like a partner. It reads and sees what the owner sees, and as long as the suspect remains in the owner's line of sight, the laser knows where to travel. It will bypass other living beings and objects and track the subject until it strikes."

"It won't hurt anyone else?"

"No. If the owner loses sight of the target, the pulse dissipates so as not to injure innocent bystanders or property."

"Wow. So, do I get one of those?"

"No."

"Why not?"

"Because if you held one in your hand it would do nothing. Each *plikor* is connected via the owner's brain waves. If I picked up Sev's, it would not discharge for me."

"Do they stun or kill?"

"Depends on the intent of the owner. I can use it to stun a suspect, or if there is imminent danger, the *plikor* senses my intent to terminate the lifecycle of the criminal."

"Scary fucking piece of technology," she said, more awed than she cared to admit.

"Not really. There are built in safeguards so that criminals cannot take it from an officer or hunter and use it against them. As I said, it can only take commands from the person to whom it has been calibrated for."

"I still don't like the idea of me not having a weapon. What about the *tolk*? I can use one of those."

"No. You don't need a weapon."

"I want a weapon."

"Too bad. You're not in charge here."

Mia's eyes darkened and Ric swore he could hear her cursing at him in her mind. But he'd rather have her angry than injured using a weapon she couldn't control.

"Quit treating me like an idiot."

"I'm not treating you like an idiot. I wouldn't give a weapon like this to anyone not from our planet."

He saw the change in her immediately. Where a few seconds ago stood a seething female, now stood one seductively batting her eyes in his direction.

He wondered if that trick worked on Earth males.

"Ric," she pleaded in a sexy voice that, despite his resolve, affected him. "I'm a police officer and a very good one. Please don't put me out there without being able to protect myself."

It would be so easy to deny her, but she was, in fact, right. He supposed he'd have to trust her.

He sighed and nodded. "Very well. I will instruct you as to its use and have one issued to you."

In less than an hour they were out of the Enforcement Unit. They'd changed vehicles into some type of big hulking military machine, a cross between a tank and a super Hum-Vee.

"Why this vehicle? And does it fly?" she asked.

Ric shook his head. "We're coming in on the ground instead of air. They have radar capabilities but nothing that can detect us on the ground. It takes longer and the terrain is rough, but it keeps the element of surprise alive."

The planet was like a paradise, full of blue lakes and greenery. Flowers like nothing she'd ever seen grew tall, their myriad of purples, yellows and blues waving along the road they traveled.

"Your planet is beautiful," she murmured, feeling like a kid with her nose pressed to the glass.

"Thank you. If we had time I'd stop at one of the lakes."

"I can see them in the distance, and I'd love to stop. How cold are they?"

"Some are more than one hundred degrees below zero. Others are warm enough to take a swim."

"How?"

"We have had volcanic activity from several of our mountains over the centuries. Many lakes are fed by hot springs and warm the lakes."

Considering how frigid the planet was, she couldn't imagine stripping naked and taking a dip in the water.

"If you like, we'll camp near one of the heated lakes this evening. Then you can bathe before we enter warrior territory."

She liked that idea, although bathing wasn't quite what was on her mind. The thought of being alone with Ric again tonight had her thoughts wandering to much more than sleeping.

But she wouldn't use the phrase to hypnotize him. She wouldn't. No matter what. She'd already compromised her principles once, and she refused to do it again, no matter how tempting he was.

Besides, she was just a boy according to the M'Loran women. She wondered if Ric thought the same thing.

"Do you think I look like a boy?"

He glanced at her. "No. Why do you ask a question like that?"

"Because those women said so."

His lips curled in a smile that made her damp between her legs. "They're not used to seeing women as small as you, that's all. Take no offense. They meant none."

Oh sure. Easy for him to say. How would he like it if he were on Earth and someone referred to him as a girl? She nearly laughed out loud. Yeah, right, as if someone could make that kind of a mistake. UlRic Lor was *all* man.

Her thoughts wandered through the afternoon and evening hours. Everything from the plan to capture Vad to the feelings of inadequacy she'd never felt before, coupled with her growing desire to straddle Ric and fuck him senseless.

None of her thoughts would do her any good. She'd simply have to concentrate on the mission and getting back to Earth when it was over. Then she could go back to her life.

Her boring, mundane, non-exciting life.

By the time the blue moon rose in the sky and a breathtaking dusk of purple hues heralded the quickly setting sun, they'd reached their destination for the night. Ric pulled the tank into a valley surrounded by grassy knolls and fields of flowers. Centered in the middle was a clear, turquoise lake, steam rising off the glassy surface.

Mia helped Ric unload their supplies, including a structure he indicated they'd be sleeping in tonight. What she thought was a folded up tent surprised her. Ric laid the object on the ground. Waves of shimmering light rose up and the object spiraled upward, changing shape and texture. Within minutes, a one room house with firm walls was set up next to the lake.

She stepped inside, awed to find a bed with what she assumed was an air current since no mattress sat on it. A fire roared in a small hearth next to the bed. Not too far away was a small eating area and a cleaning chamber.

"All the comforts of home. How'd you do that?"

He shrugged. "I told you. Our technology is advanced and it would take me weeks to explain it to you. Even I don't understand it. Something to do with molecular restructuring and minimalization."

"Well, it's damn handy to carry around in your vehicle."

He nodded. "There is much distance between cities on M'Lora, and we don't have temporary places to stay as you do on Earth. This house will provide shelter, food and warmth for us this evening."

They fixed the meal in the makeshift kitchen. Mia was once again surprised at her voracious appetite. She ate nearly as much as Ric and yet didn't feel overstuffed. He'd even brought along a bottle of *Rlok,* the sweet alcoholic beverage they'd shared the night before.

"Would you like to swim in the lake?" he asked, watching her over the rim of his glass.

"Sure." Figuring this was her one chance to experience M'Lora, she'd better take advantage of whatever exploration she was afforded.

"I will go with you. I've always enjoyed swimming in our lakes."

The thought of Ric in the water with her made her body tingle with excitement. Excitement she had no business feeling. Nothing was going to happen tonight. She repeated the silent mantra over and over again as Ric instructed her to undress and throw on the fur wrap.

She should have blushed or objected when Ric stood in front of her and undressed, but his unveiling of that magnificent body took all power of speech and any capability of protest away.

Naked, he motioned her outside and into the chilled night air.

Mia stepped carefully through the grass. The lake was only a short distance from the house, so before long she stood in front of the steaming water. Night was upon them now, the blue moon full in the sky overhead, casting Ric's face in its azure glow.

"What do you look like in your M'Loran form?" she asked, her gaze fixated on his firm ass as he descended into the steamy water.

"Similar to this, only taller." With a smile, he added, "And blue, of course."

For a moment, she hesitated, then dropped the fur cloak, unable to tear her gaze away from his watchful eyes as she quickly slipped into the water.

It was heaven. Warmth enveloped her like a liquid blanket. A slight current swirled around her body like tiny fingers caressing her skin. She swam out toward Ric and stopped, treading water mere inches from his body.

She wanted him. Whether it was right or wrong, she wanted him. "Ric, do you think I'm beautiful?"

His smile died and his face went blank. She waited to see if the code would work, but of course she already knew it would. She'd never failed in hypnotizing a subject yet. What happened with Vad was a fluke, a guard error or something. She knew the hypnocode should have worked on him.

Just like it worked on Ric.

"Ric, can you hear me?"

"Yes."

"Do you remember what happened between us last night?"

"Yes."

"Tell me."

"We fucked."

Her nipples tightened hearing the words from his lips. "Yes, we did. And did you enjoy it?"

"Oh yeah," he said, his lips curving into a wicked smile.

"Would you like to do it again?" she asked.

"Yes."

"The same rules will apply as last night. You will speak and act as you normally would, but if I tell you to stop you will drop into a deep sleep. Is that understood?"

"Yes."

"Good." She turned to swim toward the shore, but Ric's hand on her wrist stopped her. She turned. "What is it?"

"Come with me. We can make love under the J'Sol moon."

He turned and swam away. Intrigued, she followed him. He led her to a smooth mini-island of rock jutting up from the center of the lake. Once he'd climbed out he reached for her. She slipped her hand in his and allowed him to pull her onto the banks of the island. The unusual moss covering the ground felt like the warm fur of a blanket under her feet.

She felt no cold, marveling at the heated grass, the steam from the lake like a protective blanket from the frigid air.

Ric led her to the center of the island and pulled her toward him, lowering his face.

She stopped him, pushing at his chest. He paused and frowned. "Something wrong?"

Yes, everything was wrong. She shouldn't be doing this again. But at the same time everything was right. And besides, she simply had to satisfy her curiosity. "I want to make love with you in your M'Loran form."

"Are you sure?"

"I think so."

"We are not built...the same as human males."

A shiver passed through her, whether from fear or excitement she wasn't certain. "How are you different?"

"Perhaps you should just see for yourself."

His body shimmered like heat on asphalt. Almost like a thin blanket shielding her from the actual transformation, Mia could see nothing but lights pouring out of Ric's body. The lights grew brighter, then dimmed.

Within seconds, Ric's height had grown another six inches and his skin turned completely blue. His shoulders, waist and legs were virtually the same as in his human form—still muscular and well defined. And in between his legs—

"Oh my God!"

Chapter Eight

"You have two cocks!" Mia exclaimed.

Ric rested his hands on his hips and arched a brow, trying to gauge her reaction. "Obviously."

"Holy shit! Two cocks!" Then she frowned. "One's longer than the other."

"Yes."

She stared down at his dual shafts and licked her lips. He shuddered, imagining what her sweet mouth could do to them.

"Do you...um, that is, can you...I mean when you climax do they...?"

Ric laughed at Mia's struggle for words. "You mean can I ejaculate with both of them?"

She nodded.

"Yeah. The second depends on where and when and if I feel like it."

Her eyes widened. "You mean one's optional?"

Her childlike curiosity set his cocks blazing hard. "Yes. If for some reason it's...not in use, I don't let it come. If it's somewhere tight and hot and squeezing me, then ejaculating is pleasurable."

Just describing the potential scenarios set him off, made him twitch to be inside her. Everywhere inside her. With both his cocks.

Mia worried her bottom lip with her teeth. "You mean, for example, if one was in my pussy and the other in my ass, you could come in both places."

He sucked in a breath. "Yes. Would you like that?"

Her eyes darkened with desire. "I don't know. Maybe."

"There's more."

"There is? What?"

"One shifts shapes."

"No shit."

"Yes, shit."

She stepped forward hesitantly.

"Go ahead," he said. "Touch me."

Her nipples puckered and hardened to sharp points. With a tentative reach, she trailed the ridges of his primary cock with her fingertip, eliciting a rock hard awareness of her. It sprang to life, fully hard.

Her gaze met his. "It's long and thick, just like your human cock."

He nodded. "That one is exactly the same as my human form."

"So, the other one…does stuff?"

He could have laughed had he not throbbed incessantly under her scrutiny. "Yes, *J'mun*, it does *stuff*."

With her other hand she traced the outline of his secondary cock, and it, too, hardened against her palm. When she grasped it fully in her hand, the tip blossomed outward, flowering into a tulip shape.

"What the fuck is that?" she asked, jerking her hand away.

"It's transforming, anticipating giving you pleasure."

Mia frowned. "I don't understand. It looks funny now. "

Ric smiled, not at all offended by her confusion. "It's probably better that I show you what it can do for you."

Her voice lowered to nearly a whisper and she said, "Yes, I'd like that."

He held out his hands and she slipped hers into his palms. Stepping backwards, he pulled her onto the soft bank of grass and lay down, pulling her next to him.

"They feel so strange, pressing against me like that," she murmured.

"Does it bother you? I can shift back to human—"

"No! Don't change anything. I want this. It's just...new...unusual."

He pushed the wet strands of hair away from her face and smiled. "I know the feeling. You are different than what I'm used to."

"Yes, I know," she answered, dropping her gaze to his chest. "I'm repulsive."

He tipped her chin up with his finger, forcing her eyes to meet his. "No, you are not repulsive. You have one of the most beautiful faces I've ever seen. Wide, expressive eyes. They're like windows to your heart. They spark with anger, widen with curiosity and burn with passion when you're in my arms."

A sigh escaped her lips and he bent his head forward, capturing her mouth under his. He slipped his tongue inside, thrilled at her eagerness as her tongue twined with his. The curve of her hip under his hand was silken delight, a near liquid sensation.

"You're gaining weight already," he murmured against her lips.

"Must be M'Loran food. I'm always hungry."

"I like it. In the short time you've been here your hips and ass have expanded." He squeezed her firm buttocks, delighted with her quivering shudder.

"On Earth I'd feel fat."

He laughed and nibbled at her neck, feeling the bumps of pleasure pop up on her skin. "On M'Lora there is no such thing as fat. Women are revered for their size here."

"Good. I'll keep eating then." She rolled onto her back and he half covered her with the top of his body, pressing his mouth against one swollen nipple. She arched her back, whimpering when he flicked the bud with his tongue and rolled it gently between his teeth.

She reached for his primary cock, grasped the shaft and stroked, squeezing him between her folded fingers.

His secondary penis opened at the tip and covered the top of her hand. Its sensitive nerve endings sent shocks of pleasure throughout his body at the mere touch of her skin.

"Damn, that's hot, Ric," she said, her movements harder and faster. He thrust his swollen primary shaft against her hand.

It was more than he could stand. He needed to be inside her. He rolled onto his back and pulled her on top of him until she sat astride his cocks.

"I don't...tell me what to do with them," she asked, her eyes glazed with passion.

"Whatever you'd like to do."

Mia thought about all the things she'd like to do with Ric. Two cocks. She had no idea. She'd studied their planet, their customs, but for some reason their anatomy had remained a secret.

Curiosity warred with impatience as she pondered where to begin. She leaned over and lightly licked his bottom lip, marveling at the face of the Ric she'd grown accustomed to, except now he was blue. Instead of making him ugly, it only made him more attractive to her. The unique had always fascinated her. Even as a child she'd stared at alien visitors to Earth, smiling up at them and trying to capture their attention.

One particular alien's attention focused on her right now, and she planned to enjoy every minute of it. She traced his firm jaw with her fingertips. He reached for her wrist, pulled her fingers to his mouth and rolled his tongue around them. She tilted her head back and closed her eyes, remembering the feel of his mouth on every part of her body.

Unique didn't even begin to describe Ric and her response to him. Beyond a physical reaction to his touch, his very nearness, emotionally he tugged at her in ways she couldn't fathom. Her mind was awash in the sensations of his mouth on her, and yet she also felt the emotional connection, that desire to draw him close and hold him, to assuage some mysterious pain she saw in his eyes and yet he never revealed.

No, not now. She was not going to let him touch her that way. She'd allowed him access to her body, but no way would she let him into her heart.

Concentrate on the physical, Mia, only the physical. Her nipples brushed against his chest, sparks of aching need shooting between her legs. She kissed his neck, licking a trail over his collarbone and chest until she found a flat, male nipple. The rest of his anatomy was human. She didn't think she could handle much more than the surprise of finding out he had two penises.

When she sucked one of his nipples, he hissed in a breath and mumbled something in M'Loran. Pleased that she excited him, she slid down his body, marveling at how big he was…everywhere. Big, hard and well muscled. Clearly more than she could handle.

Yet she'd handled his huge cock last night. Liquid desire seeped from her onto his leg as she recalled the skyrocketing climax he'd given her. She wanted that again. And again.

But right now she had to explore. His stomach was hard and flat. Ric groaned and threaded his fingers in her hair when she ran her tongue along his ridged abdomen, traveling lower to the thatch of dark hair curling above his cocks.

She grasped the longer shaft in her hand and stroked, marveling at its firmness and length. Turning her mouth toward the other one, she nearly jumped back when it morphed back into a normal penis. When her gaze met Ric's, he smiled and said, "Thought that might make it easier…more normal for you."

There was nothing normal about this entire situation. Then again, she had no complaint. It was like a fantasy adventure, a thrill ride that she took for the first time, not knowing what was around the next curve or at the bottom of the steep incline.

She licked the tip of his smaller penis and he thrust his hips up as if asking without words for her to take more. Which she did, gladly, fitting her lips over him and sucking him deep inside her mouth.

"*L'nons, J'Mun,*" he said between clenched teeth, his voice a guttural groan.

When she released his shaft, she asked, "Ric, I've been meaning to ask you what *J'Mun* means?"

"Baby, darling, honey, my love. It's an endearment. Now suck me," he commanded, his hand reaching for her head to drive it over his swollen cock.

She smiled, somehow pleased he would call her that. Then she took him again, thrusting her mouth down over his shaft and swirling her tongue over the soft head. She kept up the stroking motions with her other hand, caressing his main shaft while she tasted the smaller one. What must that feel like to him? Was it equally exciting from one cock to the other? She had so many questions to ask, but not right now. Now she focused on taking him up and over the edge.

But he wouldn't let her. With a swift turn he sat up, pulling her up against him and covering her mouth with his lips.

Her damp mound pressed against his main shaft and she moved against it, her clit rubbing the ridged underside until she felt ready to climax right then. But she didn't want to come that way. She wanted to experience both his cocks, in what way she wasn't quite certain, but she figured Ric would show her how they worked.

"Are you perplexed about something, *J'Mun*?"

"Sort of. What do I do?" She sat on his thighs, her pussy throbbing with the desire to have him inside her.

"It's simple. Slide down over the main shaft and I'll do the rest."

Those were instructions she couldn't wait to heed. She lifted her hips, positioning his stiff cock between her labia, her moisture readying her for the invasion of his shaft. Their gazes locked. Even in the darkness she read his passion, his need for her, and it equaled her own.

She knew, somehow, that she'd be forever changed by this encounter. Sucking in a deep breath, she eased herself over him. His thick shaft stretched her inch by inch as she slowly covered him.

He tensed and clenched her hips to guide her. Mia watched his eyes glaze over to a midnight black, watched him shudder when she had him fully sheathed inside her.

Unable to believe she'd taken nearly all of him in, she stilled. He pulsed deep within her. Her body responded by contracting against his flesh, tightening around his engorged penis.

With deliberate motions she rubbed her clit against his skin, the sensation a scorching fire along her already taut nerve endings.

Ric grabbed her hands, twining his fingers with hers as he lifted his hips up and down. "Close your eyes, *J'Mun*," he said. "Feel the pleasure I'm about to give to you."

Near breathless with anticipation, Mia did as he asked, wondering who had really mesmerized whom. She was the one under *his* spell, unable to think beyond the spasms between her legs, the brush of his skin against hers, the elemental scent of their arousal.

"Lean back, Mia," he whispered.

She reached behind her, her palms connecting with the soft grass. Then she waited. And waited.

"Ric?" she asked, eyes still closed.

"Yes, *J'Mun*?"

"What are you doing?"

"Looking at your pussy."

"Oh." She squirmed a bit, knowing he was examining her most intimate of places. And yet wondered why she would be shy considering what they'd already done.

"I'm going to touch you there," he said.

"Okay." Already her clit throbbed with the need for release, her body taut and ready for a trip over the edge of ecstasy.

And then it happened, and she nearly shot off the ground. A warm, wet...something...surrounded her clit, squeezing and warming the surrounding area like a wet cloth soaked in a thick fluid.

The sensation seeped inside her core, where Ric's cock was buried deep and lightly thrusting.

"What is that?" she asked, whimpering as it lightly squeezed, almost like lips gently sucking the distended bud.

"My secondary *inson*," he murmured, his voice seemingly far away.

It was incredible, like nothing she'd ever felt before. She'd touched her clit herself while a man was inside her before, but this—this was like being sucked and fucked at the same time. Like a supercharged taser blast, the dual sensations rocked her body completely. She gasped out a keening wail as the flowery tip of his penis squeezed and suckled her aching nub.

"Open your eyes now, Mia."

The first thing she focused on was his heated gaze fixated on her face. He was so beautiful, his body like a cloud-laden sky in the summer, darkened by the night and mist surrounding them. Then he looked down, and her vision traveled to where he focused.

His secondary cock had somehow moved upward, now resting above the main one. It surrounded her clit, pulling at her pleasure center while his shaft thrust hard and fast inside her.

"Oh my God, Ric...I've never felt anything like this before." Her fingers dug into the soil and she arched her back, rocking her mound further into the hot, moist center of his second cock.

"Let go, Mia," he urged. "Come for me."

She needed no further prodding. Already the spasms swirled up inside her until she couldn't hold back. The motions of his cock hitting her deep inside her core, coupled with the gentle warmth of the tulip licking at her distended bud sent thousands of sparks shooting between her legs.

A keening wail escaped her lips as her climax turned her world over. She grabbed for Ric's thighs, scratching his skin with her nails as her orgasm intensified, catapulting her into the darkness of the night.

With a loud roar Ric followed her into the abyss, plunging deeply inside her as he shot jets of hot come that mingled with her own juices and poured out of her.

Her body bathed in sweat, she fought for control of her breathing, blowing out with her mouth and slowing down her rapid pulse. It took more than a few moments to recapture her sanity.

She watched, transfixed, as he withdrew, his secondary cock seemingly disappearing for a moment and then reappearing to the side of the larger one. Ric sat up and pulled her close, his lips covering hers with a kiss that was way too warm, way too filled with unspoken words and emotions for her liking.

He lay back on the grass and placed her head on his shoulder, wrapping his arms around her. She felt safe, and yet more frightened than she'd ever been before.

This was a man she could spend an eternity with. Strong enough not to put up with her bullshit, instinctively gentle when she needed him to be, fiercely intelligent, strong, gorgeous, and the best damn lover she'd ever had.

And she was falling in love with him.

Damn, damn, damn!

Chapter Nine

Mia quieted after Ric pulled her close against his body, and he wondered what went on in her head. Was she at peace, satisfied and exhausted, or did she regret what just happened?

Had he disappointed her somehow? Or hurt her?

And more importantly, why the hell did it matter to him? Why did *she* suddenly seem to matter to him?

This was not good, not good at all. The last thing he needed was to feel emotion for a female. Specifically, a human female. They had nothing in common. She was a ball busting pain in the ass who didn't even want to be on M'Lora with him, and made it clear she didn't care one bit for him. She even had to hypnotize him for sex.

And yet when he looked into her eyes when they were joined, he saw much more than sexual heat there. Did her eyes mirror his, had he developed some kind of feelings for her?

Impossible. M'Loran men didn't get emotional over women. Women were for sex, breeding and to partner with in work. That was all. Love and emotion were for others, not for M'Lorans.

Not for him. Not ever. He'd seen what love had done to his parents, what it had done to him as a result of being the child of two different cultures. He'd never bring children into the world who would suffer the pain and humiliation he had suffered. He was a mutant. If he bred children with Mia, their children would be mutants.

Children? Now he was really losing it. He dragged a hand through his hair and said, "Mia. Are you awake?"

"Yes," she said, her voice shaky and fragile.

"What's wrong?" He was almost afraid to look at her, fearing what he might see in her expression.

"Ric, listen to me and follow my instructions in the order they're given. First, change back to your human form. Then, I want you to fall asleep for a few minutes, and when you wake, you will remember nothing of what just transpired here. We took a swim, and that was it. You will swim to the other side, and we will go back to the shelter. Do you understand?"

His heart fell, disappointment shadowing his thoughts. Emotion, feeling. What a fucking idiot he was. She had no more feeling for him than she did for the rock behind her. "Yes, I understand."

He shifted back to his human form, closed his eyes and feigned the deep breathing of sleep. Mia sighed, almost wistfully he thought, then corrected himself. No, she was using him, she didn't care for him.

What a fucking disaster this had turned out to be. She manipulated him, he lied to her. Hardly the basis for a healthy relationship.

After mentally counting out a few minutes, he opened his eyes, followed Mia to the water and swam to shore. She was silent the entire time, including when he picked up the coverlet and threw it over her shoulders. Then she stepped inside the shelter, closing herself in the cleaning chamber immediately.

Ric laid on the bed, the air currents undulating against his back. Normally they would relax him, but he didn't feel relaxed right now. An ache centered in his chest, a feeling as foreign as the woman in the chamber.

Enough! He forced his body to relax, knowing he needed the sleep to perform his mission tomorrow. That's where he needed to center his mind—on capturing Vad and nothing else.

But he knew sleep would not come easily tonight. His mind was filled with too many questions and recriminations to settle.

* * * * *

Mia shuddered as the drying air of the chamber blew soft caresses against her skin.

Skin that Ric had touched, kissed, licked. She wrapped her arms around herself and tried to focus.

She'd created a mess of epic proportions. Not only had she lied to Ric, forcing him to have sex with her against his will, but then she had to go and develop feelings for him.

And just what the hell was she supposed to do with those feelings? She couldn't very well tell him she cared about him considering he had no clue they'd had wild sex the past couple nights. It wasn't like he expressed any interest in her when he wasn't hypnotized, so whatever she felt for him she knew wasn't returned. If she did tell him, what would he say?

He'd be furious. She'd feel the same way if someone had done to her what she had done to Ric. Theirs was a relationship based on lies, and that would never work. Coupled with the fact that only one of the parties even knew there was a relationship happening.

She stepped out of the chamber and grabbed the one piece underclothing Ric told her would keep her warm under the leather gear. It looked like long johns, only made of a material she'd never felt before. Soft and amazingly warm.

When she went in search of Ric, she found him on the bed, apparently sound asleep. She slipped in beside him and kept to her side of the bed, not wanting to touch him.

That wasn't exactly true. She did want to touch him, wanted to curl up against him and feel his strong arms around her. But that wasn't going to happen. Not now, not again. She was through with lying—to herself as well as to him. She might have fallen in love with Ric, but he'd never know it.

Sleep came, but fitfully. She chilled against the night air, finally giving up her little corner of the bed and snuggling against Ric. He slipped his arm around her and pulled her against his chest without a word. Was he asleep or awake? She knew he was no longer hypnotized, and frankly she didn't care if he objected to holding her or not. She was freezing and this was merely common sense sharing of body warmth.

Finally warm, sleep began to take over and she couldn't keep her eyes open.

"Mia, wake up."

Ric's voice penetrated the haze of slumber. She grumbled and scooted closer to his heated body.

"Mia, if you're going to hold on to my cock like that then you'd better be prepared to do something with it."

She opened her eyes, shocked to find her hand wrapped around his fully erect shaft. She bolted upright, dropping his shaft like it had burned her.

"I'm...I'm sorry," she stumbled, nearly jumping out of the bed. "I was asleep and I...I...I'm sorry, I don't know what happened there."

Ric's lips curled in a smile. "You weren't hurting me, you know. As a matter of fact, it was quite nice to have your hands on me."

Shit. He was naked. She supposedly had never seen him naked. She'd slipped in bed with him last night without thinking. "I was cold."

"I didn't mind warming you last night. Stop worrying about it. Nothing happened."

Wanna bet? "Good."

They dressed and ate a hurried breakfast, then Mia helped Ric clear supplies out of the shelter. With a wave of his hand over the sensor at the doorway, the shelter dematerialized into its small canvas shape and Ric threw it in the back of the vehicle.

Not once had he mentioned last night, or this morning. She felt like a fly caught in a spider's web, only she was the spider, too. She'd spun this web of lies and deceit to the point that even *she* didn't know what was true anymore.

"We're crossing into K'Mor land now," he said, reaching behind him for his weapons. He handed a *tolk* to her. She adjusted her hand around it, familiarizing herself with its weight and feel, then searched for the sensor to emit the shock. Somehow she felt better now that she was armed.

"How difficult is this going to be?" she asked.

"Finding Vad? Not very. I already know where he is. Getting past those who will guard his safety will be the hard part."

"They'll protect him even though he's a criminal?"

Ric nodded. "K'Mor do not take to having their kind extradited to other planets to serve punishment. They are warriors. To them, killing is a way of life. They see no crime in it, therefore feel they are above interplanetary law."

"But the Molkor, the mutant culture, are even more vicious than the K'Mor's, correct?"

"Yes. Mutants are a breed unto themselves."

"Explain this mutant thing to me." She hung on to the handle of the vehicle as they careened over a vicious hump in the road.

"Many years ago, K'Mors and J'Sols were at war for control of M'Lora. During this war, several of the warring sides mated, creating children of both species."

"And those are the Molkor."

"Some are."

Now she was confused. "What do you mean, some are? There are other types?"

Ric let out a deep breath. "Molkor are the product of an intellect female and a warrior male. They are cunning, vicious and fiercely intelligent. But their warrior side is dominant."

"Right, I knew that."

"But there were others—Soloras, that are products of intellect males and warrior females. They have the same characteristics, are well versed in warfare, but their intellect side is dominant, therefore they are not savages like the Molkor mutants."

"What's the difference whether the male or the female is the intellect? I'd imagine they'd come out the same no matter what."

"I am a Soloras mutant, Mia. My mother is a warrior, my father an intellect. There aren't as many of us as there are of the Molkor, but we do exist. We are the hunters, the ones who track the Molkor throughout the galaxies."

"Because you are more like them than anyone else on the planet."

"Yes."

Why did she feel like this revelation upset Ric? "Does it bother you?"

"Does what bother me?"

"Being a mutant—a Soloras."

"I have adjusted to the fact that I belong to neither species on my planet. I am more accepted by the J'Sols because my father is an intellectual."

"Yet he mated with a warrior woman."

"Yes."

"They're not together, I take it?"

"No. The warrior who is my mother could not bear to live on the J'Sol side, and went back to her own people, leaving my father to raise me."

Ric stared straight ahead. His mother didn't want him? How could a child survive that kind of abandonment?

"I'm sorry, Ric." Instinctively she reached out to him, then pulled her hand back, knowing she had no right to touch him.

He glanced over at her and she glimpsed the pain etched in his dark eyes. He masked it immediately with indifference. "There is nothing to be sorry for. The K'Mor culture would have killed me had my mother taken me there. She did what was best for me."

Somehow Mia knew there was more to this story than he let on, but he didn't seem to want to discuss it any further.

By the time the amber moon rose in the sky, they approached the lights of what looked to be some kind of city. Ric stopped, grabbed his weapons and stepped out of the vehicle, using a scanner to indicate their whereabouts.

"That is *Kul*, the K'Mor main city. Vad will be there."

He handed the scanner to Mia. The city was presented in greater depth and detail than she could see with her eyes. *Kul* was set up similarly to Ric's home city, only it looked more like a military compound than a place where people lived.

"We are in danger now. Stay alert, and don't leave my side. If something should happen to me, take the vehicle, set the system for reverse of destination and it will take you back to *Jolsu*. Understand?"

She nodded, chilled at the thought of something bad happening to Ric. She couldn't bear it. "Nothing's going to happen to you. I'm a pretty good partner and I'll be watching your back for you."

He turned to her, his fingers burning through her leather coat. "Mia, take this seriously. K'Mor are like nothing you've ever experienced. They aren't subdued here as they are when you meet them for hypnotizing. They're savage and will kill you before they even know who you are."

Why did she want to wrap her arms around him, pull him close and kiss him? Why had she fallen in love with the one man who would never love her?

She nodded. "Understood."

He let go of her arms and stepped back, his gaze never leaving hers. She felt the charge between them, the passion that couldn't be extinguished, the passion only she knew existed.

Then he surprised the hell out of her by grabbing her and pulling her close, covering his mouth over hers in a kiss that curled her toes. His tongue dove inside, tangling with hers in a passionate replica of lovemaking.

Mia clung to him, desperately, as if this were the last time she'd ever feel his warm strength surrounding her. The knowledge that he wasn't hypnotized right now shocked her, and yet she wouldn't question why he kissed her and held her like this.

As quickly as it started, he pulled back, his eyes blazing dark and filled with desire. His erection was outlined against the tight black leather of his pants, and she wanted nothing more right now than to drop to her knees and ease his ache, and her own, too.

"Be careful, *J'Mun*," he said, smiling down at her. "I've enjoyed your body too much to let anything happen to it." Then he motioned her up and over the hill toward Kul.

She followed mutely, her lips still throbbing from his passionate kiss, her mind scrambled between desire and his confusing statement. Then she stopped, adrenalin pouring through her as the truth hit.

He knew.

About them. About the lovemaking they'd shared. He'd never been hypnotized. He'd been fully awake each time. But how? And more importantly, why had he allowed her to believe she'd hypnotized him?

Ric was at least three meters away before he noticed she wasn't following. He stopped and motioned her toward him, but she was frozen to the ground. Anger and humiliation overrode any sense of urgency to keep up with him.

He stormed over to her, his brows knit in confusion. "Why did you stop?"

"You knew," she whispered.

"Knew what?"

"About the hypnosis, about everything. You've been awake the whole time, haven't you?"

Ric inhaled quickly and blew out a breath. "Yes, *J'Mun*, I knew. Now let's go."

"I'm not going anywhere with you."

Chapter Ten

Ric knew she wouldn't take it well, but he couldn't help himself. Should something happen to him, he'd wanted to kiss Mia one more time, feel her warmth wrapped up in his arms and breathe in her sweet scent.

And he knew as soon as he'd done it, she'd be aware of the lies he'd told.

"We can argue about this later, Mia. Now we have to go. We could be spotted here."

"How could you do this to me?" she sputtered, stomping the ground behind him.

"Stealth, *J'Mun*. If you're going to stomp around in the dirt we might as well drive in and let them know we're here."

"Don't call me that."

"What?"

"That endearment word. Dammit, how could you do this to me!"

He stopped and turned abruptly, grabbing her by the shoulders. "I did no more than you attempted to do to me by hypnotizing me into fucking you."

Her face blushed crimson under the full moonlight. "You could have told me straight off that you weren't hypnotized. Then, none of this would have happened."

"So this is my fault?" he hissed. "Granted, I played along at first, intending to tell you that it was not possible for me to be hypnotized. Since I'm frequently privy to interrogations on Earth, I wear a chip inside my head that prevents hypnosis."

"Bullshit. Why wouldn't I know that?"

"Because there is no reason for you to know."

"I'm a unit officer and a hypnotist. I should know."

"Take that up with your superiors who felt only *they* needed to know. Anyway, you lied to me."

"You lied to me."

"Then we're at a stalemate. Can we go now or would you like to yell a little louder and call attention to ourselves?"

"I don't know. Maybe."

Disgusted, he said, "Fine. Go wait in the vehicle. I will retrieve Vad and return shortly."

"No fucking way, M'Loran."

"I don't need you to give a code. I can subdue him with the *tolk* or *plikor*."

"That may be, but I have orders to come with you and capture him."

"You don't listen well."

"So I've been told."

"I am your superior officer here, Mia Logan. You will not disobey my orders."

"You're just pissed off because you got caught in a lie."

"This has nothing to do with fucking you. We're on a mission. One I'd like to get out of alive. Clear your head, push whatever emotions you have to the back of your mind for now, and let's get on with this. We'll argue later."

Mia hated not having the last word in an argument. "Fine."

He turned and walked away. She fought to keep up with him, bound and determined that when he needed backup, she'd be there. She might want to kill him right now, but that didn't mean she wanted anyone else to.

They walked for an hour, skirting the front of the city and coming in from the back. The buildings faced away from them. It was late and no one seemed to be about.

"Vad will be at the Gaming Center," he said, motioning to a tall building in front of them. "This is where they play, drink and have sex."

"How do you know he's there?"

"I can smell him."

"Seriously."

"It's where he lives. In the rooms to the back of the main center."

He grabbed her and pulled her behind him when a couple warriors passed by. Mia got a glimpse of them, though, surprised to find they looked different than M'Lorans. They were blue, and very tall, but their heads were overly large and their faces bore scars that looked like a ravaging disease had taken hold of them. Their bodies were wider, too, all their features at least twice the size of J'Sols.

When the warriors left, she said, "You don't resemble them."

"No. I took on most of my father's genetics."

"What's wrong with their skin?"

"The sun's radiation on this side is more powerful. Plus, it's warmer over here. Warriors don't care about covering up, so their skin burns and scars. We are in no danger being here at night, nor would we be in the daylight if we took precautions."

She hoped they wouldn't be around long enough to see the sun rise. She wanted to get out of there and quickly.

They entered the back of the building. Ric cut through some type of force field in the doorway and they walked quietly in. Mia had to rely on hand signals from Ric to know where they were going.

Laughter and shouts roared in front of them, signaling people approaching the darkened hallway.

Ric pulled her into an open room, shutting the door quickly and pressing her against the wall.

She grabbed his shirt and held still, her heart pounding against his body. She fought to still her shaking hands. "Why can't you shapeshift into one of their forms?" she whispered, her heart slamming against her chest.

"All M'Lorans can see each other's natural form. It's pointless."

"Where are we now?"

"Next to Vad's room. Stay here while I step outside and see if he's there."

"No, I'm going—"

Ric covered her mouth with his hands. "I'll be right back, I promise. Think of this as reconnaissance. Cover my back."

Reluctantly, she nodded and he stepped through the doorway, leaving her alone in the darkness. She heard rustling outside the door. Her blood roared in her ears as fear overtook her. She slipped the *tolk* into her jacket, using both her hands to move against the wall. Feeling her way, she slid through the darkness until the back of her knees hit a hard object. A bed, judging from the whirring air waves ruffling her hair.

She froze when the door slid open. She couldn't see who entered. Someone very tall.

Oh please, God, let it be Ric.

"Ric?" she whispered, hoping against hope that it wasn't someone else.

He paused, then said, "Yes, it's me."

Finally exhaling, she stepped toward his silhouette, throwing her arms around him. "I thought something happened to you."

He grabbed her and laughed, low and husky. His hands traveled lower, cupping her buttocks and pulling her against his erections. He'd transformed into his M'Loran shape. Mia shuddered, her body instantly awakening to his touch. Then it hit her. Why would he be touching her this way, and especially now?

"Stop, Ric," she said, pushing against his chest, wondering what the hell he was thinking trying to seduce her in the middle of the warrior's city.

"I don't think so," he responded, roughly grabbing her breasts and squeezing. Tears sprang to her eyes at the sharp pain. He pushed her against the bed and she lost her balance, falling onto the air current. His huge body covered hers.

"Ric! Stop this! No!" she cried. What was happening? How could he do this to her? "You're hurting me!"

"You'll like it soon enough," he answered, licking the side of her face. A foul stench assailed her nostrils and she knew it emanated from the man holding her. She fought to see in the darkness, but knew whoever had her pinned to the bed wasn't Ric.

Oh, God, where *was* Ric? Had he been caught? Or even killed?

She reached inside her coat, searching for the *tolk* while struggling against the stranger as he fought to unzip her pants. His rank breath made her gag. Waves of nausea assailed her. She forced the rising bile back, trying to think clearly so she could get out of this before this person raped or killed her.

He yanked the zipper on her pants down, then reached for the waistband. She kicked at him, but her size and strength were no match for the giant. He only laughed at her and rocked his erections between her legs.

Mia knew if she continued to hyperventilate like this she'd pass out and he could do whatever he wanted to her. Her hand fumbled inside the jacket and finally closed around the *tolk*.. She went still, forcing her breathing to regulate, and waited for the opportunity to pull the weapon out and use it.

When the stranger felt her muscles relax, he laughed and yanked her pants down over her hips. Then she whipped out the weapon and struck him with it. He howled and pulled away, cuffing her on the side of her head with his huge hand before he dropped to the ground.

The blinding shot of pain was excruciating, and she fought against the blackness threatening to overwhelm her. If she passed out now, she was done for. He'd only be out for a few seconds and then he'd be on her again. She yanked up her pants and struggled to stand, but dizziness dropped her back onto the bed.

A light came on, faint, but enough to see the outline of the man who pulled himself up from the floor. His image wavered in front of her and she blinked several times, trying to restore her vision. She could barely think let alone function, but she knew who it was.

Vad. His body shimmered and he shifted from Ric's form to his own, his face a tangled mass of scars. Hatred marred his features even more, twisting them into a frightening visage. "You are UlRic Lor's woman, that idiot hypnotist."

She couldn't speak, her mind a muddled mass of pain and nausea. The subdue code. She had to give him the subdue code.

What was it? She couldn't remember.

"You die now, bitch!" he snarled. His hands reached for her throat and she knew in seconds he'd crush her windpipe.

His smile was pure evil as he wrapped his fingers around her. Tears sprang to her eyes as she thought of dying, of the things she'd wanted to do with her life and hadn't.

Suddenly the hands around her throat disappeared. Vad was gone and she inhaled gulps of fresh air, her hands reaching for her neck to massage the pain.

Mia gasped, still too dizzy to do anything but lie there in wait for the next K'Mor to descend upon her. A blur of activity occurred in front of her and she forced herself to focus.

Finally, her vision cleared enough to see Ric and Vad engaged in hand-to-hand combat. Their bodies were nearly matched in size.

Ric's muscles bulged underneath his shirt as he struggled with Vad. Vad merely smiled at his adversary, a sick, twisted grin that made his mouth look lopsided.

Where were Ric's weapons? He had physically pulled Vad off her, that much she remembered. Why hadn't he used the *tolk* or *pikor* on him?

Vad managed to get behind Ric and grabbed him around the throat, his huge arm cutting Ric's breath off. With an elbow to the midsection, Ric broke free and turned, his fist connecting with Vad's nose. Seemingly impervious to the assault, Vad laughed at him, blood streaming down his face.

With a low growl, Vad pushed Ric against the nearby wall. He crashed against the heavy steel of the barred window and slid to the floor, stunned. Vad stood there for a few seconds, then approached Ric, picking up a stone artifact from the table and lifting it over his head. Mia knew in seconds he'd smash the heavy object on top of Ric. Surely it would kill him.

She needed to do something to stop Vad. The code! She had to remember the code. She struggled, reaching into her hazy memory, watching in horror as Vad drew closer to a nearly unconscious Ric. Closing her eyes, she murmured a prayer for some clarity and then it hit her.

"The valley of the shadow of death," she croaked, her voice hoarse.

Vad stopped instantly, dropped the stone and stood immobile.

It worked! Mia slid onto the floor, crawling on her hands and knees past Vad until she reached Ric. Blood poured down his neck and she reached behind, searching for the source. She found a deep laceration near the base of his skull. She searched the room and found a shirt lying on a chair. She bundled it up and pressed it against Ric's head to stem the bleeding.

Tears pooled in her eyes as the full impact of their situation hit. She'd nearly lost him. "Ric, wake up," she urged, whispering to him in the voice she used for hypnosis. "Listen to me. We have to get out of here now."

How they'd managed such a ruckus without being discovered was beyond her to understand. All she knew was they needed to escape, and immediately.

She breathed a sigh of relief when his eyes opened.

He shook his head and winced. "What hit me?"

"The window."

He looked beyond her to Vad, who stood docile and unmoving. "Remembered the code, did you?" he said, smiling.

Mia nodded, relief flooding through her at the knowledge he seemed all right. He stood, easily lifting her into his arms. She reached around his neck, craving his strength like never before.

"What about Vad?"

"I don't care. I'm taking you out of here. I'll come back for him."

"Where is everyone?"

"I created a dam of sorts. They won't be getting through any time soon."

"But—"

"Shh," Ric whispered, kissing the top of her head. "Your work is done, *J'Mun*. Rest now."

She laid her head on his chest and let the darkness take her.

Chapter Eleven

Ric hovered over a sleeping Mia, pressing his palm to her forehead again.

No fever. The medic examined her after Ric brought her back to his home. She'd suffered a slight head injury, but no serious damage. Ric breathed a sigh of relief while wanting to wrap his fingers around Vad's throat and squeeze the life from him.

He hadn't even used the *tolk* or *plikor* on Vad. If he had, their battle would have ended sooner. After he'd dammed up the entrance to the hallway, he'd heard Mia and had run to the room. His blood boiled when he saw what Vad was doing to her, and all he could think of was getting the warrior's hands off Mia.

His emotions took hold of him and all his years of training had vanished in an instant. What he should have done was kill the bastard for daring to harm the woman he loved.

But he hadn't. Vad was destined to return to Earth, and that's where he'd go, to hopefully rot out his days in one of their prisons.

Mia, once she was well, would be accompanying Vad, as would Ric as guardian of the prisoner.

And then what? The thought of never seeing Mia again created an emptiness inside him that he'd never experienced before. They'd shared much in the past several days and he'd grown accustomed to her sense of humor, her unusual looks and her obstinate nature.

How was he going to live without her? And more importantly, did he want to?

She moaned and stretched, the coverlet shifting to reveal one small, upthrust breast. His cocks stirred, remembering the feel and taste of the tiny bud in his mouth.

Tamping down his desire to lick the small, pink crest, he said, "Mia, wake up."

Her eyes fluttered open and she smiled. "Where are we?"

"Back in *Jolsu*, at my home."

"Where's Vad?"

"In our holding cells awaiting transport to Earth."

"How'd you get him back here?"

"I took you to the vehicle, then went back to retrieve Vad and my weapons."

"What happened to your weapons? I remember watching you struggle with Vad, and you didn't use them on him."

"They were taken from me during a fight with several warriors," he lied, not ready to admit that his feelings for her had affected his judgment.

She shifted to sit up, then winced. "I feel like a hovercraft ran over me."

"You suffered head injuries when Vad struck you."

Her eyes narrowed. "Bastard fucker."

"Indeed. You should get some rest now."

She yawned and shook her head. "I've rested enough. Besides, we have things to talk about."

Ric waited for the expected tirade, wondering when she'd remember how he lied to her about the hypnosis. "Go ahead. Say whatever you will."

Her gaze shifted to her lap, and then she looked up at him, her eyes luminous pools of turquoise that never failed to take his breath away. He'd miss her, but knew his lies had cost him the chance to have Mia in his life.

Then she surprised him and said, "I'm sorry about the hypnosis."

That he did not expect. "I'm sorry I lied about being hypnotized. I wasn't going to, but then you asked me to touch you and I couldn't resist the opportunity to feel your skin."

Her already pink cheeks darkened. "I wanted to touch you, too. I know I shouldn't have. I do have ethics, you know. It's just where you were concerned..."

Her lashes drifted against her cheeks and he tipped her chin, forcing her to meet his gaze. "Where I was concerned?"

"I couldn't resist. I just had to know what it was like to make love to you."

His chest swelled with the knowledge that maybe there was some hope for them. "That is why I allowed the deceit to continue. But I shouldn't have lied to you. I should have been man enough to tell you I wanted you and let you decide if you wanted me."

She sat up, the coverlet dropping to her waist and revealing breasts he now thought perfect, despite the fact they were nothing like the M'Loran women he used to fancy.

"Clearly, I *did* want you."

He sat on the bed, his hip pressing against hers. "Then at least we had the opportunity to discover each other that way." He pressed a soft kiss to her lips. She opened her mouth and he slid his tongue inside, taking in her sighs of pleasure.

"When do we leave for Earth?" she asked, her fingers trailing up his arms and over his shoulders.

He shivered at the scrape of her nails against his skin, his shafts fully erect and throbbing with the need to be inside her. "As soon as you're able to travel. You look a bit weak to me right now, though," he said, pressing her into the mattress.

She grinned at him. "I feel a little weak. I think I need a little more bed rest."

"Oh, you'll get the bed all right, *J'Mun*," he said, cupping her breasts and flicking the nipples with his thumbs. "But you'll get no rest."

Mia arched her back, filling Ric's palms with her aching breasts. Her pussy dampened with desire for him, desperately needing him to fill her. She pulled at his shirt and he yanked it over his head. Quickly discarding his pants, he slid onto the bed with her, dragging her against him. His cocks brushed against her mound and she spread her legs, lifting one over his hip. When he nestled closer and rubbed her clit with the head of his main cock, she whimpered.

"I want you, *J'Mun*," he murmured, licking her neck.

"Fuck me, Ric," she commanded, desperate for his touch. She needed to feel connected to him, knowing this would be the last time she'd be close to him, the last time he'd touch her. This moment would have to last a lifetime in her memories.

He parted her folds and positioned his shaft against her, teasing her with gentle strokes against her aching nub. Her body responded as always, by moistening and readying for him.

"I'm wet, Ric. I need you inside me."

Smiling down at her, he shook his head. "Not yet."

Frustrated, she grabbed his arms, digging her nails into his muscled flesh. He laughed, nipping at her throat. She whimpered when he bit into her shoulder, shuddering with his thrilling possession of her.

That's what was so different about him — his complete mastery over her body and her mind. She'd never been so attuned to a man before. Sex had been perfunctory...somewhat enjoyable but not earth shattering. Making love with Ric was like a galaxy explosion, and she knew then that she was connected with him, that he'd always be a part of her.

"Now, Ric," she begged, too impatient to wait any longer.

He grasped her chin and forced her gaze to meet his. His eyes were dark pools of desire, mesmerizing her with their depths. With one quick thrust he plunged inside her, stretching her sensitive flesh until she cried out in ecstasy.

He moved gently, his secondary shaft sliding against her sensitized clit.

"Ric?"

"Yes."

"What are you going to do with your second cock?"

"What do you want me to do with it?" he asked, nipping at her lower lip.

Breathless with anticipation, she already knew. "I want to try something. Something I've never done before."

He stilled, his gaze meeting hers. "What is it?"

"I want it in my ass, Ric. I want you to possess me completely."

He frowned and caressed her cheek. "Are you certain?"

His tenderness swelled her heart to near bursting. "Yes."

A soft smile curved his lips and he took her mouth in a heart-stopping kiss. Then, a vibration ruffled the thatch of down between her legs as his secondary penis shifted positions.

"I'll make this pleasurable for you, *J'Mun*." He licked his fingers and probed between the cheeks of her buttocks, searching and finding the puckered entrance. He slid his fingers over her without entering, enticing her sensitive nerve endings. All the while he slid his cock gently in and out of her pussy.

She relaxed against him, too caught up in the feel of his huge sex inside her to even notice when he slid his moistened fingers past the tight entrance to her anus. He gently eased inside, then paused, waiting for her body to accommodate to the intrusion. She moved against him, the intimacy of his touch spurring her own, making her shiver with the quest for completion.

When he moved his finger in and out of her, she cried out with the pleasure.

"Now, Ric," she urged.

"I will be gentle. If you feel pain, tell me, and I will withdraw."

She nodded, mindless of anything but his huge cock thrusting slowly enough to drive her mad. With careful movements he slid the tip of his secondary shaft against her ass, probing gently until he eased it past her defenses.

Mia felt no pain, only sparks of unbelievable pleasure.

Ric began to move inside her, both cocks rhythmically stroking her. She was filled completely, possessed by this man she'd come to love so deeply.

She dug her nails into his back. "Harder, Ric. Faster."

He complied, quickening his pace and capturing her mouth in a heated kiss, his tongue mimicking the movements of his cocks. He reached between them, searching through the down of her sex until he found the distended bud. With gentle strokes, he thrummed her clit. She whimpered, bucking back against the cocks buried deep inside her.

Mia was one with him, in every way. Completely joined. Tears streamed freely down her cheeks as she let herself experience the ecstasy of her love for Ric.

The simultaneous stroking catapulted her over the edge. Her climax washed over her like a thunderous wave, the contractions squeezing Ric's cocks inside her.

He tensed and grabbed her close against him as both cocks came inside her, filling her. He thrust one last time, then stilled. His heart pounding as hard and fast as hers, Ric kissed the top of her head and cradled her against him.

Now, in the quiet aftermath of their lovemaking, she wanted to tell him she loved him. She wanted to ask him to be a part of her life. But she knew she could never be the type of woman he wanted to be with. What they had together was sex and that wasn't enough to sustain them.

So, where was the gutsy Mia Logan? The one who feared nothing, the one who took risks to get what she wanted? Had she buried that person under her job, hiding away where it was safe?

What was the worst thing that could happen? He'd laugh at her and tell her she wasn't near enough woman for him? That she was fine for sex, but the fun and games were over now and it was time she went back to Earth?

She took a deep breath and said, "Ric, I wanted to ask you—"

"Stay with me, *J'Mun*," he whispered before she could finish her sentence.

She stilled, uncertain if she understood. "What did you say?"

He lifted up on his arm and gazed into her face, his eyes filled with an emotion she dared not hope was love. "Stay with me here on M'Lora. We'll take Vad back to Earth and then you can come back here with me."

She swallowed, her throat gone dry. "You want me to come back with you?"

He nodded. "Yes."

"Why?"

"Because you're infuriating, obstinate, you try my patience and drive me crazy."

"I see. Good reasons."

He laughed. "And because I love you, Mia. I want you to stay here with me, if you're willing. Be my mate."

Stunned, she couldn't form words to respond. A newly discovered joy filled her heart. She didn't have to make that leap because he'd just done it for her. Now it was her turn. "I love you too, Ric. I just didn't think you wanted me permanently."

He kissed her deeply. "Of course I want you. Granted, you're too skinny, but we're working on that. With your appetite here, we'll have you looking like a M'Loran woman in no time at all. Although there's no hope for your tits," he teased.

She laughed and threw her arms around him. This was what she'd craved, what had been missing in her life all these years. Now she'd have everything she wanted. A new life on a new planet with the man who'd mesmerized her with his captivating eyes, fierce intelligence, warrior's heart and a body to die for.

He kissed her, then pulled back, his dark eyes void of humor. "Our children will be mutants. It won't be easy."

She reached for him, caressing his bottom lip with her shaky fingertips. "Not mutants, Ric. Multicultural. And they'll be beautiful."

"Like their mother."

"Like their father," she countered.

"You've made me feel like I'm part of something again, Mia. Like I could have a family—even happiness. I never thought that possible."

"Stick with me, M'Loran, and all things are possible."

He pulled her close and kissed her deeply, bringing to life her passions in a way that she now knew only he could.

She might be the hypnotist, but she'd fallen under Ric's magical spell. And she planned to stay mesmerized for the rest of her life.

About the author:

Jaci Burton has been a dreamer and lover of romance her entire life. Consumed with stories of passion, love and happily ever afters, she finally pulled her fantasy characters out of her head and put them on paper. Writing allows her to showcase the rainbow of emotions that result from falling in love.

Jaci lives in Oklahoma with her husband (her fiercest writing critic and sexy inspiration), stepdaughter and three wild and crazy dogs. Her sons are grown and live on opposite coasts and don't bother her nearly as often as she'd like them to. When she isn't writing stories of passion and romance, she can usually be found at the gym, reading a great book, or working on her computer, trying to figure out how she can pull more than twenty-four hours out of a single day.

Jaci welcomes mail from readers. You can write to her c/o Ellora's Cave Publishing at P.O. Box 787, Hudson, Ohio 44236-0787.

Also by JACI BURTON:

- Passion In Paradise 1: Paradise Awakening
- Passion In Paradise 2: Paradise Revival

Why an electronic book?

We live in the Information Age—an exciting time in the history of human civilization in which technology rules supreme and continues to progress in leaps and bounds every minute of every hour of every day. For a multitude of reasons, more and more avid literary fans are opting to purchase e-books instead of paperbacks. The question to those not yet initiated to the world of electronic reading is simply: *why?*

1. *Price.* An electronic title at Ellora's Cave Publishing runs anywhere from 40-75% less than the cover price of the <u>exact same title</u> in paperback format. Why? Cold mathematics. It is less expensive to publish an e-book than it is to publish a paperback, so the savings are passed along to the consumer.

2. *Space.* Running out of room to house your paperback books? That is one worry you will never have with electronic novels. For a low one-time cost, you can purchase a handheld computer designed specifically for e-reading purposes. Many e-readers are larger than the average handheld, giving you plenty of screen room. Better yet, hundreds of titles can be stored within your new library—a single microchip. (Please note that Ellora's Cave does not endorse any specific brands. You can check our website at www.ellorascave.com for customer recommendations we make available to new consumers.)

3. *Mobility.* Because your new library now consists of only a microchip, your entire cache of books can be taken with you wherever you go.

4. *Personal preferences are accounted for.* Are the words you are currently reading too small? Too large? Too...ANNOYING? Paperback books cannot be

modified according to personal preferences, but e-books can.

5. *Innovation.* The way you read a book is not the only advancement the Information Age has gifted the literary community with. There is also the factor of what you can read. Ellora's Cave Publishing will be introducing a new line of interactive titles that are available in e-book format only.

6. *Instant gratification.* Is it the middle of the night and all the bookstores are closed? Are you tired of waiting days—sometimes weeks—for online and offline bookstores to ship the novels you bought? Ellora's Cave Publishing sells instantaneous downloads 24 hours a day, 7 days a week, 365 days a year. Our e-book delivery system is 100% automated, meaning your order is filled as soon as you pay for it.

Those are a few of the top reasons why electronic novels are displacing paperbacks for many an avid reader. As always, Ellora's Cave Publishing welcomes your questions and comments. We invite you to email us at service@ellorascave.com or write to us directly at: P.O. Box 787, Hudson, Ohio 44236-0787.

Printed in the United States
30094LVS00001B/106-117

9 781843 604969